# THE PASSIONATE VICTIMS

By LANGE LEWIS

*Murder Among Friends*
*Meat for Murder*
*Juliet Dies Twice*
*The Birthday Murder*

# THE
# PASSIONATE
# VICTIMS

By *Lange Lewis*

THE BOBBS-MERRILL COMPANY, INC.

*Publishers*

Indianapolis                                    New York

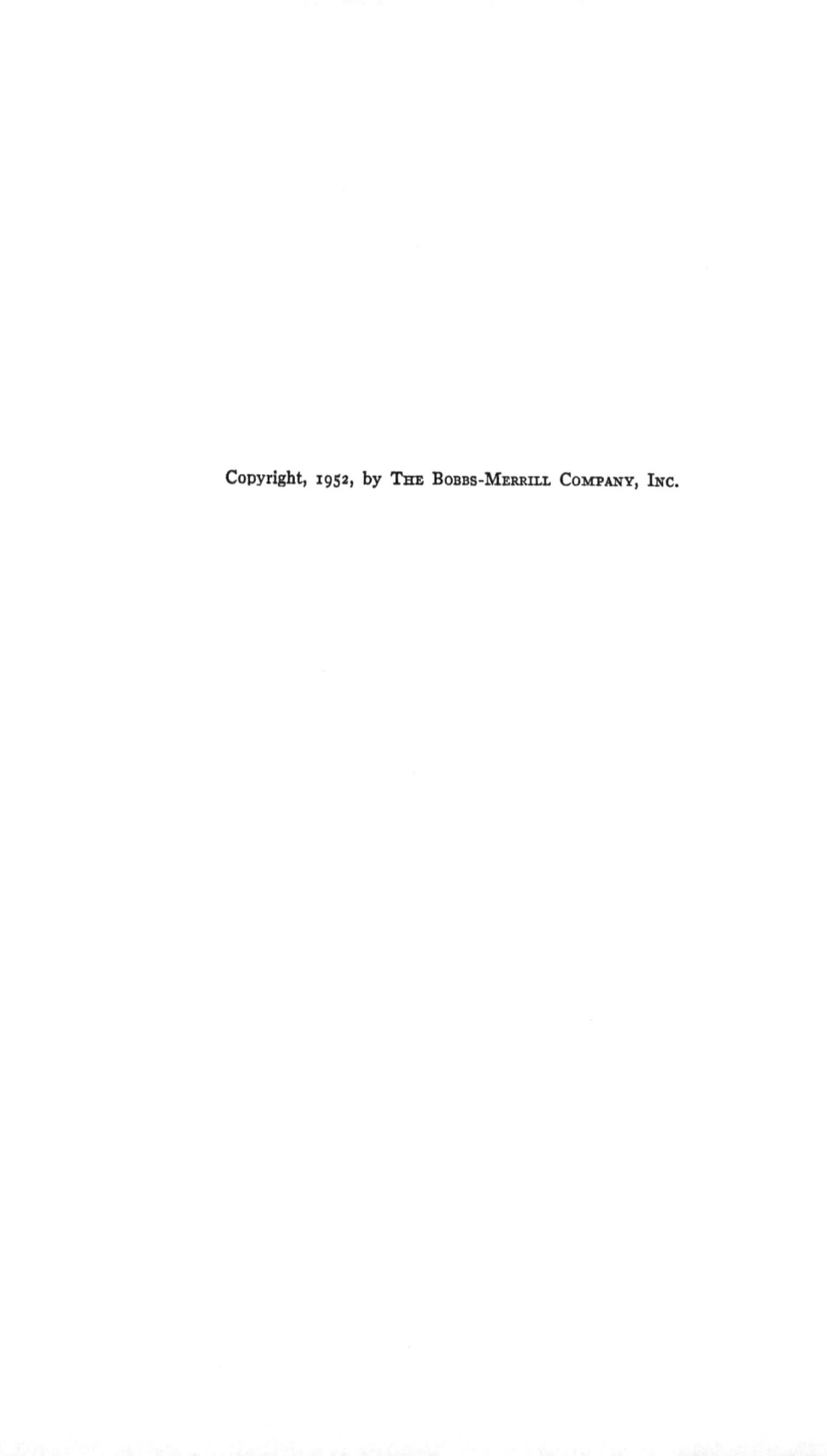

We are all passionate victims of our own prejudices, for these support the illusions about ourselves without which we believe we could not exist.

—Mordecai Fentwill

# CONTENTS

# PART ONE

*The Glove*

# 1

JUST BEFORE sundown on the day the careful pattern of her life began to shatter, Clare Crone picked five early-blooming irises from the garden. She arranged them in a flat pewter bowl with several of their long leaves, as pointed as the blades of knives. The tender, precise flare of their petals pleased her until she saw how some had been bruised by the rising wind. She frowned toward the dining-room window as it rattled faintly in its frame. There hasn't been a wind like this in years, she thought. Not since . . .

The doorbell rang. Passing through her Early American living room she paused to straighten an ash tray. The smell of roasting lamb was rather strong in the front hall. She had forgotten to close the rear door opening into the kitchen.

The last person she expected to see was her daughter. Beside Helene was a rich brown leather suitcase. A yellow taxicab was pulling away from the curb. Helene wore a fleecy white coat over the gray flannel slacks which Clare Crone detested; her puffed eyes revealed that she had been crying.

It was typical of Clare Crone that she ignored the signs of tears and the suitcase as well. She embraced her daughter with a formal gesture like one seen on the stage, pressing her older cheek against the round, firm young one. "Why, Helene, this is a real surprise! And to think that quite by chance I'm having leg of lamb tonight. You were always so fond of lamb. You can stay for dinner, can't you?"

With a faint, hard smile Helene picked up the suitcase. "I'll probably be around longer than that. I'm going to get a divorce."

Controlling her inner stab of shock and annoyance, Clare Crone allowed extravagant surprise to show on her face. Then she smiled reprovingly. "Helene!" She took the suitcase from her daughter's hand and set it down by the telephone stand. The two women entered the living room side by side, Helene looking about at familiar objects almost gratefully.

"I'll just set another place," said Clare Crone. "Sit in one of the wing chairs by the fire, dear. Would you mind lighting it? Your hands are like ice." As she chattered Clare Crone hurried through the wide arch to the dining room. The table, with its glossy linen, its centerpiece of iris, its silver dish of jam, looked almost as well as it did when company was expected. Mrs. Crone believed that dinner should be a gracious meal. With her back to the living room she placed well-polished silverware on the table and asked, "What seems to be the trouble, dear? Do you want to tell me?"

"The trouble seems to be another woman," said Helene flatly.

"One?" asked Mrs. Crone as she put a napkin beside the forks. "Or more than one?" She turned and went to her daughter.

Helene was slumped deep in one of the wing chairs flanking the fireplace, her hand arrested in the act of striking a match. One corner of her mouth smiled. "There are times, Mother, when you really shock me. Isn't one woman enough?"

12

Straight-backed, Mrs. Crone sat down in the chair facing Helene's. Both chairs were upholstered in a pattern which showed red-coated figures riding to the hounds. On the hearthrug a life-sized white-china cat was curled in a pose of extravagantly blissful slumber. Clare Crone picked up the embroidery hoop on the arm of the chair and began to draw a needle in and out of the large curly initial with which she was decorating a pillow slip. "Most men," she said, "are very much alike." There was complacence in her voice. "If it weren't for the fact we have children to consider, I doubt if we'd be able to put up with them as forgivingly as we do."

"Fortunately I have no children," said Helene and blew a puff of smoke at the ceiling, her mouth wry and hard.

"Don't try to be sophisticated, Helene. It's not your forte."

"I'm not. I said 'fortunately' because I have certain ideas about marriage. I don't happen to believe that its only function is to provide a home for offspring." Her voice became faintly noble. "A man named Comte said what I feel about marriage so well I memorized it. 'Between two beings so complex and so diverse as man and woman, the whole of life is not too long for them to learn to know each other well and to love each other worthily.'"

"You are talking fairy tales. I am trying to speak of facts. You are twenty-four years old. Most, if not all, of the eligible young men you knew at college have married or are involved with fiancées. If you abandon your husband . . ."

"He seems to have abandoned me."

"This woman," asked Mrs. Crone, resuming her sewing with an effort, "is she anyone we know?"

Helene gave a hard little laugh. "No, Mother. At least I didn't recognize her voice on the telephone and I've heard it several times."

"How did you happen to talk to her on the telephone?"

"Oh, she calls up and asks for him—just like that! Both times she said, 'Tell him the same time and place.' And how do you like *them* apples, Mother dear?"

"Some women have no shame whatever," said Clare Crone mechanically. "But that's beside the point. If I were you, before deciding rashly to throw away a husband only too many young women would be quite anxious to acquire, I would find out a few things. Do you have any idea where he's meeting her?"

"Yes. He's meeting her tonight at six in the Blue Grotto."

"That dark, ordinary bar down on the boulevard? The one near the foot of this street?"

"It's not only dark, but it's also conveniently located if she lives at this end of town, which is what I'm presuming."

"Is that why you came here?"

"Because the Blue Grotto is conveniently located?"

"You know what I mean! Were you so foolish as to leave your home because you found he was meeting this woman again?"

"That's it in a nutshell. She phoned him again this afternoon after about a month of silence. I knew who it was at once, because her voice is so unusual, more like a man's. So I eavesdropped, and I heard him say, 'The Blue Grotto at six sharp.'"

"Are you sure it's *this* Blue Grotto?" asked Clare Crone. She had always thought that her son-in-law possessed very good taste, and to conduct a flirtation (the only word she would allow her mind to use) in such vulgar surroundings did not seem like him at all.

"There isn't any other Blue Grotto, because I looked it up in the telephone book."

"How do you know it *wasn't* a man?"

"Because her name's Miss White. He admitted that much the second time she phoned."

14

"It was very unwise of you to flounce out. You should have prevented his seeing her—told him you had planned to meet friends for dinner."

"Evidently we're more alike than I thought, Mother. That's just what I did. He got very evasive, said he had to meet a business acquaintance at six. He seemed rather sorry about it all. It was just as though something were drawing him to the Blue Grotto while part of him wanted to have dinner with me."

"Well," said Mrs. Crone, "in your place I should certainly find out more about this Miss White. The whole relationship may be entirely innocent." Her tone, she was aware, did not carry much conviction.

With sudden violence Helene pitched her cigarette into the fireplace. "I'm tired, tired, *tired* of living with a man who doesn't love me any more, if he ever did."

"Love," said Clare Crone, "wears many faces." In that instant her face looked to her daughter like a bad portrait of itself, with the shadows on one side crudely and darkly painted, and ending too sharply at the chin, as a mask ends.

"I'm going to my room," Helene said abruptly.

"Take a shower, dear. You'll find it will soothe you. And do change those slacks. And you might take one of those little pills Dr. Ferris gave me. They're on the second shelf of the medicine chest. You're very tense. You *must* relax."

Suddenly Helene was standing with her legs spread like a young boy's, her fists balled on each hip. "Don't get the idea this will blow over! I'm going to have a talk with Dad tonight. I think he'll see it my way."

"I have little doubt of that. You and your father are just alike in some ways. There's a blundering, destructive element in both of you." Clare Crone pressed her lips firmly together, stabbed the needle so inaccurately through the cloth that it jabbed her finger painfully. She dropped the

15

embroidery, snatched away her thumb and squeezed a small bead of blood to the surface of the pink, whorled skin. Then she blotted it up with the handkerchief drawn from the pocket of her neat, powder-blue shirtmaker dress.

Helene went upstairs to her girlhood room. Only as she opened the door onto that frilled and chintzy and now lost sanctuary did she realize that she had left her suitcase in the hall below. She started to go back for it, then paused at the threshold of her mother's room, thought for a long moment and went in to where a four-post bed with a spread of white eyelet muslin stood as though never slept in amid the faint smell of hidden sachet.

When Clare Crone heard the back door close softly after her daughter she smiled to herself. She knew that Helene was going to the Blue Grotto to learn more about Miss White. But, being Helene, she had to be secretive, had to maintain her sense of independent action by not acknowledging that she had taken her mother's advice.

The cuckoo clock said a quarter to six. In three quarters of an hour the lamb would be done. Before she put on the rice and peas Mrs. Crone went upstairs to freshen up. This was part of her evening ritual and meant that she cleaned her white, even teeth, combed her crisp, dark, short hair, powdered her face and armed it with fresh lipstick. She comforted herself with the knowledge that many wives never seemed to learn the importance of offering no target, however small, for husbandly criticism. An unkind word or look can bring out a sharp response, and then, before either knows it, bitter truths are being spoken.

But when she entered her bedroom she found the closet door opened wide, the box which had contained her black hat open and empty on the bed. A glance showed her that the new dress she had intended to wear to the Third Thursday meeting was gone from its pink padded hanger. Her Persian-lamb coat was also missing. Her first dazed notion was that a thief had broken in, her next that the coat was insured, and then she realized that Helene had gone to the Blue Grotto wearing the only disguise at hand. She relaxed, smiling faintly. After all, her daughter's happiness was more important to her than a new coat or hat. Only she did hope Helene would not tear the delicate veil!

It was a quarter to seven when the front door opened and Helene entered as though thrust into the house by the wind. She looked oddly mature in the bulky coat, and the puff of dark veil across her eyes made them seem mysterious. "Well, did you see her?" Clare Crone demanded.

Helene shook her head and took the hat off slowly. Her short brown hair was rumpled, and she smoothed it awkwardly. "No, I didn't see her." She sounded puzzled. Then, realizing that her mother knew without having been told where she had gone, she looked more alert and put on a smile of bravado. "Thanks for the hat and coat. Isn't Dad home yet?"

"Your father telephoned to say he'd be a little late tonight. Fortunately I hadn't put on the rice and peas. Tell me what happened."

"I got there first and went straight back to the short corridor where the washrooms are. There's a phone booth, and through the glass I could look down the length of the place and see the entrance. He came in only a couple of minutes later. He took the third booth back from the door and ordered a bottle of beer. I went quietly down to the booth next to his. As I sat down I saw that he was reading a copy of *Time*. In exactly twenty minutes he got up and left. He did not, I may add, look like a gent who's been stood up. He looked, in a vague way, kind of pleased with himself."

"You see?" demanded Clare Crone. "It wasn't this Miss White he went to meet at all!"

Helene slumped wearily in the chair facing her mother's. She shook her rumpled head. "It was her voice on the phone this afternoon. It's a voice you don't forget. A deep, phony voice, a sly voice, but with a peculiar assurance to it. No, he went out to meet Miss White, all right. But why wasn't she there?" She wound her forelock around her finger, a gesture which Clare Crone remembered from Helene's childhood. "The only answer I get—and it's perfectly crazy—is that there is no Miss White at all—that the whole thing's a gag cooked up with one of his screwball friends solely to torment me!"

"I wish you wouldn't use expressions like 'screwball'!"

The cuckoo clock said ten minutes to seven, which meant that Helene's father might be expected in half an hour. Clare Crone was seized with the desire to see her daughter depart for her own home before Eric Crone returned to confuse matters by what he would regard as his objectivity but which Clare Crone knew would consist of his dislike of his son-in-law, plus his atrocious partiality to Helene's point of view. Remembrance of them allied against her, as they had been too often in times past, aroused a flutter of anger in Clare Crone's chest. The thought that with Eric abetting her Helene might literally begin divorce procedure released in her a scurry of panic and dismay. Two swift images crossed her mind: a moment when guests had seen a mouse scamper across her clean kitchen floor, and the face of the president of the Third Thursday Women's Club as she sharply rapped her gavel to still the gossip which preceded each meeting.

But she smiled. "You'll never guess who I met today in Magnin's. Joan Able! I never saw her looking better. She isn't engaged yet, though. I wonder why?" Joan Able had once been flagrantly in love with Helene's husband and as a

18

bridesmaid she had kissed the groom with more warmth than good taste. The meeting had actually occurred three weeks before, but appreciation of literature had endowed Clare with a knowledge of the emphasis to be gained from proper juxtaposition of events.

"Oh? Has she lost any weight?" There was a faint glitter in Helene's brown eyes.

"Pounds. With her height she looks like a model. She really does."

"Then her taste in clothes must have improved one hell of a lot." The glitter in Helene's eyes was more noticeable.

Clare Crone chose this as the right moment to lean forward, her face firm and serious. "If you leave your husband, do you think for one moment he'll sit home pining? No, you'll do that, added to which will be the pleasure of hearing from your friends that he's been seen here, there and everywhere with girls like Joan! Oh, your young women friends will be full of sympathy. And pity! When a marriage as truly enviable as yours suffers a break, no one ever believes this was something the woman wanted. Whatever you say, people will think that *he* got tired of you—a thing his carefree behavior will do nothing to deny."

Helene's silence was very thoughtful; her narrowed brown eyes now looked like her mother's. "But I can't go back now," she said. "I can't make such a fool of myself. You see . . . I left a farewell note."

"Oh, Helene!" This sudden barrier to her plans was felt by Clare Crone as a dull jolt inside her chest, as though a little door had slammed. She could feel her blood backing up behind the closed outlet, a sensation much like one accompanying a mild heart attack; she had suffered three such attacks. "What did you say in the note?" Clare Crone demanded, and heard the thin strained tone in her own voice.

"Just that I was going to spend a few days here thinking

over certain intolerable aspects of our marriage." Helene sounded relieved that she had limited her rage and hurt so well.

"Pooh!" Mrs. Crone dismissed the letter. "If you get back before he does, he won't even see it!"

"But I want him to see it! I want him to know just how I feel about this White woman. Maybe then he'll come through with a reasonable explanation!"

To Mrs. Crone her daughter's mental antics were like those of a child of five. "But what if he has no reasonable explanation! Do you want to force a situation which, with a little cleverness on your part, could be skirted and in time forgotten?"

"I want to know what I'm up against," said Helene, squaring her already square jaw.

"Stop that! You look like a pugilist!" The cuckoo clock released its shrill wheezing bird which defiantly announced the hour of seven. Each "cuckoo" echoed twice inside Mrs. Crone's head, and the swift passage of thrice-recorded time occasioned in her a faint, falling sensation of despair. She felt she could not face for a moment longer the stubborn child in the chair opposite hers and stood up sharply, turning blindly toward the sofa.

Without prior thought, almost without conscious volition, she lay down, one hand dangling limp, one clenched on the pale-blue wool covering her chest. Her eyes became fixed on the ceiling as though she were listening for something.

"Mother! What's wrong?" Helene stood over her, then bent forward with anxiety.

Very calmly Clare Crone said, "Bottle. Spoon. Table by my bed. Top drawer. Bring them." Her eyes lingeringly watched her daughter run out of the room and up the hall stairs. It may or may not be an attack coming on, Clare

Crone told herself, but there's no use whatever in taking chances. She closed her eyes.

In no time at all Helene was again beside the sofa. She read the doctor's instructions on the medicine bottle and carefully poured a spoonful of the liquid. Mrs. Crone raised her head stiffly and swallowed it.

"You never told me there was anything wrong with your heart, Mother!" Helene sounded hurt, accusing.

"It's not serious," said Mrs. Crone in almost her usual tone of voice. "Hide the bottle and spoon in the secretary. I don't want your father to see them."

"He doesn't know?" Helene obeyed, but sounded aghast.

"He has enough to worry about. You don't seem to realize that since he's been an assistant district attorney in charge of juvenile cases, he's had to carry a far greater load of responsibility than when he was a mere investigator. I'll tell him, in time, but I'll pick the right moment to do it."

"And I come and dump my troubles on you," Helene said.

She's a dear, good child in spite of her college education, thought Mrs. Crone. She reached out her hand—a thin hand, but large-boned, capable. Helene's warm, plump hand took it. "Don't my irises look lovely?" asked Mrs. Crone with brave gaiety. "The first of the season. In the East they wouldn't be blooming for months yet!" Her tone changed. "When your father comes home, say nothing of any trouble. Not tonight. He's under a great strain, and he's so apt to lose his temper. Not with *you*. With me. To say nothing of your husband." She smiled ruefully, reminding Helene of past conflicts between the older man and the younger.

"I've thought things out," Helene said. "I've decided that this time you're right. I'm going home. If he's seen the letter . . . well, he's seen it. At least it will give us a starting point from which to discuss things. If he hasn't, I'll toss it into the fire. And then I'll wait and pick the right time for a discussion of our problems."

"You're being very mature, Helene. A woman has no weapon better than just waiting for the proper time. Because, you see, if a man's shortcoming is hurled in his face with tactless crudity, his guilt merely turns to hatred. But if a wife has the self-discipline to wait for a moment when his actions show that he has realized how wrong he is, a few gentle questions can usually bring out the truth. And he's grateful, truly grateful, to get rid of his sense of being in the wrong."

"But how do you know when a man realizes he's been wrong?"

"Your father used to buy tickets for a play he knew I wanted to see. With a great many it's flowers or candy. You'll know when the right time comes. Now hurry, dear. Because it would be so much better if you could get home before he reads that silly, impulsive note you left."

"It seems, well, sort of devious, Mother. But you've been married for twenty-five years, and I guess you've learned something."

"More than you, perhaps, will ever know," said Clare Crone. It struck her daughter that the words concealed some sad event of which her mother would never speak.

The cuckoo abruptly announced the hour as seven-fifteen. Clare rose quickly from the sofa. Now the blood was pumping normally in her chest, and she felt the strength that comes from having commanded a delicate, potentially dangerous situation. "I'll call a cab while you go up and change. That black hat looks very well on you, dear. Keep it, if you'd like."

While Helene tried on the hat, peering judiciously at her reflection in the hall mirror, Mrs. Crone dialed the cab company. "As quickly as possible, please. The address is 1900

Acacia Street. It's the two-story Colonial house on the east side of the street. Please hurry. It's rather an emergency." On the last words she smiled at her daughter, a cheerful conspirator against their common enemy, the male of the species.

"And, darling," she commanded as she turned from the telephone, "don't wear those slacks. Whatever men may say, they like a woman to look womanly."

"Even when she's not?"

Clare Crone smiled. "Then even more."

"Then it's really a game, marriage. A very serious masquerade." Helene spoke thoughtfully, but then her gaze sharpened and her face looked impish. "Is that what you and Daddy have been up to all these years? Putting on a good show?"

"Certainly not!"

Helene saw how sharp and angry her mother's face had grown, and this reaction to her light words made her a little uneasy. "I was only kidding, Mother."

But her mother's face seemed withdrawn from the present, a trick which Helene had felt keenly as a child when it had had the power to fill her with a queer panic and turn the ordinary secure objects around her into insubstantial phantoms out of a nightmare. She reminded herself that her parents were ordinary, middle-class American people, that there was no important part of their lives she did not know.

"I don't think I'll take the hat, Mother. But thanks anyway. It somehow makes me look much too respectable." Her mother's smile was distant, and the next few minutes did not re-establish their brief rapport. Even through the sound of the wind outside they both heard the taxicab squeal to a stop, and went to the hall. Helene picked up her suitcase, and they turned to each other like automata to kiss and part.

Halfway down the front walk Helene glanced back and

smiled a farewell. Her mother waved from the doorway. The taut look of some nagging inner strain might have been less apparent in a kinder light; but bathed in the clear sad glow of a greenish sky from which a huddle of low purple clouds and a last orange glimmer of sunset was fading, she seemed, for just an instant, a faintly tragic figure bearing with reserve some secret anguish which made her remote from the conventional beliefs and gestures to which she clung.

# 2

Eᴙɪᴄ Cᴙᴏɴᴇ looked to many people like an inspector from Scotland Yard. A bear-shaped man in his middle forties, he wore the roughest of tweeds and a man-sized ginger-colored mustache. He also smoked a pipe with a curved stem. In his big ruddy face his small brown eyes appeared lidless and seemed to indicate a shrewd, calculating brain. He was given to faint half-smiles. Juveniles who were engaged in peddling marijuana, stealing cars or robbing small store-keepers got the uneasy impression that he knew everything about them, and he occasionally did. But when he left his office for the day, when he entered his home, he took on the patient, discouraged slump of a man long used to making explanations, whether called for or not.

"I'm afraid the lamb is cold," said Clare Crone as her husband began to carve. Her tone made the comment less an apology than an accusation.

"A couple of the boys brought in Figueroa Rose," explained Eric Crone. "A *muchacha* of seventeen who's been understudying the Little Flower of Temple Street, right down to the knife in her pompadour. The question was whether to book her on hypo marks, or for following the oldest profession, or to let her loose on the chance she'd lead the narcotics boys to the peddler she's getting her caps from."

"Your office jargon always bewilders me . . . and I can't say I'm sorry," said Clare Crone. "Los Angeles used to be such a nice city. I can't understand where all these vicious youngsters come from."

"They are born in the usual fashion," Eric Crone said dryly. "Slums make criminals of them. We condone slums."

"I certainly do nothing of the kind. Ignorance is what condones slums. But how can those of us fortunate enough to possess intelligence and education change the fact that the poor are always with us? Though I don't believe that the poor of other times further aggravated their condition by smoking marijuana and cocaine."

"You don't smoke cocaine," said Eric. "It is usually injected with a hypodermic needle."

"Shall we talk of something else?" Clare Crone suggested brightly.

After a moment of silence Eric Crone turned to a new topic. "Have you heard from Helene? I've been kind of worried about the kid. I thought she looked pretty beaten down when we were out there two weeks ago."

"Oh, she's all right. They both stay up too late, go out too much. And I wouldn't be surprised if a little too much drinking goes on."

"Helene said a funny thing to me last time I saw her. I told her I thought she was looking pretty thin and pale. She said not to worry—if anything really went wrong, she knew she could count on me." He added hastily, "Of course she meant *us.*"

"There's nothing to count on us *for.* She's perfectly happy. They'll iron out their little differences, given time."

"They've had over a year."

26

"The first year's the hardest."

Eric spoke reflectively. "Oh, I don't know about that."

"They have everything," said Mrs. Crone. "A lovely new home, a private income, a beautiful car, and it looks as if his little cosmetic business is going to do remarkably well."

"I never thought I'd have a son-in-law who manufactured goo for women's faces."

"When I consider how little we had I just can't worry about Helene." Clare Crone looked at their present possessions with approval. "Which reminds me, the taxes on the house are due. There's not enough in the checking account to cover them and the month's expenses too. I suppose I'll have to dip into my savings. Unless your salary's raised this year, I'll have to forget about turning in the convertible on a new one. Oh, well. We're lucky my mother was a good businesswoman."

"Are we? We *could* have got along with a smaller home . . . *and* no convertible." Eric spoke with heavy jocularity, under which was a hint of malice.

"You never liked my mother."

"She was a remarkable woman. Is there any more peach jam?"

Clare Crone looked at the empty jam dish with polite incredulity. "You're exactly like a child about sweets. You know that Dr. Ferris warned you to watch your weight."

She heard Eric's feet shuffle under the table. "Oh, it's about the same as it was last year."

"It certainly is not. The coat of your brown suit is so tight you can't button it. And it was a perfect fit six months ago."

"It probably shrank some at the cleaner's. And anyway a small amount of jam isn't going to make any difference. If there isn't any more jam, say so."

"There are at least two dozen jars in the cellar, thanks to my having canned for a solid week last summer when you in your air-conditioned office came home groaning about the heat."

"It isn't air-conditioned!"

"It's entirely up to you, Eric." Clare Crone rose with dignity, her narrow, rather flat-chested body held elegantly slim in its sheath of pale-blue wool. "If you want to ruin your appearance and endanger your health gobbling sweets, go right ahead."

"Oh, forget the jam." He looked disconsolately at the half biscuit on his bread-and-butter plate. "Don't trouble yourself."

"I'm thinking only of you. It's not the trip to the cellar I mind."

He started to get out of his chair. "I'll go down for it."

"You wouldn't know where to look. I doubt that you've been in the cellar once in the last ten years." As she left the table he started to carve himself another piece of meat. "Lamb is rather fattening, Eric. There are a hundred calories in one small slice."

The door leading to the small cement-walled cellar was under the hall staircase. Clare Crone always kept it locked. After she snapped on the naked electric bulb she went lightly down the narrow steps, pausing halfway down to glance at a high shelf which held such rarely used paraphernalia as a picnic basket with a broken handle, two large thermos bottles, a tennis racket with broken strings and an ancient portable victrola.

The peach jam was on a lower shelf; but she decided to take down a jar of watermelon pickles which was out of reach, and briskly set up the small stepladder. Her hand had just touched the jar of pickles when the telephone shrilled imperatively in the hall above. For no reason she could later explain to herself she was sure that it was Helene calling. She scrambled lightly down the ladder and ran to

28

the foot of the stairs. But before she had started up the steps she heard her husband's deep voice, and stood with her head tilted, listening.

"Well, well, well! How are you, Helene? . . . What? Talk slower. What? . . . Oh. Go on. . . ." During the long pause Clare Crone felt herself stiffening with anxiety. "Oh, so that's the lay of the land, is it? Now listen, Helene. Stay right where you are. I'll be out for you as fast as I can make it. I'm leaving right now. Don't worry. Let me do that for a while."

Clare Crone heard the telephone crash into its cradle. Her husband's heavy footsteps thumped to the top of the cellar stairs. His voice roared down like a wild beast's. "Why in hell didn't you tell me Helene was here today? Why did you tell me everything was all right?"

"Before you leave there is something I would like to discuss with you," Clare Crone said calmly. The blood was pounding thickly in her throat and ears.

"Make it snappy! Where did you hide my overcoat?"

"In the hall closet." She turned, went to the ladder and moved it three feet. It now stood below the high shelf where the picnic basket and thermos bottles were stowed. She climbed the ladder with spry agility, reached behind the basket and drew out into the glaring light a third thermos bottle with a white "X" chalked on its blue side. Her hand started to unscrew the chromium cup, paused, drew away. Just then something heavy crashed to the floor of the hall closet upstairs. She was sure it could only be her husband's revolver.

The menace of the sound startled her into action; she twisted the cap from the bottle, upended it. Her thumb and forefinger pried into the narrow mouth. From the clean glittering interior she pulled out a white glove. The fingers were stained with dried brown blood.

29

She could feel disgust settle on her face, grooving the creases at either side of her mouth deeper, making her jowls leaden. Before she went up the stairs she stuffed the glove into the deep pocket of her dress, picked up a Mason jar in either hand and by an effort not new to her smoothed her face into its normal expression of ladylike composure.

Eric, enormous in his camel's-hair overcoat, was walking up and down in front of the hearthrug, his hands plunged into the pockets. When she came in with the two jars he glowered. His face was ruddier than usual, and even his eyes seemed to have a reddish tinge.

"What did you drop in the closet?" Clare Crone asked.

"A flashlight. Say what you have to say fast."

"Kindly lower your voice, Eric. Because I did not want to worry you with what seemed a trivial matter, I do *not* deserve to be treated like a criminal."

"I just don't get it! Helene came here today to ask us for our help and understanding. Apparently you talked her into going back to that bastard she married. And then lied to me about it!"

"I did nothing of the kind!" With thinning restraint Clare Crone set the jam jars down on the whatnot table, whirled to face her husband. He was standing beside the chair Helene had occupied earlier in the evening and on his face Clare could see the same childish stubbornness, the same kind of stupidity. She thrust her hand into her dress pocket, clenched it around the glove. Maybe I won't have to, she thought. I hope not.

He looked coarsely sure of himself. "Helene came here today and told you her husband was involved with another woman. You don't deny that, do you?"

"I do not. What you don't know is that this other woman is a voice on the telephone, no more. Helene has no proof that he's carrying on with her."

"I'm not going to argue with you, Clare. I don't know yet exactly what's happened, but I know Helene's close to hysterics. She needs a rest from that playboy, and she's going to get it. And if she needs a divorce, she's going to get that too. She was a healthy, happy girl when she married him. In a year she's turned into a neurotic wraith! That's enough for me!"

"She looked remarkably healthy when I saw her two hours ago," Clare Crone said in a hard voice. "Helene's main trouble is that she's spoiled, and you spoiled her. For the last ten years every time an issue arises, you take her side and refuse to see mine."

"I was damned if I'd see her pumped full of your false values!"

"My values are very standard ones!"

"They still stink. It all dates from when your mother left you that money. It used to make me sick every time Helene drove that damned Cadillac convertible to high school, looking like some rich man's kid. And you watching from the window, smiling your pussycat's smile!"

The venom of her husband's tone first hurt, then deeply angered Clare Crone. How cruel, how unfair that she should be blamed for wanting their child to have the best! "I notice you were perfectly willing to drive my car when it was available," she said with a cool smile.

His thick hand pointed at his barrel chest. "Me? How often did I drive it? When my sedan was in the garage for an overhaul!"

"You drove it the night Ruth Ann Briggs was killed, I remember."

He stared at her stupidly. With apparently genuine puzzlement he asked, "What the hell does that have to do with what we're talking about?"

"Nothing. I was merely pointing out that my car was a

convenience, at times, to both of you. For which I was glad."

"You're getting kind of far from the issue. We were talking about Helene—a waste of time, because I'm going out there to get her—now!"

He started for the front door, but she stepped in front of him. "I won't stand by and watch you destroy my daughter's marriage!"

"She's my daughter too. And it's not her marriage you're thinking of so much as the fact that she happened to marry into a rich family."

"That's not true!"

"Look. I happen to love Helene. I know she's miserable, and she's asked for my help."

"Love! You will forgive me if I say you have entertained such peculiar affections down the years that I can no longer trust the word *love,* coming from you."

"We haven't time to discuss the women you believe I've slept with. I'm going!"

As he started to pass her, striding toward the front hall, she took another quick step toward him, once more arresting his flight. An alien strength was pounding through her body; yet she felt very light, as though she could run faster than the wind was blowing, as though she could fly. "If Helene knew what you are, Eric, she wouldn't want your help!"

His breathing was very heavy, but his voice came out light with insolence. "You sound looney. You look like a crazy woman."

"Do you think I don't know?" she cried. "Do you think I haven't known for six long years that you killed Ruth Ann Briggs?"

His small eyes had widened between their thin lids. They were fixed on hers as though they could never stop looking. She saw his heavy arm in its big tan sleeve go up to strike her with a balled fist. Before she could display the glove in

32

triumphant proof his hand opened and swept her out of his path. The power of the thrust was so enormous that it was not like being hit by a human being, but by the huge impersonal force engendered by an explosion. She was swept toward the fireplace, clutched air, struck her arm against the stand which held the fire irons. There was a muffled crash of falling metal, and the front door slammed. She felt the first spasm of an entirely genuine heart attack and with it the terrified knowledge that the anger on her husband's face could well have been a look of righteous wrath. Her head thudded on the fallen poker, rolled on the brick hearth. Blackness swallowed her.

# 3

BRIGIT ESTEES was the only woman on the Los Angeles Homicide Squad. She had bright-red hair, an innocent face, and she was five feet eleven inches tall in her stocking feet.

Richard Tuck, also of Homicide, was six feet five inches tall. His length was topped by massive shoulders, a long, doleful face with eyes the color of black coffee and straight brown hair which had the shine of a wet seal. The deep grooves bracketing his big firm mouth gave his face a granite look until he smiled and showed that dimples had once been there. He had been reared on a farm where apple pie usually topped a breakfast of cereal, ham, eggs and hotcakes, but Brigit Estees' capacity for victuals at times astonished him. One windy February night he watched Brigit ponder the chessboard between them while she ate, almost absently, a large wedge of banana-cream pie.

"I wouldn't mind watching you put away three pieces of pie after a full-course dinner if you would just admit that you like pie, instead of pretending that you eat it for its nutritional value," Tuck told her.

Brigit Estees' blue eyes opened wide and blinked twice. Tuck saw this look as that of a child accused of a subtle dishonesty far beyond her intellectual powers. "Maybe I do eat a little more than an average-size woman. But you've got to take into account, there's a lot more of me to nourish! Should I be ashamed because I can't live on lettuce sandwiches and fruit salad?"

Tuck saw that she was utilizing her height to justify her appetite. He wondered whether some slight guilt lay behind a dogged pairing of facts only slightly related; Brigit, in other regards, had an honest brain. An explanation occurred to him. "How much do you weigh, Brigit?"

"One hundred and fifty on the nose."

"What did you weigh before you joined the force, when you were a model?"

Brigit evaded his eyes by putting the pie plate aside and reaching for a cigarette. He held out a light, and her candid eyes met his over the flame. "I weighed a hundred and twenty-nine. And most of the time I felt as if a good breeze would blow me away. I woke up hungry. I went to sleep hungry. I thought of food all the time in between. What cooked my career as a model, though, was getting my face on the front page of a fashion mag. My mother decided I was going to be a big success, one of those models that marry millionaires—for love, of course. If I gained three ounces, to her I was throwing away my future happiness. She began to count my peas and figure my calories with a slide rule. Even so, she said I ate too much! So . . ."

Brigit's voice trailed off as she realized that her monologue had done a tricky full circle, right back to the question of her appetite. "I never liked being a clotheshorse anyway, Tuck. Too much sham. I like feeling I'm doing something useful for society." Her tone was faintly smug. She moved her white knight and placed Tuck's queen in hazard.

"And a lady dick can weigh what she pleases," added

Tuck, moving his queen to black's fourth rank. "Check." As though to emphasize the white king's jeopardy, the wind rattled suddenly at the windows.

Brigit paused with her hand out to move her king from peril, her eyes on the wind-filled night beyond the pane. "You know what this blow makes me keep thinking of?"

"The night when Ruth Ann Briggs was killed," said Tuck matter-of-factly.

"So you were thinking of her too!"

"Once in a while I wonder who hit her on the head. Whether the wind's blowing or not. . . . Your king's still in check."

As Brigit moved it to safety the telephone rang. Pondering her next move, she answered it. The hoarse voice of Gufferty, head of Homicide, demanded, "Tuck there?"

"Yes."

"Good. Get over to 1900 Acacia Street right away. Woman on the floor, blood on the poker. A neighbor reported it as murder, telephoned down here to headquarters a couple of minutes ago. I told her to call the doctor. A little bit of blood makes people jump to conclusions."

"Acacia Street!" said Brigit. "That's funny!"

"What's funny about it? The woman who was attacked is Mrs. Eric Crone. Her husband's that fellow in Juvenile Division. The neighbor is a Mrs. Macabee. She'll be at the scene. She says, by the way, that she knows you two. From the Briggs case. So long."

The room wore the disheveled air of a place which crime has entered. Fire tongs, poker, brush and bellows lay scattered in brassy chaos. The stand which held them had been knocked over, narrowly missing a white-china cat whose pose of blissful slumber seemed bizarre. The poker lay apart from the other implements, and its iron shaft showed a

36

small dense bloodstain. More blood made a small pool on the brick hearth. An embroidery hoop, needle thrust through an unfinished initial, reposed on the arm of one of the wing chairs, as though set there to display the injured woman's handiwork.

For Mrs. Crone was not, after all, dead. She lay on the sofa, an afghan drawn up to her white closed face. Blood showed on the gauze bandage around her head.

Seated on a hard chair drawn up to face the sofa was a small, dignified, pewter-gray doctor. He looked extremely grave as he took his patient's pulse and watched the shallow rise and fall of her breathing. "I must say, Mrs. Macabee, that it's lucky you found her when you did and telephoned me. She was nearly gone. She's never had so severe a heart attack before, although that blow on the head was no help."

"I didn't know there was anything wrong with her heart," said Mrs. Macabee a trifle guiltily. She looked up at Tuck and Brigit. "But I did the right thing calling you. It's plain someone *tried* to kill her!"

"Not quite," said Tuck. "Suppose you tell us why you think so."

Mrs. Macabee wore a brown beaver coat which made her look like a plump, domesticated animal. Her graying hair was wild under a small feathered hat, roguishly tipped. The shocked look on her face seemed to perch there unfamiliarly. "A woman's not safe in her own house any more!" she announced. "These goons and degenerates pop right in on you!" She sat down nervously on the ladder-back chair by the antique secretary, her plump hands clasped on the narrow shelf of her lap.

"Well, it was around ten-thirty when I rang the doorbell. The reason was, Clare didn't show up at Third Thursday meeting tonight, and I thought maybe something was wrong.

37

As a matter of fact, I noticed her daughter Helene getting out of a cab with a suitcase late this afternoon. Mr. Macabee says I'm nosy. I guess I am. Anyhow, the lights were all on, but no one came to the door. That's funny, I thought, and went around to the driveway to see if Clare's car was in the garage. It was, though Mr. Crone's was gone. I went around to the front again and peeked through the living-room window. The Venetian blinds weren't quite closed, and through one of the cracks what did I see but Clare Crone's legs! They were sticking out into the room from behind that wing chair to the right of the fireplace—the one with its back toward the front hall. At least I know now they were Clare's legs. I couldn't see the rest of her at the time. I was real upset, but I didn't think of murder—I mean attempted murder. I thought of a fainting spell, an accident, something like that.

"I went around to the back door hoping it was unlocked, and it was. So in I rushed. And stopped dead when I saw the fire things thrown all around and then the blood by her head. I just plain wanted to scream and run. But I took myself in hand, told myself whoever did it wouldn't be apt to hang around the scene of the crime asking for trouble. I went closer and bent over and felt her hand. It felt cold as marble. And she didn't seem to be breathing. So I marched to the hall phone and called the Homicide Department and asked for you. Then I called Dr. Ferris. He's her doctor, and mine too.

"I forgot to say, I locked the kitchen door. Oh, and just as I started to phone I noticed a funny thing. The door in the hall leading down to the cellar was part-way open, and I know Clare always keeps it locked tight because the stairs are so steep. It sounds silly now, but I got the awful feeling that whoever tried to kill Clare was hiding down there in the dark. I slammed that door fast and locked it."

38

"Excuse me," said Tuck, and left the two women.

"Dr. Ferris came right away," continued Mrs. Macabee, speaking to Brigit. "He gave Clare an injection and after a few minutes it kind of brought her around. But she couldn't talk yet. She just looked at me in a vague way, and then over toward the fireplace. That brought something back, because she seemed to be terrified and tried to get up, but the doctor wouldn't let her."

Tuck returned. "There's no one in the cellar, Mrs. Macabee. And no window he could have got out by. Thank you, Mrs. Macabee. We won't need you any more if you want to go home. Oh, one thing. You said it was ten-thirty when you rang the bell?"

"Yes." She rose, gathering the bulk of her coat about the bulk of her body. "I'll just phone down the street for Mr. Macabee to meet me," she said. "These goons and degenerates pop right out of the bushes! Ever since the war. I won't say a lot of fine people haven't come to L. A., because they have. But there's no feast without some crumbs."

On the flowered hearthrug, in the heavy shadow cast by the wing chair bearing the embroidery hoop, Brigit found it—a white cotton glove, a woman's glove, palm up. It had a gauntlet cuff. Small stitches outlined the seams of the fingers. For half their length they were soaked with dry brown blood as though they had once probed a wound. To Brigit the sinisterly stained glove seemed both macabre and obscene.

Tuck took it more calmly. As he outlined its place on the rug with white chalk he said, "It's just as well Mrs. Macabee didn't see this. We'd have a homicidal maniac to look for, sure as feasts leave crumbs."

"What in God's name is that?" asked Dr. Ferris. Brigit turned, saw the doctor staring at the bloodstained glove in

39

Tuck's hand with what in anyone but a man of science she would have called revulsion.

"Perhaps Mrs. Crone can tell us," Tuck said.

The doctor's voice had a ramrod in it. "I cannot allow any further shock or exertion tonight."

At that moment a key scraped in the lock of the front door. As they all turned to stare toward the front hall Eric Crone came into the house. He moved wearily. To Brigit the big man looked much older than when she had last seen him and in some way defeated. When he saw the two detectives and the doctor a look of surprise flooded his full face, to be replaced by agonized concern when he saw his wife lying on the sofa. He moved toward her woodenly, his open camel's-hair coat hanging from a body that suddenly seemed to have the stiff, mechanical limbs of a robot.

The doctor's spare neat form stepped to Eric Crone's side. "There's nothing to worry about. Your wife has had a very narrow escape, but she's going to be all right. She was apparently struck by a prowler, and this brought on a heart attack of considerable severity. Whether there is a fracture in addition to concussion I cannot yet say."

Eric Crone's head turned to the doctor slowly. "I didn't know there was anything wrong with her heart."

A weak voice spoke slowly from the sofa. "A man got in by the back door, Eric. About an hour after you left. I think he tried to kill me."

In unison Tuck and Brigit stepped toward Mrs. Crone. "Did you see him?" Tuck asked.

"No." With her dark eyes raised to her husband's face Mrs. Crone asked anxiously, "Is Helene all right? Isn't she with you?"

Eric Crone sank suddenly into the chair the doctor had occupied. He looked down at his dangling hands as he

40

spoke. "She's with Mrs. Ames. She wanted to go to a motel, but I suggested Ruby's."

"You did the right thing." Eric Crone raised his head in a dazed way at the sound of his wife's gentle voice. One of her hands was reaching out for her husband's; he took it numbly. Brigit was surprised to see that tears shone in Mrs. Crone's eyes. "Oh, Eric, I've been so wrong, so wrong about everything!"

"Could you give us some idea of what happened?" Tuck asked.

"I'm in the dark," said Eric Crone faintly.

While Mrs. Crone spoke she looked up at her husband. "After you went out to Helene's I was very upset and sat by the fireplace sewing. You know how that calms me. It must have been about half an hour later that I heard a sound in the kitchen—a faint scrape, like someone bumping into the table in the dark. I sat very still, I remember, listening, but there was no other sound. I decided that I was imagining things. The wind was making such queer noises. And I thought the back door was locked. I realize now that Helene must have left it unlatched when she went for a walk at six this evening. So I went on with my sewing. Then I realized I had to clear the table and do the dishes. I put my sewing down on the arm of the chair—that chair." Her eyes, beginning to fill with remembered terror, moved to the wing chair which stood to the right of the fireplace, its broad high back to the hall doorway. "And then, as I stood up I was suddenly sure that someone was standing in the front hall, behind me. It was a dreadful moment. I knew the sound I'd heard in the kitchen was not the wind and no trick my mind had played. I screamed. I think I screamed. I think I remember quick footsteps behind me. The last thing I saw was the cuckoo clock. It said nine-thirty exactly. I don't

41

remember being hit, or falling, or anything else at all until I opened my eyes and saw Dr. Ferris bending over me and heard Mrs. Macabee saying something about a prowler." Mrs. Crone shut her eyes, as though the recital had wearied her. Her hand still gripped her husband's tightly.

"When you came to, did you notice this?" asked Tuck quietly and held out the white glove.

Mrs. Crone opened her eyes, turned her head slightly on the pillow. The long stare she gave the glove seemed to Brigit to exaggerate the ghastliness of the dried brown blood on its fingers. Eric Crone was looking at the glove with amazement; he turned his head from it to his wife's face.

"Was that glove *here?*" asked Mrs. Crone stupidly. Tuck nodded. Her face as white as the glove's clean cuff, Mrs. Crone asked, "But why would he leave that *here?* Was it some kind of horrible joke? Or did he drop it by accident?"

"Why do you say 'he'?" Tuck asked.

"Because it was a man who attacked me. I'm certain of that much." She met their watching faces with a puzzled, faint smile. "I'm sorry I can't tell you why I know this." She frowned and her voice became petulant, unsure of itself. "I just don't seem to remember." As her white eyelids came down, her slender body seemed to flatten on the sofa.

Dr. Ferris stepped between his patient and further questions. With his cold gray eyes on Tuck he spoke to Eric Crone. "Mr. Crone, I want you to telephone to the Good Samaritan Hospital for me. Tell them I said to have a bed ready for your wife. She will be there at least two days for observation and rest."

Eric Crone moved like a big trained bear toward the lighted hall. He paused for a moment in the doorway to glance vaguely upward as the wind roared sullenly in the chimney, blew fine ashes out of the fireplace over the white-china cat, the bloodstained hearth, the fallen fire irons.

Then, after a quick look at the blood on the iron shaft of the poker, he stepped into the hall, turned mechanically toward the telephone stand.

As Tuck slipped the glove into its Manila envelope he said matter-of-factly, "To brief matters, Mrs. Crone, you do not remember seeing the man who attacked you, and you did not see this glove until I showed it to you?"

"That's right," said Clare Crone in an exhausted voice.

The doorbell pealed. It was the police photographer, a fingerprint expert and a young, eager-looking reporter.

As Brigit and Tuck left the Crones' house the wind tried to flatten them against the closed door at their back. Far down the street the two rows of lumpy black trees were moving strongly in the gale, menacing yet impotent. Brigit thought of another windy night, six years before. Ruth Ann Briggs had lived on Acacia Street. But she had not, to anyone's knowledge, worn white cotton gloves on the night she died.

"It may not be human blood at all," said Tuck as they went down the front walk, the porch light pushing their long shadows ahead of them. "We'll leave the glove with the lab boys. The stain is an old one, but they should be able to tell us that much."

As they got into his long black sedan he added, "If that blood is human, we're face to face with the possibility that the man who hit Mrs. Crone is a most peculiar gent. And not a novice at attempted murder."

"Or murder, perhaps," said Brigit Estees.

The roar with which Tuck started the car showed that he was somewhat disturbed. He turned it toward the lighted boulevard and said, "Brigit, you are creating a mental trap into which you are falling fast. I admit the Briggs girl and Mrs. Crone were both hit on the head. I admit both lived on

Acacia Street when this happened to them. I admit there's a strong wind blowing tonight. But don't you see this makes it all the more preposterous to suppose there's any connection between the two crimes?"

"Oh, it's preposterous, all right," agreed Brigit. She was staring in fascination at the bland round moon riding serenely above the wind and the city. She was remembering that rain clouds had blotted out such a moon on such a night so many years ago. Do our lives depend on things like these? she wondered. If that moon had gone on shining, would a girl named Ruth Ann Briggs still be alive?

One thing was sure. The rain which fell that night had been the first factor which had helped her killer to escape them.

# 4

Y<small>OU MUST HAVE HAD</small> some reason to suspect me of murder," said Eric Crone to his wife.

After a bright warning that his visit must be brief, the nurse had departed with the air of conferring a favor on both husband and wife. Now they were alone, behind closed doors, in the blank impersonal hospital room where a shaft of pale afternoon sunlight fell on antiseptic surfaces.

Clare Crone had dreaded this visit all morning. Her husband looked strange from her nearly horizontal position on the high narrow iron bed, a giant staring down with the flat shielded eyes of cold, uneasy anger. "You must try to see this from my point of view, Eric," she said in a moderate tone.

"I am trying to, believe me," he remarked dryly. "It is not an easy job. As far as I can see, you have believed for six years that I killed a girl by bashing in her skull. The motive I find it impossible even to guess at. As for opportunity, that's a little clearer. I suppose it was the fact that I used your convertible that night, and that such a car was seen going toward the scene of the crime?"

"Not that alone. But you lied to me. You said you went to the library, Eric. But you didn't. Because two days later

45

the library sent a post card saying your books were overdue. To save you bother, I went over with it and told the librarian there must be a mistake, that you had been in night before last and certainly would have returned the books. The older librarian . . . what was her name? Miss Jellicoe, wasn't it? The thin one who was always so nice?"

"It doesn't matter."

"Well, anyway, she, Miss Jellicoe, was quite upset and began to check. And then a snippy young assistant librarian, the one with the long blonde hair, said, 'I'm afraid you've been misinformed, Mrs. Crone, because I happen to know your husband by sight and he wasn't in at all night before last, because I was on duty the whole evening and I didn't see him.' "

"I see," Eric Crone said dryly. "So you left the library realizing that I had murdered Ruth Ann."

"Certainly not! Why must you be so unkind? It's difficult enough without that. I decided that you had stopped in at the Blue Grotto." She saw his face change subtly. "But when I tried to find out if you had, the bartender, the fat one, said oh, no, you hadn't been in for a long time."

"Good old Jenkins," said Eric Crone in what seemed to his wife affectionate exasperation. "He was trying to do me a favor."

"And then there was the mud on the car," said Clare Crone quickly. "When I took it to be lubricated a few days after the murder I saw it up on that high thing, and all under the fenders and the lower side of the pan it was caked thick with splashes of mud. I hadn't been anywhere muddy and you know where they found her."

"We seem to have established the matter of opportunity. But what about motive? Why in God's name did you think I would kill a girl I'd spoken to at most three times?"

"How did I know that? How did I know what kind of a

46

girl she really was? How did I know whether you'd been seeing her secretly for months or not? I did know that on several occasions you had lied to me about where you'd been. She might have been one of these precocious creatures who carry on flirtations with older men and then threaten to blackmail them!"

"You have a mind like a sewer," Eric said conversationally.

"Eric! How dare you talk to me like——" She recalled that she, not he, now had explanations to make and cut off her sentence, at the same time pruning the anger from her voice. "And then there was the andiron," she went on calmly. "You took it down to the Fix-it shop to have it mended that night, remember? Only it was closed. So the two broken halves of the andiron were right there on the front seat of the car. And they said she'd been struck with something smooth and heavy."

He stopped staring at her, turned his wide back and walked to the window where he pretended to look out at the flat sprawl of the city merging out into a vague haze. He turned slowly. "There's a good deal you're holding back, Clare." He took a step toward her; it seemed a slow and rather menacing step. She gave a frightened glance toward the door. If only the nurse would come! "Those two detectives from Homicide may have swallowed your story about a prowler in the kitchen, but you can't expect me to. And that glove. What about that glove?"

For an instant her mind wavered between the truth and a falsehood. Looking up into her husband's bitterly angry eyes, she decided she preferred the doubts she had lived with so long to the certainty which the next few moments might reveal to her. "My story about the prowler happens to be the truth," she said with dignity. "I wish you'd go now. I don't care what you believe."

47

His face began to look puzzled. "You mean to tell me that on the very night I knocked you down for the first time in twenty-five years of marriage a screwball broke into the house less than an hour later and let you have it with the poker?" He began to shake his head—a slow, aggravating motion. "You must admit, Clare, that sounds somewhat unbelievable. But let it pass. Where did you get that bloody glove? What did you intend to prove with it? That I killed the Briggs girl, I presume."

Her mind wavered on the brink of a fateful act of candor. Once again she very vividly saw her gloved right hand force its way into the crevice at the bend of her car's red-leather seat, probing for her missing key ring. Once more she felt her fingers plunge into moisture, and once more she jerked them out, angrily certain that her husband had left her car open in the rain the night before. Again, in memory, she stared at the clear, bright, somewhat diluted blood on the glove's fingers. "Since you don't believe that I was hit by a prowler, there's very little use in my telling you about the glove," she said calmly. "You wouldn't believe that, either."

"I'll try," said her husband.

"Last night I was too upset to notice things closely. But I've been thinking about that glove all morning. Eric, I'm sure it's exactly like a pair Helene gave Ruth Ann Briggs for Christmas."

His face showed that she had confounded him utterly.

"As to why anyone would leave it on our hearthrug I have no idea," she added. "Have you?"

He frowned down at her with vacant eyes, his mind evidently trying to make sense of what she had just told him. At last he said slowly, "Tuck and Estees will have to know about this. They can check on the truth of it. My guess is that it's only a coincidence. After all, there must be thousands of white gloves like that one."

48

"That's just what I keep telling myself," said Clare Crone. "But just the same, as you say, they should know. Only I simply will not tell them, Eric, about our argument just before you left for Helene's. There is nothing to be gained from washing dirty linen in public."

He grinned down at her rather mirthlessly. " 'Argument' is rather an understatement. But it's a bad time to tell the world that our marriage isn't exactly happy. It won't help Helene, and it could put me in a mighty false position." He gave her a quizzical look. "Is your mind still a blank on the prowler angle?"

"I'm afraid so, Eric," she said. There was in her voice a faintly apologetic tone.

The nurse, exuding false professional cheerfulness, came in then on soundless white shoes to tell Eric Crone that it was time for him to leave. "I peeked in on you a few minutes ago," said the nurse, "but you were so busy chatting I hadn't the heart to interrupt you."

Clare and Eric Crone searched the woman's eyes and found them guileless; then they exchanged a brief glance with each other. It said that the pattern of many years would continue uninterrupted; they would behave in public as society expected them to, letting no stranger know of the latest clash between their unlike souls—a clash which again had illustrated a bitter lesson they had long since learned: If marriages are made in heaven, some seem destined to be lived on the outskirts of hell. But in that locality they were far from alone.

And each of them knew, in his own fashion, how foolish it was to speculate about the person he might have become had he married someone else. Choice of each other they saw as fated, and if young Eric at twenty-three had seen the young Clare's dainty coldness as virginal delicacy, and if she had mistaken his forthright sensuality for manly vigor,

those wishful illusions had died without drama, were long
forgotten—or nearly so.

"It was so fantastic," said Clare Crone to Richard Tuck
and Brigit Estees that night at seven o'clock. "But when I
woke up this morning I remembered where I had seen a
glove like that before. As my husband may already have
told you, my daughter gave poor little Ruth Ann Briggs a
pair like that for Christmas, just a little over a month before
she died." In the moment of silence that fell, Brigit saw
Clare Crone look at Tuck's long impassive face, then at her
own. It was a bright, intelligent look. "I happen to remember
those gloves because I selected them. They were 'Cre-
scendos.' I bought them at Bullock's a week before Christmas."

Brigit felt that Tuck was forcing himself not to look at
her, just as she was avoiding a stare at him.

"You people seem very calm," said Mrs. Crone. "I suppose in your type of work nothing is amazing. But to me,
the idea that the man who tried to kill me was carrying in
his pocket one of Ruth Ann's gloves . . . with her blood
on it . . ." She raised her thin shoulders in a nervous
shrug.

"The glove we found is a 'Crescendo,' all right," said
Tuck. "But you mustn't jump to conclusions, Mrs. Crone."

"That's what I keep telling myself," said Mrs. Crone in
a voice which tried to be matter-of-fact and failed by a slight
quaver—the sound that issues from a throat when it is tight
with fear.

To a stranger Tuck might look as impassive as ever, but
Brigit, who knew his face better than her own, saw that
he was faintly dazed by Mrs. Crone's story. She herself
could not speak for picturing a figure crouching over a dead
girl to steal a trifling bloodstained token which would re-

mind him of his moment of death-dealing and triumphant power. . . .

"I suppose," said Mrs. Crone, "that such a person is definitely insane."

"That's the most obvious explanation," Tuck agreed a little hollowly.

When the two big detectives had left her Clare Crone relaxed against her pillows, spent. I did what I could, she thought, to save him. To save all of us. There isn't anything I can do now but wait.

The moment when she had first seen the bright wet blood on the fingers of her white glove seemed distant and unreal to her. She found that she was overpoweringly sleepy. Her eyelids closed of their own enormous weight, blotting out the impersonal bareness of the hospital room and with it the grotesque events of the past twenty-four hours.

But she could not at once blot out a recurrence of the conviction that her husband had struck down, in an instant's blind violence, a precocious young wanton who had tempted his vulnerable heart only to laugh at his middle-aged ardor at last, killing his foolish dreams, wounding his manhood, and ending all sense of security forever. She slipped from these thoughts into a waking dream which had offered sanctuary a thousand times since the Briggs girl's murder. In fantasy her husband moved once again through a series of actions which exonerated him of guilt, explained the blood on the glove and made Ruth Ann's killer an unknown maniac, one of the thousands of degenerates who haunt big cities and who on a certain windy night had prowled Acacia Street.

"That's a good girl!" said the nurse's voice very far away. "We'll just go beddy-bye!" Safe in magic darkness, Clare Crone smiled faintly and slept at last.

# PART TWO

*The First Victim*

# 5

Ruth Ann Briggs had been halfway through her first
year at Hollywood High School, an "A" student, secretary
of her class, and without demerits. The neighbors said she
was a "good" girl. A few admitted that she began to act a
little "wild" after her father was inducted into the Army
and her mother went to work in an aircraft factory. But they
hastily added that she was not in the least "fast." After
all, many athletic girls affect a boy's tight blue jeans, many
pretty girls use lipstick too lavishly. And sweaters are
standard attire, although perhaps Ruth Ann's had revealed
too clearly that she was unusually well developed for a girl
of barely fifteen.

No one had the slightest notion why Ruth Ann's body,
one side of the skull crushed in, lay gently sprawled on lush
grass in a canyon twisting into the hills behind Hollywood.
But there it was found at noon on February 2, 1945, by three
Boy Scouts.

The discovery saved her reputation. She had been missing since eight-thirty the night before, but the news of her
murder came in time to still the rumor that she had run off
with a man. If she had, he had killed her—such exaggerated
punishment for the immorality of which neighbors on Aca-

55

cia Street had barely begun to suspect her that by dinnertime her killer had been labeled a homicidal maniac. Everyone agreed that his innocent victim had been a nice girl—an average, decent American high-school kid.

Acacia Street began at Hollywood Boulevard, was level for two blocks, then sloped gently northward to a cleft between two low, scrub-covered hills. The houses on the level stretch were solid frame structures built more than a quarter of a century before by uninspired carpenters. Their lawns were well tended and the sidewalks were thickly shaded by sullen flowerless acacia trees which held out massive clumps of narrow leaves the color of olives.

But most of the newer houses on the slope tried to be grander or more quaint. A nearly Colonial demimansion, two Spanish haciendas and a half-timbered Tudor establishment democratically mingled with smaller dwellings suggesting Cape Cod, provincial France and Anne Hathaway's cottage. There were also several houses suggesting nothing more remote than Los Angeles, and the Briggses' was one of these. Of pallid stucco, it gestured vaguely toward charm with bright-blue shutters and a roof of Mexican tiles. Before it stood an adolescent tree with too much sky showing between the branches. Like all the trees on upper Acacia Street it cast a frail and insignificant shadow. Brigit Estees and Richard Tuck soon learned that had such trees grown on lower Acacia Street, Ruth Ann Briggs might have entered her lighted house unharmed. For the black shadows below had conspired with her murderer.

On the night she died Ruth Ann returned later than she had intended from a British film at the Hawaii Theater on Hollywood Boulevard. She rode homeward on a red streetcar with a girl friend she had met at the theater late that afternoon. It was just eight-thirty when she got off at the foot of Acacia Street, waved back at her friend and walked into the heavy shadows of the trees, whose thick-leaved branches were twisting in the rising wind.

Just after the streetcar lumbered off Eloise Carewe noticed Ruth Ann's flowered scarf on the floor and picked it up. When Eloise got home she telephoned Ruth Ann to report that the scarf was safe. Mrs. Briggs answered, a little angry because Ruth Ann had said she would be home by seven. But Eloise Carewe explained that they saw the picture twice and stopped for hamburgers. "Tell her I've got her scarf," she said. After she hung up the receiver Eloise realized that nearly a quarter of an hour had passed since Ruth Ann got off the streetcar and began a walk which took only five minutes. But the notion that any harm had come to Ruth Ann never crossed her mind.

Mrs. Briggs had just started to mend Ruth Ann's green sweater. She had decided to make a good job of it by raveling some strands of yarn from a castoff sock which was exactly the same color. With a tired woman's obsession she became lost in the operation of pulling out several long strands of wool, then found herself half listening for the sound of her daughter's key in the lock. She was filled with a vague uneasiness which she attributed to the strange sounds created by the wind. Poinsettia stalks rapped against the side of the house, a windowpane rattled, and suddenly a draft sucked a door shut with a loud slam. Mrs. Briggs jumped up, her uneasiness congealed into awareness that Ruth Ann should have reached home by now, that too much time had passed.

With a sharp motion Mrs. Briggs put the sweater to one side, hurried to the hall and slipped on her coat. No longer tired, she stepped out into the riotous wind. As she hurried down her front walk she looked up and saw the moon gulped by a long black cloud. After it swallowed the moon the edges of the cloud grew brilliant, and the cloud was outlined in

57

silver against high dark space where other clouds were swiftly massing. Walking down Acacia Street to meet her daughter, Mrs. Briggs wondered when she had seen so queer a cloud before.

She did not encounter Ruth Ann. When she emerged from the shadows of the writhing trees and stood on the empty corner of the busy boulevard she found her mouth open in a limp "O," her icy palms pressed flat against her cheeks. A closed gasoline station glared bleakly on the opposite corner; the drugstore at her back contained no customer resembling her daughter, and beyond it stretched the dark windows of small closed shops, punctuated by the cobalt neon sign of the Blue Grotto. Inside the bar a piano jingled, a woman sang. Mrs. Briggs heard the distant mumble of rare thunder.

As she turned and hurried homeward her stomach felt as though a giant fist were squeezing it. Knowing that she would telephone the police unless she found at once that Ruth Ann was safe, she told herself that nothing could have happened in a few minutes on a quiet residential street.

But somehow, from that place and in that brief space of time, the girl had vanished.

Since the initial search by a squad car from the nearest police station led to no clue whatever, the Juvenile Division assigned Eric Crone to the case. He lived on Acacia Street and knew the dead girl by sight. It was ten when he answered the emergency telephone call, crossed the street and plodded up the slight slope. Even then, he later told the investigators from Homicide, even while he tried to calm the distraught mother and attempted to learn whether there was any youth with whom the girl might have eloped, he had been filled with the premonition that a much greater disaster had occurred.

58

"I had talked with her only a couple of times," Crone said, looking down at Ruth Ann's body, "but I got the impression of a sensible kid. And it takes very clever faking to fool me on juveniles. It seemed to me out of character for a girl of Ruth Ann's type to rush off with some young Romeo and leave her mother worrying all evening. From the first I was afraid that she had been abducted. I had hopes, for a while, of a description of a loitering car. No luck. Cars were seen passing, none stopping. For that we have those damned thick trees to thank."

"We don't know yet that there was a car," Richard Tuck pointed out.

"No, we don't, do we?" Crone admitted, rubbing his forehead wearily. "Well, this is one girl's disappearance that won't take much of Juvenile Division's time. I wish you luck, Tuck. If I can help you and Miss Estees in any way, let me know." He turned away, a tired man in need of sleep and a shave, and in a moment drove off in his heavy maroon sedan.

The only woman detective in the Homicide Department stood watching him go. It was plain to Brigit Estees that the murder of the young girl across the street had moved Eric Crone quite deeply, used as he was to violence among the young. She looked up at Tuck, but he did not share her interest in Crone. He was looking down at the body of Ruth Ann Briggs, his long face sad, his brown eyes full of wonder.

A light wind stirred tall February grass around a girl who did not stir. Blue eyes stared up with the vacancy of small wet flowers. The livid face was ghastly only at first glance; then it looked like the pallid clay of a statue discarded for rain to fall on, weirdly clad in a schoolgirl's yellow sweater, plaid skirt, open tan coat whose lining was mottled with dried rain. A red purse spilled trivial objects which gleamed in the waving grass.

59

There was no blood. The broken skull and drying wound did not seem real until a fly buzzed to a stop on matted hair and began its tiny exploration.

Tuck's long hand swept an arc above the fly. It buzzed away, an angry iridescence in the shallow grassy gully beside the canyon's earth road. The body lay only a quarter of a mile from the point where the asphalt of Acacia Street stopped as though chopped by a cleaver; yet the spot had a peculiar lonesomeness, isolated from sight and sound of the city by barren slopes without trees or houses.

Tuck turned slowly from the dead girl to take a big step out of the small gorge onto the road above. He pointed down at the road without comment. None was needed. Except for the marks of his tires and those of Eric Crone's sedan the moist soil was blank.

"That rain last night was sure a windfall for the killer," remarked Brigit. "That is, if he drove her here in a car."

"Which seems more likely than a helicopter, motorcycle, or surrey with the fringe on top," Tuck elaborated with heavy humor.

"Death was instantaneous, or nearly so," snapped the medical examiner half an hour later. A small man, Tuck's six feet five inches of height always seemed to bring out the doctor's acid side. "The distribution of post-mortem lividity is absolutely normal for the position of the body, no deviation whatsoever."

"That means she was killed here, doesn't it?" Brigit asked.

The little doctor gazed up at her as if he disliked amazons even more than giants. "It means, young woman, that since the blood begins to settle at once, and since it takes about four hours after death for the blood to reach the body's lowest level, and since to alter the body's position during

60

that four hours is to cause certain deviations in the distribution of lividity which I do not observe, there are three possibilities: The girl was killed right here in this gully, or she was placed here immediately after death, or she was brought here more than four hours later."

"No blood," said Tuck.

"I beg your pardon!"

"No blood. And that wound on her head must have bled."

"I'll say it did!" The medical examiner began a scholarly explanation involving a major, mangled artery.

"When did she die?" asked Brigit.

"I'd say between eight last night and two this morning."

"She died," Tuck corrected gently, "between eight-thirty last night and half-past nine."

"May I ask how you arrive at that hour?" With throttled violence the doctor snapped shut his black bag and rather impressively signaled the ambulance attendants.

"She was seen alive at eight-thirty by a witness we have no reason to doubt. It rained last night for about fifteen minutes between nine and half-past. It did not rain again. Therefore that was the rain which washed the blood away, and she must have been lying here when it fell."

"Two more facts," said the medical examiner. "The weapon was heavy and blunt and very smooth at the point of contact. And there are no signs of any violence aside from the fracture on the left side of the cranium, toward the back. Now here's something a little peculiar: Only one blow was struck, and on one of the stronger parts of the head. It was a blow of unusual violence, therefore. Yet there are no signs of violence aside from the smashed skull." As though rather pleased at presenting them with this complication he added, "As a rule, this degree of damage is caused by many blows and is almost always accompanied by other bruises and contusions. It's as though something fell on her out of the sky, like a meteor."

He turned to leave, then paused. "That was quite a wind last night, wasn't it! Blew my wife's hat clear down the street. My daughter went after it. Got it, too." He smiled a little. "A kid of sixteen can run as if the Devil's at her heels." His eyes slid to the body being lifted into the gray police ambulance. "Why the devil didn't she run?" he asked of no one.

"Since there aren't any signs of a struggle, she couldn't have been raped," said Brigit. "Was she seduced?"

"If you think I can answer that at this point, you somewhat overestimate my powers," the medical examiner snapped. But both Tuck and Brigit forgave his sharp reply, for they knew that Ruth Ann's youth had linked the dead girl with his own young daughter who had run blithely after a hat while Ruth Ann approached the last moment of her life.

The body gone, Brigit and Tuck turned their attention to the dead girl's purse—of red leatherette simulating alligator skin. The wide scattering of its hoard of small objects suggested that it had been flung into the ditch. Inside the handbag they found a tooled-leather wallet, a yellow lead pencil, a crumpled handkerchief and a change purse containing forty-two cents and seven bobby pins. Around the handbag lay a tube of lipstick, a gold compact, a comb, a fountain pen, a key chain and a hard green plastic cigarette case which contained a package of Lucky Strike cigarettes. One third of the foil at the top had been torn away neatly, revealing that only one had been smoked.

The key chain held two keys, one for a Yale lock, the other a tiny gold key only half an inch long, plainly belonging to a diary. In the wallet were three dollar bills, a student identification card and a photograph of a man about forty who wore the uniform and insignia of a technical sergeant in the Army of the United States.

The bloody chamois was discovered by Tuck, lying only a few yards from where the body had lain—a wad of dingy tan that was barely discernible against the earth showing between two patches of grass. The outer part was stiff from rain, but when Tuck spread it open he looked down at a solid stain of still-moist blood.

"There *was* a car," he called to Brigit and strode toward her holding up his find.

"And she was killed in it," Brigit whispered. She saw a faceless form wiping red hands in a gesture as ordinary as that of a garage mechanic, then bending to cleanse the seat of an automobile which a few minutes before had looked like any other.

Mrs. Macabee was a stout, middle-aged woman with a crisp tongue, a falling bosom and flobby arms which seemed designed solely for the kneading of dough, the rolling of pie crust. She lived in a large comfortable house which stood just above the last acacia tree, at the point where the sparse-treed slope began to rise. On the night of February first she had stood looking out her front window from 8:25 until 9:00. She had recognized Mrs. Briggs when she passed under the street light; she saw Mrs. Briggs return up the street out of the tree's shadow a few minutes later; she did not see Ruth Ann at all. And she was prepared to swear on any number of Bibles that exactly six cars, no more and no less, went up Acacia Street.

She had been watching with controlled anguish and boiling rage for her husband, having just learned by telephone that Mr. Macabee had spent two hours imbibing immoderately in a bar near his office, from which he had departed singing "The Road to Mandalay."

"When he gets to *that* stage he can't steer the car up the driveway without running over the flower bed alongside the house. And I spent two whole afternoons putting in pansies and petunias and they were coming along so nicely! My plan was to gallop out and stand right in the middle of our driveway with my arms out so he'd *have* to stop, and then I'd take the wheel. Which is what I did. But it was nine o'clock before he got here, and by then I was more worried than mad. So I said to him, 'Mr. Macabee, move over!' And let me tell you, he moved!"

"I'll say he did," said Mrs. Macabee's brother, who had appeared just after the telephone call which had revealed Mr. Macabee's deplorable state and had remained, as he frankly admitted, to act as umpire. "A fly couldn't of crawled past her," he stated.

Mrs. Macabee remembered three of the passing cars very clearly: a hopped-up Ford like the one driven by the boy up the hill, a large dark sedan which could have been the one belonging to the old gardener whose house stood at the mouth of the canyon, and a long gray convertible like the one driven by Mrs. Eric Crone and her daughter Helene. The other three cars had registered on Mrs. Macabee's mind only as anonymous shapes passing swiftly in the windy darkness and not containing her husband.

In farewell Mrs. Macabee said, "It seems silly now, worrying over those pansies and petunias. She was such a sweet girl, such a nice girl! And her mother working so hard, and her father in the Army. Oh, I hope the murderer's hung high as Hamen!"

The hopped-up Ford had indeed belonged to the boy up the street; he had reached home the night before at twenty minutes to nine and had spent the next three quarters of an hour talking to his girl friend on the telephone—a fact his exasperated family recalled all too well. The old gardener

64

had not used his black sedan the night before, having been ill in bed with influenza—a fact attested by his wife and the doctor who paid a house visit at seven-thirty. And when they questioned Mrs. Crone she said that her gray convertible had been in her garage from five in the afternoon of the day of the murder until two the following afternoon when she went shopping. "It was for a wedding gift for the daughter of an old and dear friend. I wouldn't have gone if it hadn't been vital. I was terribly disturbed by Eric's horrible news at lunch. That poor girl!" Her drawn face attested to a greater concern than her words.

The balance of that first afternoon of the investigation revealed that the little gold key most probably belonged to a diary which Ruth Ann's aunt had given her for Christmas. It was not found. The photograph in the wallet was of her father. The bloody chamois was of a make which could have been bought in almost any gas station in California and a number of other states as well.

The fingerprint expert was not very hopeful. Even had the murderer handled the purse or its contents, all but a few objects had lain out in a heavy downpour.

The medical examiner said that Ruth Ann had died chaste; he made an obvious pun about that.

Two of the city's newspapers managed sly suggestions of a secret rendezvous with a sweetheart of murderous disposition. The majority favored a reckless ride with a maniac previously unknown. Neighbors, friends and relatives all said that they did not believe Ruth Ann would have gone riding with a stranger. For a time the innuendoes of snide journalism had no effect on them. Monotonously, sincerely, carelessly or with tear-filled eyes they continued to say, "She was a nice girl, a sensible girl. She wouldn't have got into a stranger's car, not in a hundred years—she just wasn't that kind."

But she had got into someone's car unless the gale itself had blown her to that dark ravine, unless the black cloud the mother saw had dropped down and swallowed the daughter as it had swallowed the moon.

## 6

Ruth Ann wasn't allowed to date boys," said Eloise Carewe. "Not until she was sixteen, her mother said. But she'd of liked to." A pretty, brown-eyed blonde, Eloise fought tears. "If one of the fellas she knew at school had of driven up after she got off the streetcar and offered her a lift, she might of taken him up on it. The wind, the way it was blowing last night, it made me feel kind of zippy. Like I wanted something different to happen, right out of the blue!" She recalled what had happened out of the blue, and her tears fell as suddenly as had the brief rain of the night before.

But Eloise could not or would not name any high-school boys who might have offered a ride to the dead girl. "Ask Helene Crone," said Eloise. "She used to drive Ruth Ann home from school when she had the car. And Ruth Ann might have got kind of chatty with Helene or maybe asked her advice about some fella, Helene being on the Girls' Senior Council and all."

In her chintz and flounced room Helene Crone lay stretched across the bed on her stomach, a schoolbook open to the play of *Macbeth*. A pertly pretty girl, she wore faded blue jeans, scuffed saddle oxfords and a boy's white cable-knit sweater which was many sizes too large. With her chin cupped in her hands she blinked wisely up at them. "Ruth Ann was no angel," she said. "No one drives a girl to a dark canyon except to pitch the woo, and Ruth Ann knew that as well as I do!"

"Helene!" said Mrs. Crone, entering with a pale shocked smile. "These people will get the wrong impression of you!"

The glance Helene gave her mother strove for cynicism. "That's better than getting the wrong impression of Ruth Ann. Who, I'll remind you, is lying on a marble slab. Someone put her there, and it won't help any to go on insisting that she was 100-per-cent angel."

"She was a *very* nice girl," stated Mrs. Crone as if this remark erased all her daughter had just said. It seemed to Brigit that Mrs. Crone was unduly shocked by the fact that a girl who had ridden home from school beside her daughter was now violently dead. "A very nice girl indeed," she repeated.

"What you don't know about nice girls would fill a book the size of Shakespeare," said Helene.

"I don't know what I'm going to do with her," said Mrs. Crone to Brigit, then gave a slight start as her husband silently appeared in the doorway just behind her. He was puffing a pipe, and his large and tawny mustache helped to conceal his expression from her. "Helene's right, I'm afraid, Clare," he said somewhat diffidently. "Pretty generalities aren't going to help much." As he looked at his daughter Mrs. Crone could see a slight change come into his eyes, an almost negligible change, but it seemed to create a rapport with Helene.

"I wash my hands of you both," said Mrs. Crone with a thin, false smile.

"Speaking of washing hands," said Helene, "I sure think Macbeth is a corny character!" She looked up at Tuck.

"Real murderers don't slop over with remorse, do they?"

"It seems to me, Helene," said Mrs. Crone with brisk distaste, "that we have discussed morbid irrelevancies quite long enough. I suggest that you answer the questions these people want to ask you and then go on with your homework."

The questions drew from Helene the information that the night before she had gone to a dance with a college boy who was a drip, that she had driven Ruth Ann home from school the previous afternoon and that Ruth Ann had behaved exactly as usual. Helene agreed with Eloise Carewe that the dead girl might have accepted a friendly lift on such a windy night, but she said she knew of no boy who had been friendly with Ruth Ann Briggs. "Not that friendly anyway, because, as I said, she wouldn't have gone riding up the canyon with someone she didn't really go for in a large way." After a brief pause she added, "And I know for a fact that Desmond Grover isn't any cradle snatcher. He told me so—" she dimpled—"the last time he phoned me and asked for a date!"

"Who is Desmond Grover?" Tuck asked.

"Oh, a senior out at school. Ruth Ann had a crush on him, I think. I've gone out with him a few times. He's a nut, but definitely attractive." Her dimples showed again, then she sobered. "If you ask me, I think you should find out where old Mr. Bugg was last night. Ugh, but he's a nasty old man. I remember when I was younger he used to try to give me bags of candy. He's got a screw loose somewhere, but definitely. And the Buggs live at the top of the street, right by the entrance to the canyon, too."

There was little doubt that old Mr. Bugg was a victim of senile mental decay as well as extreme deafness. He was a retired gardener, once employed by the city, and had a reputation for trying to flirt with the younger housewives whose gardens he tended. Perpetually bent as though peering for aphides or snails, he had a loose mouth and pallid, hopeful eyes under the shadow of an old visored cap. Mrs. Bugg was a wide, stately German lady with a broad pale face from which tiny gray eyes stared flatly. Her hair was braided across her large head and looked unnaturally tidy. So did her house, filled with calmly ugly furniture. "He don't hear so goot," she explained unnecessarily, and then she added, "I think maybe I seen de car of de fellow dat killed de Briggs girl."

It was a few minutes after nine the night before when Mrs. Bugg had gone to the front window, marveling at the fury of the wind. The three tall thin palm trees before her house had been swaying to and fro uneasily, but the central one had executed a wider swing, its dry fronds rattling menace. She had remarked to her husband that it was probably rotten at the root and should be taken out as soon as he was well. It was as she had stood watching the palms' eccentric dance that she saw a long convertible coupé, the top closed, pass out of the dark canyon and down Acacia Street. She was absolutely certain that the time was about five minutes after nine: A radio program which had begun at eight-thirty had ended a few minutes before. Furthermore, as she stood idly watching the car's tail lights disappear down the street the sudden, brief rain began to fall. The morning paper said it began at five minutes after nine.

When asked for a fuller description of the convertible coupé Mrs. Bugg said that it looked like the long gray car belonging to a woman down the street named Mrs. Crone.

But Mrs. Crone reiterated that her gray convertible had been in her garage from five in the afternoon until two the following day when she had gone shopping. She also stated that she had five witnesses to the fact that she had been in her home from eight-thirty until eleven o'clock. These were irreproachable wives and mothers, members of the Third Thursday Literary Committee of which she happened to be chairman.

The next morning a Mr. Helios telephoned the Homicide Department. He lived on the west side of Acacia Street, three houses from the corner. After making it clear that he was a rug dealer with an excellent credit rating he spoke of his duty as a citizen. He then said, "Night before last when that little girl up the street got killed, my car is parked out front. When I hear the rain start I grab my umbrella, run down the walk to get her into the garage. What do I see? Two houses down the street, nearly to the boulevard, this car is parked. It's a convertible coupé—you know, with a top that goes open or shut."

"Did you notice the color? The make?" asked Brigit in some excitement. More than once a call like this, from a citizen like Mr. Helios, had been the feather's weight to balance the scales of justice.

"Sure I noticed the color," Mr. Helios said. "It's gray. Late model, good condition. A big car—Cadillac, Packard, Lincoln maybe. With the back to me I'm not gonna say I'm certain. But here's the thing! This car, she's parked near the corner, out from under the trees. And the top's down!"

"You mean open?"

"Open! Down! Back! That car, she's open in the rain like a shoe, like a bucket! Accident? Maybe. But maybe, too, someone figured to let that rain wash some blood away."

When Eric Crone learned of Mr. Helios' telephone call a sheepish look settled on his ruddy face and a faint smile

71

raised the corners of his mustache. "I hate to ruin such a good lead, but I'm afraid that car Mr. Helios saw was mine. Or rather, my wife's."

"But Mrs. Crone said it was in the garage all night!" said Brigit, while in memory Mrs. Crone's face became enigmatic.

"She probably thinks it was. You see, Clare asked me to drive down to the boulevard on an errand, and I used her convertible because I'd left my sedan at the corner garage overnight for a lube job. Apparently I didn't mention this to her. There wasn't any need to, because I have an extra key to the convertible. My wife was entertaining a lot of women that night, so at about eight o'clock I stopped into the Blue Grotto for a couple of drinks. I parked at the foot of Acacia Street, the west side, just where those trees begin —just where Mr. Helios saw the convertible with the top open. Well, the top of mine was open, all right. I didn't notice the rain begin, and when I went out to my car at about nine-thirty there was the damned top back. But that's not all. I found I'd lost my keys. They didn't turn up in the Blue Grotto, and I had to telephone the auto club and have them send out a locksmith." He looked at Tuck with a faintly grim smile. "You're a bachelor, but I think you can understand why I didn't go out of my way to tell my wife all this."

"Is this what you came over to explain to us?" Tuck asked.

"No. That phone call from Helios sidetracked me. I came to tell you that the bartender at the Blue Grotto just telephoned me at my office. He said my keys were found. But he mainly wanted to ask me to stop in at the Grotto as soon as possible. He said he had something peculiar to show us. He said it might have something to do with the Briggs case. I couldn't get a plain statement from him; he just kept saying we'd have to see it. He sounded very uneasy."

72

The Blue Grotto was well named, being both blue and grotesque. Cobalt lights, half hidden by abalone shells, cast an aqueous glow on rugged brown plaster painted to resemble the walls of a cave, although not too convincingly. Fish nets were draped here and there, and from the ceiling over the bar hung a life-sized mermaid, looking as if dead.

The fat bartender looked relieved when he saw Eric Crone, and at once held up a small brown-leather key container initialed "E. C." in gold. "Found it when he swept out good yesterday. Got kicked 'way back under one of the booths. These folks detectives?"

Introductions were performed. Mr. Jenkins was not only bartender but also co-owner of the Blue Grotto. In appropriate costume he could have presided over any pub in any century. His round red face wore an almost sincere professional jollity even as he earnestly told them that the good name of his bar meant as much to him as that of his wife. Then, exuding reluctant honesty, he led them to the white spinet piano on a small dais at the far end of the long dim cave. "Since the war, business has been good, folks. So we been having entertainment. A piano player every night and on week ends a girl singer. Patriotic, you might call it. A little something extra for the boys. Well, the singer noticed this last night, late, and I phoned Mr. Crone here first thing this morning." He pointed a sausage finger at a thin red-brown smear on the piano's glazed white side. It was thigh-high just about where a person of average height would press against the piano to watch the player's nimble fingers or to join in singing "Sweet Adeline."

"College kids and our boys in uniform go for singing stuff, so I tell the piano player to strike up some college and Army songs now and then. The kids love it. They pack around this-here piano like so many sardines." His simile evidently struck him as unsuitable, for he glanced unhappily

73

down at the red mark which had been made by no sardine. "There *could* be a perfectly innocent explanation for that stain. A cut leg. Or maybe it isn't blood at all." . . .

It was blood, and could have come from the same source as a solution obtained from a matted lock of the dead girl's hair. The schoolgirl's killer had almost certainly mingled with the crowd in the Blue Grotto after the crime.

"Which is perfectly plausible," said Eric Crone. "It was a miserable night, wet and windy, and the Grotto was convenient. The killer probably washed his hands in the lavatory, but missed seeing that one bloodstain. Which suggests dark clothing. Too bad it's February instead of June."

"Too bad he didn't leave his driver's license or a key ring with his initials on it," said Tuck. His voice, Brigit noted, was jaunty, for him. She also felt cheered by Mr. Jenkins' find, which narrowed their field of operations and had given them a dim picture of the murderer's movements.

"What kind of person goes into a crowded bar right after he's killed someone?" she asked. "And why?" She looked around the Blue Grotto. "The answer's all around us. The killer knew this place would be dark, crowded, full of people watching the singer and piano player. He'd been here before!"

"Maybe," Tuck agreed. "But what interests me more is the mental angle. The absence of fear, of shame."

"Or perhaps their presence," said Eric Crone. "People are sometimes driven by fear and shame to wild acts of bravado by means of which such feelings are denied and triumphed over. At least," he added, "I have found this to be true among juveniles."

The piano player, a young man both sullen and shy, could not or would not remember anything about the patrons who packed the Blue Grotto on the night of February first. But the girl who had sung there that night and the following night was more accommodating and uninhibited.

She went by the name of Lily Tripoly. The surname was, by odd chance, her own, although she confessed that her mother had baptized her Gertrude. She was a tiny, busty brunette whose cheerfully risqué songs had given her a certain local following, particularly among the college and high-school crowds. She remembered the good-looking blond boy and the fattish redhead because she had heard the latter mention the name "Ruth Ann."

"Of course, it didn't mean anything to me at the time," Miss Tripoly said. "But the next day when I read in the paper about the Briggs kid I remembered it. The redhead was sitting in the last booth near the piano with two sailors. The blond boy was on the last stool of the bar, just opposite her. He was alone. She kept looking at him, but he didn't seem to notice her. Just after I finished singing, the red-headed girl—she was the lardy type all got up with flowers in her hair—started to go to the little-girls' room, and when she passed the blond boy she pretended to see him for the first time and I heard her say in a loud, catty voice, 'Why, Mr. Grover! All alone? Couldn't you rate a date with Ruth Ann?' "

"You're sure she said 'Ruth Ann'?"

"Absolutely. The boy handled a neat brush-off. She tried to freeze him with this grand stare, see, but he just grinned at her, and then she made an elegant exit to the can. He looked like a high-school or college kid, a classy-frat type. She was just a run-of-the-mill heifer. Looked about twenty but might have been younger. No class, no charm, no brains. And, I'd guess, a yen for the blond boy."

Mr. Jenkins' intense desire to impress on the police the fact that he never served minors any drink stronger than a cola did not agree with Lily Tripoly's statement that both

75

the blond boy and the red-haired girl had partaken generously of a stronger stimulant. "I remember that their eyes had that excited glaze kids' eyes get when they've had one or two more than they can handle," she said.

Of all the faces she had seen that night, these two alone stood out, because the dead girl's name had passed between them. It was about a quarter to ten when their encounter occurred. Lily Tripoly did not notice when either of them came in or departed.

The blood mark found on the side of the piano did not excite her. "Whoever leaned there did it either before I got here or about ten o'clock, after I finished my second vocal. The piano player gave out then with a couple of college songs—'A Rambling Wreck from Georgia Tech' for one, I remember. There was the usual mob around the piano, singing off key. But I didn't notice anyone in particular. Maybe because there were a lot of uniforms, everyone looking pretty much alike."

She ended wistfully, "I wish I could have been more help to you. Maybe it sounds hard as nails, but my picture in the paper as star witness wouldn't do me a lot of harm. Gee, this is a tough town to get a start in! Oh, well, I'll make it yet."

"Do you think you could identify the boy and girl you told us about if you saw them again?"

"Sure. And glad to help. I'm not one of your sentimental dames, but I got a kid sister who's fifteen years old."

# 7

THE GENTLEMEN of the press made as much as they could of the murder car, to which some referred as "The Phantom Auto." What face had smiled at Ruth Ann Briggs while an arm thrust open the door of an automobile and a friendly voice offered safe transport home? To what ears did Ruth Ann perhaps tell the plot of the movie she saw twice? Why did she drive with her killer up that dark street, past her lighted house and into the canyon beyond? The wind might have drowned her scream, but why had it not been backed by an effort to escape? And it could not have been, for the girl's skin bore not so much as a bruise the size of a pea, the scratch a playful kitten might have made. No bonds, no chloroform, no knockout drops accounted for her strange passivity. What, then, had been the hypnotic charm of the car's phantom driver?

"A friend," Tuck said. "There's still no other answer. It was someone she knew, wasn't afraid of and who let her have it fast. No one, not even Ruth Ann herself, knew she would see a movie twice and walk up Acacia Street an hour and a half later than her mother expected her. That suggests that the murder happened out of coincidence. An unforeseen meeting between the predestined killer and the predestined victim. I keep thinking of a mixed-up high-school kid."

"Do you know how many kids go to Hollywood High School?" asked Brigit conversationally.

Tuck's long face grew sadder. "I wish I knew something about juveniles."

"They're a lot like people," said Brigit. "Only it shows more."

Painstakingly conversational interviews with Ruth Ann's classmates revealed the names of three people who might have offered her a ride which might have been accepted. These three were Desmond Grover, Dayleen Burke and Manuel Reyes.

Desmond Grover, blond, boyish and handsome, and the black sheep of a wealthy and socially prominent family, had already been in trouble with the police.

At the age of fifteen he was found to have been the author of the five mysterious notes which for two weeks had terrified the pretty and very ignorant Mexican maid of the family next door. In the best detective-story tradition, these notes had been pieced together from words cut from newspapers. They had threatened Dolores with kidnaping by a white-slave gang unless she revealed the combination of the safe where the family jewels were kept. The first two warnings had been sent by mail; the rest were found here and there about the house and yard where the maid would come upon them in the performance of her duties.

She showed the first warning to her employers, who laughingly dismissed it as the trick of some child. They pointed out that there were no jewels in the house anyhow, as they were kept in the safe-deposit box at the bank. So the maid suffered the next three notes in silence. But the fifth one broke her nerve utterly, and she was found packing her suitcase. As servants were difficult to obtain, her employers took a different view of the matter and summoned the police. A plain-clothes man was stationed in the house and the next day apprehended Desmond Grover in the act of sliding a sixth note under the screen of the maid's downstairs room by means of a kitchen spatula. The boy was turned over to an officer from Juvenile Division. This officer happened to be Eric Crone. Although for a short time somewhat apprehensive and chagrined, Desmond Grover soon took the matter very lightly. He said he had noticed the maid's "colossal stupidity" and had wanted to see if such a kiddish trick would frighten her. Since the maid's employers were friendly with the Grovers, and since the maid was easily persuaded to press no charge, the matter was dropped.

Three years later when Desmond Grover was questioned by Tuck and Brigit about his relationship with Ruth Ann Briggs he boldly admitted to having been somewhat attracted to the dead girl. "A mighty cute little piece. Not too long on brains maybe, but gentle and sweet. I don't like these babes who go around shoving out their bazooms and trying to look sexy and hard-to-get at the same time. Ruth Ann hadn't learned that stuff yet, and that's why I liked her." With a rather annoying grin he added, "I'd have been glad to offer her a ride in my jalopy any time. Only I didn't. For one thing, I didn't have my car the night she died. My father took the keys last week on account of two tickets I got for speeding." Beyond this he offered no alibi for the night of February first. "I was just down on Hollywood Boulevard, strolling around and looking for some fun."

"You also stopped in at the Blue Grotto," Tuck said.

"So what? Sure, I dropped in around ten to hear Lily Tripoly chant a few ditties. You can't arrest everybody who goes to the Grotto, can you?"

Desmond Grover, they learned, had transferred to the public high school from a preparatory school which took a rather serious view of a prank involving dynamite. His new friends had nicknamed him "Dizzy Rover" and were half contemptuous, half affectionate in speaking of him. They saw that beneath his swagger there was a desire to be liked by those boys he considered his intellectual equals. They thought him clever beyond average, but without ability to use his brain constructively. "He's always lousing himself up, trying for an effect," said the boy who was President of the Student Body. "He thinks he's a cynical misogynist, but actually he's slightly afraid of women, I think. I don't like a chaser, but a guy his age ought to have a steady girl."

When asked about Desmond's fondness for Ruth Ann Briggs the Student Body President said, "I think he really went for her. Whenever she passed us during noon hour he'd make a pretty nice comment. I razzed him about her being a freshman, a kid, and I think it made him a little sore. 'Why not pick on somebody your own age?' I said."

"You keep your hands off Dez Grover or you'll wind up a sorry little character," Dayleen Burke had said to Ruth Ann Briggs in the girls' lavatory in Science Building at two in the afternoon, just a week before Ruth Ann's death.

As the girl's vice-principal understood the story behind the episode, Dayleen Burke had, at noon hour, approached Desmond Grover to ask him to a party at her home and he had pointedly refused the invitation. He had then rather loudly praised the face and figure of a passing girl, who had happened to be Ruth Ann Briggs. Still stinging from Desmond's rebuff, Dayleen encountered Ruth Ann in the lavatory two hours later and delivered herself of the reported threat.

Ruth Ann had been frightened and upset and had fled the lavatory believing she had encountered a lunatic, a feeling somewhat augmented when one of the girls who had witnessed the occurrence confided that Dayleen went with a wild crowd who smoked marijuana. But then Ruth Ann began to feel angry. What right had anyone to humiliate her like that? So she marched into the vice-principal's office and in a voice trembling with her suppressed sense of outrage told that lady what had just occurred.

"She said," recalled the vice-principal, " 'I'm no tattletale, but goodness knows how many of the girls who heard Dayleen believe that I'm the kind of girl who flirts with boys, and I'm not.' "

Dayleen, however, had quite a different story to tell. In a low but full voice that seemed destined one day to belong to a fat woman, with crudely feigned innocence and indignation Dayleen repeated to Brigit and Tuck what she had already told the vice-principal. In brief, she had merely tried to play big sister to an innocent little freshman. "I happen to know that Desmond Grover goes with a fast older crowd that smokes marijuana. I was just trying to warn Ruth Ann when I said, 'Listen, honey, you stay away from that Dez Grover. He's no good, and you'll be sorry if you get tangled up with such a fellow.' "

Exhibiting the heavy shrewdness which so often accompanies ignorance, Dayleen added, "Nobody can prove from what I said that I wasn't just trying to be a big sister to her!" In Dayleen's pale-blue eyes Brigit fancied that she caught that small evil flicker of secret merriment which warms the brains of those to whom the police force is the eternal enemy.

But Eric Crone, who had volunteered his services in the questioning of the high-school students, had a way with juveniles. He extracted the information that on the night of February first Dayleen had spent most of the evening in the bathroom dyeing her hair, for which she had her mother as witness. That her hair had been rather recently dyed, no one could deny. It blazed with unreal splendor, somewhere between blond and red in color.

"Did you dye it before or after you went to the Blue Grotto Café with two sailors?" asked Eric Crone gently.

Dayleen's eyes widened almost in terror—as one of her feminine progenitors might have looked on confronting what was undoubtedly the blackest of magic. "Did I say I hadn't been there?" she demanded in a loud, nervous voice. "As for those sailors, they happen to be very nice fellows! One of them asked me to marry him!"

"You were seen in the Blue Grotto at about ten o'clock," repeated Eric Crone. "Was it before or after this that you dyed your hair?"

"Before," she said promptly. "Who dyes their hair at midnight?" In departing she distributed among the investigators a jolly smile which deeply dimpled her plump cheeks and doubled the chin under her full, broad jaw. "The reason why I dyed my hair, in case you want to know, wasn't for any sailors. It was on account of my father lined up a singing job for me through an old buddy of his which could easily lead to a motion-picture contract on account of it's a place where all the big-shot producers go!" With an airy wave of plump fingers she began a departure interrupted when she added, "I also do inter-prative dancing. You know, Balinese stuff and all that." Suddenly dead pan and sultry, she spread her sturdy legs, squatted slightly and began to move her neck stiffly from left to right, while her hips went from right to left and her flattened palms shaped mysterious patterns on the air of the empty schoolroom where questions concerning a young girl's tragic death had so recently been asked of her.

"Yes," said Eric Crone flatly, "that's fine. You can go now, Dayleen."

She winked at them. "I fake it!" she confided. "I never had a lesson in inter-pratative dancing in my entire life!"

The door at last closed after her. Eric Crone sighed and mopped his brow. "The poor, God-awful, Hollywood-crazy kid."

"Yeah," said Brigit absently. She did not know why her mind had no trouble imagining Dayleen's face twisted with fury, nor her heavy arm coming down through dark windy air to bash out another girl's brains.

The door opened part way and Dayleen's round face peered in. She was smiling. "Incidentally, did Dez Grover happen to tell you he was in the Blue Grotto too?"

The third high-school suspect was scarcely that. Manuel Reyes, however, was questioned for three reasons. He had once written the dead girl a note in Spanish class which had said, to Eloise Carewe's best recollection, *"Eres la más bonita de todas las niñas en esta escuela."* He had also admitted to having borrowed his older brother's car on the night of February first for the purpose of attending a movie at a Hollywood Boulevard theater which was only half-a-dozen blocks from Acacia Street. He had stopped in at the Blue Grotto for about fifteen minutes, between eight and eight-thirty.

As to the truth of Manuel's statement, they had the word of the theater usher, who remembered Manuel because he had come out of the movie with tears showing damp on his cheeks. Pretending to look at an ad for a coming film he had surreptitiously brushed them away. The usher would not say exactly when Reyes had entered, except that it wasn't long after the start of the picture, and it had begun at eight-twenty.

Manuel Reyes was almost overcome by fear as he made his statements. The fear was, to Brigit and Tuck, quite natural. Manuel was a Mexican, and, not long before, sixteen Mexican boys had been indicted, tried and jailed for a serious crime which, as it later turned out, they had not committed and which might not have been murder anyhow.

The movie during which Manuel Reyes had wept was a French film called *Le Jour Se Lève*. It had concerned a young murderer who shot the vile seducer of the girl he purely loved.

With his warm dark eyes roving with fear, with his pale young face as sallow as candle wax Manuel Reyes stood at attention like a soldier at court-martial and said in a small, choked voice, "Yes, I wrote her a note. This was fresh of me. But you must see, thinking so much of her the way I did, I would not hurt her, no!"

Soothed by Tuck's reply, Reyes then tried to be helpful. "A month ago we had in the auditorium a lecture about marijuana. I was sitting next to her. When we went up the aisle together she told me she had no sympathy for people who smoked reefers. I think she would have turned them in."

"But that is just an opinion?"

"*Si*, yes. An opinion. A feeling."

"Manuel may have something there," said Eric Crone. "We can't overlook the fact that the use of marijuana among high-school kids has become one of the biggest problems Juvenile Division has to cope with. And it's getting bigger all the time. But I'm inclined to doubt that Ruth Ann would have turned in the name of anyone she knew who was using reefers. There's a freemasonry among kids which makes them absurdly loyal to one another in the face of adult interference. But it's possible that some kid with a guilty conscience knew Ruth Ann had the goods on him—or her—and lost control while under the influence of the stuff."

"I always thought the idea that marijuana turns a normal

84

person into a bloodthirsty monster was a lot of malarkey," Brigit said.

Eric Crone nodded. "The effect of any drug on a given personality is highly variable, though. Chemistry explains a good deal, but it does not explain why a dose of whisky which makes one person loud and jolly will make another morose and angry. Or why, to refer to marijuana, one person seems to experience merely a pleasant slowing down of the tempo of the world around him, while another feels this in a more exaggerated form and also a decided stimulation of sexual desires. This much is sure: A person high on marijuana is all ego. He feels himself beyond the laws of good and evil. Nothing within censors impulse, and the chasm between desire and fulfillment seems to narrow to a hair's width, which is apt to make frustration unbearable. As a little guy in a jive band once said to me, 'When I'm high on Tea I'm a big man, all ways. I love people and they love me. I take a solo and I'm better than Armstrong and folks break their hands off clapping, but they couldn't make enough noise to match how good I am!' Actually a person who is high on marijuana answers to the classic description of criminal insanity: he cannot, for the time, clearly distinguish between right and wrong."

"This is all very discouraging," said Tuck. "What you're really saying is that this case may be as good as closed. Because there's no way to distinguish a kid who uses marijuana from one who doesn't unless he's full of smoke."

"Or unless you find the weeds on his person," agreed Crone. "And now that the papers are starting to play up addiction among juveniles, that's going to be increasingly hard to do."

During the next week a dozen Belmont high-school students were held for questioning about the marijuana they had smoked at a jive session in the home of pretty Blanche

85

Bayles; a youth's back-yard reefer cache was found in a rabbit hutch; and a Dr. François Mezzner opined in the most conservative Los Angeles newspaper that the current increase in the use of marijuana by the young was a reflection of the troubled international situation.

And then, suddenly, the objects found scattered near the dead girl's purse yielded a clue.

This was not the thumbprint which an expert found on the cellophane of the package of Lucky Strike cigarettes. It was what Tuck found inside the package.

While the expert explained that the thumbprint belonged to a man—but no man with a local criminal record, and not Desmond Grover nor Manuel Reyes, and possibly only the druggist or grocer who had sold the Lucky Strikes—Tuck half-absently picked up the pack of cigarettes and began to slide them into the green plastic container in which they had been found. The unopened side of the pack felt slightly limp, not square and hard as it should. On impulse he tore open the government seal and tin foil to look down at a dozen small brown marijuana cigarettes, neatly hidden in the space where mere cylinders of tobacco should have been.

Mrs. Briggs said she had never seen the green plastic cigarette case. "But then," said Tuck, "she wouldn't have." She also said, with some wrath, that her daughter had never smoked cigarettes and had certainly never smoked ones made of marijuana. "But then," Tuck said later to Brigit, "she would certainly not have smoked them in front of her mother."

Eloise Carewe and Helene Crone said they had never seen the green cigarette case either. When pressed, Eloise said, "A girl doesn't go poking into another girl's purse. And what's so important about a pack of Luckies anyway?"

Tuck and Brigit sought each other's eyes. They had

agreed to say nothing of the marijuana cigarettes until they had established whether or not the green case had belonged to the dead girl. "For," as Tuck said, "the idea that an apparently innocent lassie could have been a marijuana user is one of those notions which make people remember all sorts of things to support it, whether they really remember them or not."

"All right, Eloise," Tuck said. "I'll tell you what's important about this pack of Luckies in this green case. If it wasn't hers, it belongs to her killer."

"Then how did it get into her purse?" Eloise demanded.

"It was found on the ground near her body."

"Oh, now you reach me!" said Eloise. She eyed the green plastic case with excitement. "I never saw her smoke and I never saw her with that green case! It's his, I'll bet a hundred thousand dollars!"

Ultimately the gentlemen of the press had to learn of the marijuana cigarettes. They pounced on them with all the restraint of dope fiends confronted with free samples of cocaine. They had a natural and they knew it. Whatever the truth happened to be, the actual ownership of the drug-filled pack of smokes was irrelevant to a good news story. If the killer had dropped it, they had a drug-crazed murderer to serve their readers. And if it had belonged to the dead girl, so much the better! Every paper in the city broke out in a rash of stories exposing the juvenile drug traffic, how it reached out its octopod tentacles from the slums of Main and Temple Streets to the sunny western sprawl of Los Angeles; from battered old schools full of Mexican and Filipino kids to schools like Hollywood High; from scabrous tenements to nice homes like the one in which Ruth Ann Briggs had lived.

In the mysterious way of human beings, many neighbors who had defended her virtue, her innocence, now recalled a hectic look in the dead girl's eyes, a day when she had walked past like a girl in a dream, a wild burst of laughter or her secretive way of lowering her eyelids.

No one was sure he had ever seen the green plastic cigarette case in her possession, but no one was sure he had not. It was, they all pointed out to one another, a very common type of cigarette case, sold by the thousands in any drugstore or five-and-ten. They could have glimpsed it in her open handbag or seen it peeping from the pocket of a sweater or jacket without the fact registering strongly at the time. So many young girls smoke nowadays!

Mrs. Crone summed up the attitude prevalent among the good wives of Acacia Street—and a thousand other streets as well. "She seemed such a nice girl," she said with finality and regret. Her cool dark eyes were alive with horror, real or feigned, and her face showed in every line the suspicion that Ruth Ann Briggs might well have been lured down the path of drug addiction long before the violent blow ended her life.

Brigit was indignant, but Tuck showed a more philosophical attitude. "Ruth Ann isn't real to them any more. The crime itself, the newspapers they've been reading, our questions, all these have turned Ruth Ann into a creature unlike themselves. They can sincerely believe anything about her."

The twelve reefers which accomplished this also granted anonymity to her unknown killer. For if the green case belonged not to her but to him, then he had very probably been moved to violence by the strange, impersonal force of a drug used by thousands in the year 1945 in the City of Angels.

# PART THREE

*The Trap*

# 8

W<small>HITE</small> <small>GLOVES</small>?" asked Mrs. Briggs's rather sharp voice on the phone. "Sure, Ruth Ann had three or four pairs. Used 'em when she got dressed up. Church on Sunday, a show on Saturday—things like that. Why?"

The Briggses had moved to San Fernando Valley, where they now owned a small café. In the background Brigit could hear the faint sound of voices and laughter, the clash of china and silverware. "Do you know if one of her gloves was missing after she died?"

"She lost gloves right and left. Sure, a couple were gone. Why?"

"What size did she wear?"

"Six and a half. She had big hands, like her dad. Why did you call up to ask me about Ruth Ann's gloves?"

"Could she have worn white gloves when she went to the movies, the day she died?"

"She could have. I don't know if she did. I was still out at work when she left the house to meet Eloise."

"But do you think it's likely that she would have worn white gloves?"

"Well, she had on high heels and nylons. And she changed from her brown school skirt to her new pleated plaid. Sure, she might have worn her gloves, or taken them in her purse."

"I'll be out there in half an hour, Mrs. Briggs. I want you to tell me if a certain glove looks like one of Ruth Ann's."

"O.K. But make it in an hour, will you? We serve dinner till eight-thirty, and for some reason we got a rush of late eaters tonight."

The small square café was named "The Mollie." Through the big front window it would have looked a little like an aquarium even without the large pictures of tropical fish which adorned the walls. Mrs. Briggs, who had lost the look of youth which American women are taught to prize, filled two cups with coffee from the silex and said, "I guess you two wouldn't remember that little aquarium Ruth Ann had. Her favorite fishes were these little fellows she called Black Mollies. I wanted to name this place 'The Black Mollie,' only Jim said it would make people think of the black widow, the poison spider, you know, and that wouldn't be good for business. So we compromised on 'The Mollie.' Anyway, there's a real classy place called 'The Red Snapper' not far from here, and it might have sounded, you know, like we were copying." Brigit noticed for the first time, on the shelf above the cash register, a square glass tank in which small black fish swam among flexible seaweed above a scattered hoard of shells like those a child might once have gathered.

"Now what about that white glove?" asked Mrs. Briggs as she began to mop the counter with automatic vigor.

Without saying anything Tuck drew the glove from its envelope, laid it beside his cup. Mrs. Briggs paused in her work to stare at it with pale surprise, and then horror masked her features. "Take that thing off my counter! Where did you get ahold of a thing like that?"

"It was found," Tuck said, "beside a woman who was apparently struck on the head from behind. Her name is Mrs. Eric Crone. She lives on Acacia Street."

"I read about that in the paper this morning. Mr. Crone's wife. But what's that brown stuff on the fingers?"

"Blood," said Tuck. "Did Ruth Ann own a pair of gloves like this one?"

Mrs. Briggs stared at the glove held out to her on Tuck's flat palm. Brigit watched the woman's stunned face closely and believed she saw recollections dawn there. "That's just like a pair she got for Christmas! She lost them."

"When?"

"I don't know. They weren't with her other gloves, though."

"Who gave them to her?"

"I'm not sure. I think it was Helene Crone. Where did that blood come from? It's old blood, isn't it?"

"Do you know what Ruth Ann's blood type was?" asked Brigit.

"Normal, I guess," said Mrs. Briggs vaguely. Her hand, holding the clean damp cloth, rested idle on the counter of new formica and her eyes looked blankly at the glove which Tuck was returning carefully to its Manila envelope.

"Not her blood pressure, Mrs. Briggs. Her blood type. Did she give any blood to the Red Cross during the war?"

"Oh, her blood *type*. I don't know offhand. But I can find out. Because it was the same as her father's. He gave her a transfusion when she was ten."

Tuck stood up, and Brigit followed suit. Staring up at Brigit's bright-red hair, but not as though she were really seeing it, Mrs. Briggs whispered, "I just don't get this."

"Neither do we," said Tuck politely.

Suddenly, Mrs. Briggs was crying, without any sound at all.

The laboratory expert on bloodstains was a small spare man with eyes as clear as his own beakers and test tubes.

Brigit could not imagine him betting on a horse, spilling his coffee or exceeding the speed limit. But the impression of cold infallibility was shattered when he looked up from the bloodstained white glove on his neatly ordered desk over which morning light fell.

"With old bloodstains," he said in his precise voice, "we find that the red cells have been destroyed. They can no longer be seen under the microscope. They cannot be agglutinated by means of the grouping test."

"How about the properties in the serum?" asked Tuck.

"The agglutinogens are far more resistant than the agglutinins," acknowledged the expert with a slight nod. "And the Lattes method is extremely reliable if done by a capable person."

Brigit glanced at Tuck to see if he understood what the expert on bloodstains was talking about. Apparently he did. The Lattes method was as new to her as the headlines of that morning's paper. She was glad to know it was reliable.

"But," said the expert, "a positive conclusion can be arrived at only if an extract of a human bloodstain is found to agglutinate the cells of a given, suspected individual's blood. If that is the case the bloodstain tested cannot be his. Or hers."

"But she's dead!" cried Brigit.

The expert cast a glance of passing amazement at her emotional comment and continued, to Tuck: "If no agglutination occurs, there is the *possibility* that the bloodstain may have come from the suspected person, but nothing can be definitely proved. There are millions of individuals belonging to the same group. Probabilities grow stronger if the blood in question comes from a rare group such as B, of which only ten per cent of the human race so far examined belongs, or AB, to which only five per cent belongs."

Brigit leaned forward. "You see, the girl we think the

94

blood on that glove could have come from is dead. But her father has the same kind of blood. . . ."

"Type. Group, to be exact," said the expert.

" . . . so could you match that stain to a sample of his blood? Then, if it turned out it *couldn't* be that kind—type —group of blood, at least we'd know something."

"What?" asked the expert pleasantly.

"We'd know that no one's been keeping that bloody glove for six years for Lord knows what crazy reason!" said Brigit.

The expert looked at Tuck as though silently questioning him as to the mental balance of his female partner. "You didn't tell me this stain was six years old, Tuck. It's hopeless even to attempt tests. Sun, heat or putrefaction have almost certainly destroyed even the serum properties."

"Still," said Tuck, "I do seem to recall several cases—the Pelham murders in Great Britain, the Gruenwald case in Germany and the Leopardi ax killing in New York City— where old bloodstains were successfully analyzed." He added, "Of course I realize that the experts who pulled those rabbits out of the test tube were among the greatest in the world."

The Los Angeles expert's clear light eyes looked at Tuck coldly. "I don't pretend to be in the same class with them, of course, but I am perfectly willing to do my humble best." He stood up, looking down at the glove which had become a challenge. "Will you have a sample of the father's blood here as soon as possible?"

"I guess the simplest method would be to send in the father, so you can take as much as you need," said Tuck.

"That will be entirely satisfactory," said the expert.

Tuck had gone home when Mr. Briggs entered the Homicide Department at five that afternoon. He looked very little like the soldier whose photograph the dead girl had carried in her purse. He seemed, with his thinning hair and big

95

clumsy hands, to be a rather gentle person. A small strip of adhesive tape covered the tip of one forefinger.

"I don't believe in vengeance," he said after he introduced himself to Brigit, "but I do believe in justice. It's never too late for that." He peered into his inner coat pocket and removed a long and rather bulky white envelope. "Now that there seems some possibility of renewed interest in my daughter's murder, I've brought you this rather peculiar letter. It was sent to my wife three years ago, just before we moved away from Acacia Street. It's anonymous."

February 15, 1948

My Dear Mrs. Briggs:

Even at this late date I want you to know that upon reading the newspaper accounts of your daughter's death I felt deeply for you in your tragic loss. That the police were unable to solve the mystery surrounding it seemed to me inexcusable. Why, I have asked myself many times since, should supposedly able investigators have failed to arrest her killer?

The possible truth occurred to me very suddenly night before last, a windy night, you will recall, very much like the one on which your daughter died. Walking down the street, or rather half blown along by the gale, I was abruptly struck on the shoulder with such violence that I was knocked down. For a moment I believed myself the victim of a lunatic of some sort, and then saw that what had struck me was merely the branch of a palm tree, torn loose by the wind and blown through the air with great force. Had it struck a vital spot, such as my temple, I might not now be writing you this letter. As I continued on my way, somewhat shaken, I found myself suddenly thinking that fate had offered me a vivid example of what might have happened to poor little Ruth Ann. Could it be, I asked myself, that the police found no murderer because there was none? Had an animated piece of wood, wielded by no malignant arm but only by the gale, delivered the fatal blow? But in that case, how had her body got to the canyon where it was found? A plausible answer to this question at once occurred to me.

Picture to yourself a passing motorist, who glimpsed her form huddled on the sidewalk under those thick dark trees which all the newspaper accounts said had concealed from chance eyes the moment when she entered the killer's automobile. He could easily have learned from identification in her purse that she lived only a few hundred yards up the street, and would most likely have lifted her into the car to drive her home, where a doctor could be called. In the thick shadows of those trees the wound on her head could have gone undetected. Imagine this person's horror on discovering, after he had lifted her into his car, that the girl was dead! How easily he could have leaped to the assumption that murder had been done, a murder of which he himself might easily be suspected!

Panic, I believe, would have taken over. I can see this person, on foolish impulse, driving the girl past her house, into the dark canyon at the head of the street on which she lived. Certainly innocent people have been falsely accused often enough to make this action entirely believable. Psychology tells us that hidden guilts often motivate our actions; perhaps this person had some piece of wrongdoing on his—or her—conscience. I believe that that unlucky driver, desperate, must have decided to leave the body where it could be found later—by someone else.

Why this person did not come forward during the investigation is plain enough in view of the immediate assumption of murder, an assumption which would not have been made had the girl's body been found by the police where it had originally fallen.

My sole aim in writing this lengthy letter is the hope that this reasonable explanation of your daughter's death may remove all ugliness from your memories of her, leaving only the fatalistic realization that she may well have been the victim of accident. Even as a stranger to you and to her I find it pleasanter to believe that no evil killer filled her last moments with terror, nor roams at large among us, unknown and unpunished.

Yours with deep sympathy,<br>
AN UNKNOWN FRIEND

"As I told my wife," said Mr. Briggs when he saw that Brigit had finished reading, "that letter seems to me the work of a crank. It must have been written by some· do-gooder who happened to feel strongly about the murder of young girls."

"Why didn't you turn this over to us when you first got it?"

Something like a bitter smile pinched the corners of Mr. Briggs's eyes. "She had been dead for three years. The case had been officially closed for over two. Would you have laid aside the new case you were working on in February of 1948 to follow up a clue like this one?"

"No," said Brigit candidly.

"That is what I told my wife."

Brigit spoke thoughtfully. "If this was sent by a crank, it was a very unusual one. This is an intelligent, well-educated person who is able to believe in a childish theory. The two don't jibe. And if the only motive was to make you feel better, why not sign a name?"

"Yes, I see what you mean," said Mr. Briggs. "The second clue I have brought to you is more important, I believe. It came to light a year ago. My wife refused then to let you see it, but today I was able to persuade her. However, I must ask you to promise not to let any reporters have it. My wife —and I, too, to some extent—well, we feel badly about what those reporters did to Ruth Ann's reputation when they got ahold of the marijuana cigarettes." He ducked his head, and from the side pocket of his overcoat he drew a small blue book with a tiny gold key dangling from a string. He nodded. "Yes. Ruth Ann's diary. The one my wife thought had been lost. The people who bought our house on Acacia Street found it up in the attic, at the edge of the trap door in the ceiling of Ruth Ann's bedroom closet. Just where Ruth Ann had hidden it the day before she died."

Brigit reached for the little book, but Mr. Briggs gently withdrew it. "No reporters," he said firmly.

"No reporters, Mr. Briggs."

He handed it to Brigit then and rising said, "She wrote quite well, I think. English was one of her strong subjects." With a stiff little nod of farewell he turned and left. Some of his hidden sadness had been breathed out into the air of the Homicide Department.

Across the flyleaf Ruth Ann had written: "To whom it may concern. This is my *private* diary, and whoever reads it without permission is no better than a common *burglur*. RUTH ANN BRIGGS."

Jan 1, 1945

So begins another year. Perhaps this one will see the end of this dreadful war, but Dad's last letter did not sound like that. It is awful to realize this has been going on ever since I was a child.

Jan 2, 1945

One of the hands came off my wristwatch and its going to take my whole allowance getting it fixed. Mother doesn't realize that five dollars a week goes mighty fast. She says she felt lucky to get a dollar a week when she was young. I replied with dignity that a dollar was worth a dollar then, and not about sixty cents and dwindeling rapidly. She seemed impressed. So some good came out of Civics, the most boreing subject I ever had to take, includeing Algebra from that old droop Hotchkiss. I am now *sure* he wears a toupay, glued on with some sort of stickum, but why he picked auburne, I would not know.

January 3, 1945

Today Mr. C. said I looked like a rose! I know he was only trying to be kind. But it gave me the feeling of how it would be to have a man say that meaning it. Being a girl is certainly wierd. You have to wait for everything to happen to you. It will be nearly two years before Mother will let me wear Mascara or green eyeshadow.

Jan 4.

Today in Aud I sat next to D.G. He smells like bay rum.

I would have thought it was a different sort of alcohol, only Daddy used it sometimes.

Jan 5.

There is no doubt that M.R. likes me a lot, to put it mildly. Its too bad he's Mexican, because he looks like Tyrone. D.G. is more the Bob Stack type. I wish I knew a type like Frankie. When he sang at the Bowl I was too young to go, but Eloise did and she says girls fainted right and left. I, personally, do not believe the story that they were paid twenty-five dollars apiece to do it.

Jan 6.

Today there was a special Aud call, a talk about marijuana. How its being sold right here at high school, and how kids who smoke reefers are taking the first step on the sorrdid road to drug adiction, and how it isn't smart or clever to smoke it, because it takes more strength to hold out and be called a square. Also much talk on how if you have a friend who uses reefers you are doing him a favor to report this to the principal's office so the person who sold the marajuana can maybe be discovered and arrested. I did not like the hint that your name will be kept secret if you do tell on someone you know. I, personally, would not have any of same. If I was going to tell on someone, I would let them know first, and why. What never seemed to reach the man who gave this talk is that the kids who use it don't think that drug addiction will happen to somebody as smart as them. It's just one more case of what Dad calls the cynacal of the world taking advantage of the stupid.

Skimming through to the final entry, Tuck and Brigit learned nothing new except that like any decent, average American girl of fifteen Ruth Ann had been normally boy crazy. She mentioned actual boys by their initials, male movie stars by first names, and was "sent" by almost all of them. The last entry was dated January 31, 1945.

This morning I got a postcard from R.C. The first since he was drafted three months ago. He says if he can get a pass this week end he's coming down to L. A. and maybe come over to teach me to rumba like he said he would last summer! And I didn't think he cared a whoop. I guess he must have finally gotten over Helene Crone, or else realized she would never go for him. When you carry a torch like the one he did, it blinds you.


"R.C.?" asked Helene's voice when they phoned her. "I don't remember any R.C."

"He was in the Army. He carried a torch for you. He was probably a good dancer."

"Oh, that must be Dicky Carewe!"

"Any relation to Eloise?"

"Her cousin. He graduated from Hollywood High when I was a junior. Yes, he did have an awful crush on me for a while." A woman's voice spoke in the background. Helene gave a short laugh. "That was Mother, remarking that Dicky was a vacant-brained oaf. She never liked him much. I used to drive him home from school once in a while. He lived with his mother in that red-brick apartment house at the foot of the street." The background voice spoke again and Helene said wearily, "The color of his mother's hair is irrelevant, Mother." She added, "That was Mother saying that Dicky's mother used to bleach her hair."

"Do you know where he is now?"

"I haven't the faintest notion. He sent me several letters while he was overseas, and I remember that one of them said his mother had moved away from Acacia Street. Eloise Carewe would know where he is, but I don't know where she lives. She got married, and I don't know her husband's name. Say, wait a minute! Do you remember a girl named Dayleen Burke?"

"I sure do."

"Well, I ran into Dayleen a few months ago and she mentioned that Eloise lived on the same street she does. Dayleen more or less forced her telephone number on me, but I threw it away. I remember, though, that she said her married name was Pflugel. So I guess you can find it in the book."

"Thanks, you've been a big help."

"Oh, I'm always for law and order if it doesn't cost me anything."

"How is your mother feeling?"

"She says she's feeling fine."

"Has she remembered anything more about that prowler?"

"No," said Helene, her voice subtly altered. "If I didn't know my mother as well as I do, I'd say the whole thing sounded definitely phony."

Faces and voices forgotten for years had become suddenly vivid to Brigit. Desmond Grover, Manuel Reyes, Dayleen Burke—— What were they now . . . and where? There seemed little doubt that R.C. was Eloise's cousin. But why had she said nothing about him? A natural oversight? A deliberate one? Had he been in Los Angeles on the night Ruth Ann died?

## 9

DAYLEEN PFLUGEL lived in the lower half of a narrow stucco hillside house overlooking a reservoir known as Silver Lake. A porch light blazed on a vermilion door. When Brigit knocked, all sounds within stopped; the solid silence suggested eyes seeking eyes.

The door was flung open by Dayleen herself. Her mass of hair was now a more sullen red, her chin was double, and one fat hand held together a Chinese robe of pale-blue brocade, an effort which did not entirely conceal a black lace brassière upholding bosoms the color of uncooked dumplings. Dayleen's left eye had been blackly mascaraed, but the right eye was naked of make-up and stared at Brigit as cold as a bird's, as pale as a glass of sea water.

Recognition brought a slack look, then Dayleen quickly donned a big, dimpled and unconvincing smile of welcome. She admitted Brigit to a tiny room paneled in knotty pine, filled with atrocious landscapes in gilt frames, lamp bases which were black panthers, a big television set and a dense crowd of five people.

Dayleen's fat-girl voice left broken sentences dangling like streamers of confetti after New Year's Eve. "You could of knocked me over with a—— Hey, folks, I want ya

to meet Miss Estees. She's a lady detective, and she——
That grumpy guy on the sofa is Al and that's Vi in the kitchenette. She's baking a—— Come on in Vi and say hello to
—— The sailor boy on the day bed is an old friend, and his
nose isn't broken the way you might think from that bandage. He just had a—— And the guy standing there in the
middle of the rug is The Bird. . . ."

Dayleen pointed to her guests, and Brigit nodded at them.
Each reacted according to mood. Al, a dour short man in a
faded Hawaiian shirt and a day's growth of beard, said
darkly, "I'm on my second hang-over since this goddam
shindig started." But Vi beat cake batter in the kitchen
and called, "Don't pay no mind to my hubby, honey. He
just don't go for all-night parties." Then the young sailor
swung from the sofa and came toward Brigit, his hand out-
stretched. The two eyes peering at her over the thick pad of
gauze taped to cover his nose were cordial and direct. "How
do you do? It's a pleasure meeting you, Miss—I didn't
catch the name, Dayleen." His head turned to Dayleen, now
tying her robe more securely. "Estees," said Dayleen and
demanded of Brigit, "Don't Pete have the best manners?"
"It's really a pleasure, Miss Estees," said the sailor. "Forgive my appearance, but I just had plastic surgery on my
nose." "You go lay down some more," said Dayleen with
a tempered kindness. She looked, for some reason, indulgent
and pleased.

Of them all The Bird stood out, perhaps because he continued to practice golf strokes with an imaginary putter
and no ball. Brigit found herself watching him go through
all the motions of making a long putt, his eyes following the
course of the ball to the invisible hole in the corner of the
room. He was impeccable in gray flannel slacks, a pale-blue
nylon sport shirt open at the throat, white sleeveless sweater
and polished tan golf shoes. Yet the careful style of his

garments gave him the appearance of a man dressed for a role he does not fit, a fact he often suspects. He seemed to be dreamily drunk.

"Hey, Bird! Show some manners!" Dayleen commanded. "Say hello to my guest!" The Bird raised his head, looked in Brigit's general direction, gave her a brief, smiling nod. She saw an oval face with pale eyes set under downward-sloping eyebrows, a strong nose, a jutting chin and a small neat mustache above a thin mouth. At each temple wiry brown hair, cropped as close to the skull as a cap, receded in two points, Mephisto-fashion. "Greatest sport in the world," he announced and settled his attention again on the golf stick his hands were not gripping.

Dayleen's hand closed over Brigit's arm just above the elbow. It felt like a fat hand even through two layers of wool sleeve. "Come on to the bathroom," Dayleen said. "I gotta finish dressing." She slowly closed the mascaraed eye-lashes to indicate a subtle motive.

The bathroom opened off an ell of the living room, opposite an open door which revealed a littered sleeping apartment airy as a hatbox. The bathroom was shaped like a shoe box and was brilliantly lighted, cloying with the smells of unguents, powders, perfumes. "I know you didn't come here to pass the time of day," said Dayleen, shutting the door. She winked again and moistened a small mascara brush with saliva. "Now we can talk private. Also, my husband's due home and I haveta dress." Tipping back her head to the blazing glare of mirror, she began to brush black paste on light lashes. "Was it the same guy?"

"What do you mean?" Brigit lighted a cigarette to season the thick broth of perfume.

"Don't try to kid me, Miss Estees. The man who conked Mrs. Crone on the head. Was it the same guy that killed Ruth Ann Briggs?"

"We don't know."

Dayleen cast her a shrewd look from the mirror. "I read about it in the paper. It sure looks queer to me. I mean the way the wind was blowing the other night, and Mrs. Crone living on Acacia Street and all. I think it was the same guy, myself. A lunatic, see. Like the fellow Robert Montgomery played in this picture a long time ago. Not the one where he was named Danny and carried this woman's head around in this hatbox, but the other one, where he sat up in the tree in the moonlight and smiled."

"Oh, that one," said Brigit, obeying the principle that an interview should be casual and conversational and that the investigator should allow the questionee the opportunity to talk fully.

"You can't kid me," said Dayleen. "You know the guy's off his rocker as well as I do." She regarded her thick black lashes approvingly, turning her head from side to side. "You know why Pete in there had his nose lifted? I said it was too big. Can you feature that? Oh, he's been nuts over me for years. Always bringing me things. Electric toaster, electric waffle iron, electric mixer, electric percolator—things for the home, see. Also a portable radio and a television set!" In her triumph and gratitude she faced Brigit for a girl-to-girl chat. "Ray—that's my husband—he just don't have the *go* Pete does. With a car salesman, unless he's got *go,* it's dough today, starve next week. My dad don't go for Ray. He says a girl like me oughta *get* more outta life. He sure gave my husband a dirty look when he saw the television set Pete gave me, but Ray was busy giving the television set a dirty look and missed the point entirely. Ray looks a lot like Frank Sinatra, is why I ever fell for him."

A booming knock threatened the door's hinges. The door then burst open to admit a dark, small, alert young man who gave Brigit a hard stare and commanded, "Get some clothes on, Dayleen. We're going out to dinner."

"I got *guests,* Ray! What about them?"

"They can jump in and pull the chain, for all I care," Ray announced. "Snap it up. I'm hungry."

As he turned to go Dayleen warned him: "I won't eat in any joint!"

Carelessly he showed her a big wad of bills.

"What did ya do, rob a bank?" Then Dayleen's indulgent smile vanished. "I was only kidding," she said quickly to Brigit. And to Ray, "This is Miss Estees. She's a lady dick."

Ray nodded up at Brigit sourly. His unpleasant smile and utter composure showed her that he had not, at least, robbed a bank. "She meets the damndest people," he confided with candor if not complete graciousness. "What do you want with her?"

Dayleen faced Ray with a broad and moist lipstick smile. "She wants to ask me some questions. About a murder."

Ray's eyes narrowed. "You making up lies again?"

"It happened before I knew you," Dayleen said loftily. "Long, long before."

Ray gave up with a shrug. "I'll be waiting out front in the car." He nodded at Brigit, who watched him cross the small living room to the front door with no glance right or left. The sailor seemed asleep, sweet Vi and sour Al were looking at television, and the thick smell of baking cake was almost visible. When Ray flung open the front door to go out the Bird was standing on the small porch, knuckles raised to knock. Over one shoulder was a golf bag and clubs. Behind him the jet lake glittered small reflections.

"Hi, Bird," said Ray and brushed past him into the night.

The Bird gave Ray only a passing glance. His smile beneath the small mustache was superior. He leaned his bag in a corner and began to practice with an actual putter, but no ball. In his hip pocket was a pint of whisky, on his lips a secret smile, as though he were a magician doing a wonderful trick whose cleverness only he could truly appreciate. . . .

When Brigit returned her attention to the bathroom she found that Dayleen had put on a sleeveless knit blouse of white and silver and a gray gabardine skirt. "Women always go for Ray," Dayleen admitted indulgently and picked up a plastic bathroom glass, full of whisky. A half-filled fifth of bourbon now leaned drunkenly out of a drawer which also contained towels. "Care for a swig?" She politely extended the glass to Brigit, who declined. Dayleen looked at once properly offended. "You came here to ask me something. Start asking." Her peremptory tone suggested that Brigit had used a pretext to intrude on the dregs of her party.

"Where does Eloise Carewe live?"

"Right down the street. She's Eloise Adolph now. Is *that* all you wanted to know?"

"That's all. What's her exact address, please?" Brigit held pen poised over her notebook while Dayleen frowned.

At last Dayleen shook her head negatively. "I never could remember numbers. You go down the street until you come to a cement wall with steps going up like these-here, only her door's in the side of the house. It's downstairs, like this."

"How far from here?"

"Oh, five, six houses. You can't miss it. Say, wait. The Bird can lead the way! *Hey, Bird!*"

In a moment The Bird stood in the doorway. Although he reeked smiling assurance his eyes looked oddly shy under their lugubrious brows. "I always went for *big* broads," he confided to Brigit.

Then The Bird was pushed aside like a curtain and little Ray strode into the bathroom, took Dayleen's thick wrist in his thin hand and hauled her after him, past Brigit, past The Bird, his face expressionless. Dayleen seemed pleased by this attention. "O.K., Hot Pants, lemme get a coat." Ignoring her, Ray dragged her into the living room, across it to the front door. By clinging to the edge of the doorway with one hand she was able to yell to The Bird: "Show her where Eloise lives, will ya, Bird?" Her grasp weakened, and she suddenly disappeared, like a puppet jerked off stage.

"By now," said The Bird in a loud voice, "Eloise is high as three kites. I was there tonight, earlier. She drinks like a fish, is her trouble. I tell her it'll ruin her looks, but she don't pay attention to me. I'm just The Bird, see? A dope. A clown. Good for a loan now and then. But just The Bird." His gay voice lowered. "They *think!*"

"You folks leaving so soon?" the sailor asked in his mannerly voice. He was holding an ice cube to his bandaged nose.

"Yeah. Take care of that beezer," said The Bird from the doorway with disinterest. Then he led Brigit down the steps and down the dark street to Eloise.

The Adolphs' living room was dim, hot and reeked of paint. The Bird opened the screen door and strode in confidently. Furniture stood awry, newspapers were spread everywhere, and asleep on a sofa was a young man wearing a pair of blue jeans. He was snoring monotonously, and in the dimness his obese pale torso made Brigit think of slugs.

The dining room was three steps above the living room. It was lighted by a standing lamp with a rakish shade that cast glare down onto a large oblong table spread with newspapers. Facing them across its width was a young woman with harsh yellow hair, huge brown eyes, a thin face. She wore white slacks, a flowered brassière, several splashes of paint, and clutched a glass of straight whisky. Her chin was propped in one hand. "Oh, it's you again," she said flatly to The Bird. "Who's that with you?"

"Listen, Baby," said The Bird in an authoritative voice, walking up the steps toward Eloise with the menacing, slow tread of Hollywood's most popular private detective. "I want you to come up outta that whisky fog, see? She's a dick, see? And she wants a few words with you."

Eloise turned her head sulkily away from The Bird, her chin in her hand. "Ah, you're high again. Go soak your head."

"The Bird may be high, but The Bird knows what's what, see?" Not the fake menace of his tone, but a closer view of Brigit Estees made Eloise straighten slowly. Her bent arm dropped to the table with a soft thud, like wet putty. She stared with blank brown eyes at Brigit, who saw for the first time under this older face a pretty blond student named Eloise Carewe. This woman, who was not over twenty-three, looked nearer forty. The smooth young shoulders contrasted strangely with the haggard rouged cheeks, the hard sad eyes, the mouth slack with some obscure self-pity.

"I remember you," Eloise whispered.

She started to rise and be a hostess, encountered gravity, thought better of her notion. "Have a chair, if you can find one. That thing in there on the sofa is my husband. Mr. Julian Adolph. Every Saturday it's the same deal. Golf with the boys, drinks at the nineteenth hole. Gulps his dinner down and then snores his big fat head off. Oh, it's a great life!" She poured more whisky into her glass thoughtfully, broodingly. A tear suddenly stole down one cheek. She averted her head, blew her nose in semisecret. Then she rose, wove into the kitchenette, came out with two glasses, planted them on the table, reeled, caught her balance, reached her chair and sat down with a thump. The Bird matter-of-factly poured whisky, pushed one drink toward Brigit and swallowed half of the other. Then he pulled up two dining-room chairs, waited while Brigit sat on one, and straddled its mate next to her.

"Whatdya wanna know about pore lil Ruth Ann?" asked Eloise. Now, for some reason, her tongue was thicker, her words blurred. A sentimental look mourned from her big eyes, and her mouth displayed a sweet, false tenderness, unappealing, like stale pastry. "She was a real buddy to me. True-blue. Not like most girls who'll be your buddy till some man comes along and then the hell with being real, true-blue buddies any more!" She dropped her chin into both hands and with bitter eyes apparently recalled a girl who had stopped being true-blue.

The Bird remarked over his shoulder to Brigit, "She's the weeping kind of lush."

If Eloise heard him, she gave no sign. "I'da got a divorce if it wasn't for the kid," she remarked to no one. "The big fat slob." Suddenly she straightened and yelled toward the living room, "Big fat slob!" A look of mingled fear and expectance was on her face. At her cry a snore broke off in the middle, sofa springs creaked violently, and then the snoring was resumed.

"There's something wrong with him," Eloise confided darkly to Brigit. "With his glands. He's got a disease of some gland. Nobody sleeps like that with normal glands. He'll prob'ly drop over in a comer one of these days and never wake up." She looked at sadness ahead of her. "I'll be a widow. At my age. With a kid to raise." Tears gushed to her eyes, hung trembling on the rims of the lower lids.

"Watch, now!" commanded The Bird, touching Brigit's sleeve. "It's like somebody turned on a faucet." But Eloise's tears obstinately trembled on the edge of falling. The Bird's cropped head shot toward her. He was provoked. "Go on! *Cry!*"

"You go to hell!" said Eloise with spirit. From between her breasts she drew a crumpled handkerchief, carefully dried each eye. Automatically she drained her glass. The raw whisky might have been water. "Pour yourself a *real* drink," she commanded Brigit. "Don't act like it was rot-gut! 'S the best stuff money can buy!"

The Bird obediently poured himself a generous portion of bourbon which he drank with his little finger extended in a genteel way, glancing at Brigit from the corner of his eye to see if she noticed this evidence of culture. Then he swung toward Brigit with a brilliant smile. His off-focus glance suggested that he had forgotten where they had met, why they were here. "You look like the type who'd go for a game of golf!" he announced approvingly. He started to rise. "I'm gonna wake up Julian. I want him to meet you."

With a quick movement Brigit reached up for his shoulder and replanted him in his chair.

Eloise said, "If anybody wakes Julian up, *I'll* wake Julian up!"

Before she could get to her feet Brigit stood up and leaned over the table on both palms. "First I want you to tell me where I can find your cousin."

"My cousin?" Eloise had a look on her face which suggested that she had forgotten such remote kinship.

"His name's Richard Carewe," Brigit reminded her. "Do you know where he is?"

Eloise's face took on a slow look of frank contempt at Brigit's stupidity. She pointed. "Right there beside you!"

The Bird sat straddling his chair, looking up at Brigit

with innocent eyes and a surprised smile. "You mean it was *me* you wanted to talk to all along?" he asked as though honored.

While Eloise fought sleep, while Julian Adolph snored, Brigit questioned Richard Carewe. His age was twenty-six, his occupation was bartender, his ambition was to own his own bar, he lived in North Hollywood and was employed at the Blue Grotto Café. "My mother used to be pretty friendly with old Jenkins, so when I got outta the Army in '47 he offered me a job as relief man and I been there ever since."

"Do you remember Ruth Ann Briggs?"

"Sure I remember her. I used to run into her at Eloise's once in a while. Cute kid. Too bad what happened to her. Did they ever catch the guy?"

"No. Do you remember where you were on the night she was killed?"

"I was up at Fort Ord waiting shipment overseas."

"You didn't get a leave that week end?"

"No. I got rooked out of it. That sergeant was a bastard."

"When did you last see Ruth Ann before she died?"

"About three months before, it must of been. I also wrote her a couple of post cards from camp. Funny, when you think of it. I'd probably of dropped in to see her if I'd got that pass. Maybe if I had she'd be alive right now." He shook his head slowly and sadly, amazed by the bizarre tricks of fate. "Sure, I'd of talked her mother into letting me take her to an early show or something. She wouldn't of been walking up any dark street alone. Funny the way things work out sometimes."

"Yeah," said Eloise's voice, sudden and belligerent. "Funny like an iron balloon!"

The Bird followed Brigit to her car. "I'm gonna give you

113

a ring one of these nights soon," he told her expansively. "We'll get together for dinner."

"You do that."

"Hey!" he said suddenly, peering in at her through the open window. "How come you looked me up like this? There must of been some reason."

"Just routine, Bird."

"Don't hand me that." He sounded puzzled but amiable. The sudden flare of Brigit's match showed that his face was knotted with thought. Then he smiled. "I don't know how long they keep records at Fort Ord, but if they still got 'em for February of '45, they'll show I pulled a C.Q. that night."

"What's a C.Q.?"

"Charge of quarters. I was due for a pass, too."

"Tough."

"Yeah. That sergeant was a bastard." As her car pulled away he stepped to the center of the street, waved after her and called, "Remember, you got a date with The Bird. The Bird isn't a bad guy when you get to know him!"

# 10

A TELEPHONE CALL to Fort Ord brought Brigit, after numerous delays, the information that some nonessential records covering the early part of 1945 had been destroyed, that it might not, therefore, be possible to ascertain whether a Private Richard Carewe had been given leave on February first. The officer in charge of the files which might or might not reveal anything of value was off the post for the evening but would undoubtedly attend to the matter in the morning and communicate his findings promptly.

He had not done so when, at ten o'clock, Brigit rang the Adolphs' doorbell for the purpose of learning what Eloise might have to say when sober. It was a gray morning, and the narrow gray clapboard house clung to the slope of a hill above its narrow cement terrace as though it had long ago abandoned the niceties of appearance in a grim resistance to gravity and termites.

The door was opened by a large, plump young man who wore a Hawaiian shirt in which the colors red, yellow, green, blue and purple strove for dominance. His hair was damp from a shower, and his gray eyes seemed somewhat dissolved. And then Brigit saw that they were really hard eyes, like quartz under a film of water. At first they looked at her coldly, then they roved over her person while he engaged in some sort of mental arithmetic, subtracting her height from her red hair and adding her pretty face to the remainder. The sum was in her favor, for he smiled with grim humor. "I'm Julian Adolph. You're the lady detective that was here last night."

She nodded.

He stepped aside, holding the screen door wide so she could enter. Now his smile chided her. "Dickie's new girl friend."

"If he told you that, he's indulging in wishful thinking for reasons I don't know." She saw that the living room had been somewhat tidied; now the furniture was more or less in order and the paint cans were lined up in one corner near the rolled rug. A pretty little girl of three, in jeans and a T-shirt, was sitting on the sofa tearing pages from a magazine with a certain method, to judge by the way she first scanned each page. "Hello," said Brigit.

The little girl raised huge blue eyes, but did not reply.

"That's my daughter Susie," said Julian Adolph. "Run out and play now, Susie."

With an immediate compliance which Brigit found unusual, Susie slid from the sofa and trotted across the room to the door, stumbling a little in her pointed cowboy shoes. The screen door slammed shatteringly behind her, and she advanced into the gray-smogged morning beyond the porch.

Brigit turned to Julian Adolph and found him watching her with a wise and somehow rather annoying stare. He asked formally, "Like a cup of coffee?"

"No, thanks. It was your wife I came to see."

He relaxed into a low, chubby armchair and nodded toward another. "Sit down, why don't you? She's not up yet. She's not even awake yet. We might as well yak, if you're in the mood to wait around for her. . . . You came about the Briggs murder, didn't you?"

"How did you know that?"

He looked pitying. "I heard them talking last night after you left." He offered a cigarette, lighted one. "We're painting the joint. Save an honest dollar and take some of the lard off Eloise. Why the hell does a woman let herself go to pot? A few years back she was a reet neat little piece." He flickered an ash from his paunch, his eyes not unapproving. "You want some dope on The Bird?" he asked, his pale eyes suddenly full of good humor as he raised them, rather slyly, to her face.

"It might not do any harm. How well do you know him?"

"Well enough. Better than Eloise does, in a way. She's as blind as a bat where he's concerned. They were raised together for a couple of years when they were kids, see, and she acts now like he's her brother. I even think she *thinks* he's her brother sometimes. She's got a soft spot in her heart for him as big as her can. But me, I see him as he is—a sad sack in nylon shirts. A putty head." He laughed. "He's the local boy who never makes good. He's got all the angles, only they never work, for him. It's too bad he ever got himself discharged from the Army. He was a lot better off with someone doing his thinking for him." Julian ground out his cigarette, looking elaborately modest. "Myself, I was a captain in the last fracas. Occupation of Germany. The Bird's a lot like them damn Krauts. A heller as long as the dice roll in his favor, and chicken crap when the other guy's got the club and waves it some."

"You don't seem to like him much. Why?"

Julian shrugged his broad, plump shoulders. "I don't feel much about him one way or the other. I just know him, is all. Go on, ask some questions."

"I gather he's a Los Angeles boy?"

117

"You gather right." His tone derided her verb. "Born and raised here. Thinks the Prudential Building's a skyscraper, thinks the Coconut Grove is the last bloody word in night clubs, thinks . . ."

"I get the idea he never had much of a family life. So why do you suppose he came back to L. A. after he got out of the Army?"

"Mama," said Julian, looking both sneering and bitter. He stood up. "How about a beer?"

"No, thanks."

"I'm gonna have one." He strode ponderously to the kitchen, the full floral shirt bellying behind him. There was a scrape and gush as he opened a can; he clomped into the living room wiping foam from his chin. "Aunty Dot is a character too," he announced.

"Carewe's mother, you mean?"

"I mean." Julian nodded with the restrained look of a man who is about to tell a good if subtle joke. "Aunt Dot must be edging fifty—forty-five anyways—but she don't look over thirty-five. And she's on her fourth husband. Or maybe it's her fifth. She buried one and divorced two or three more. She's really been doing all right for herself. The current hubby, Harry Schneider, he's got a nice little nest egg tucked away and owns some fair income property. Aunty Dot plays the horses, the slot machines, in fact, anything she can lose money betting on. But once in a while she wins, and when she does she always ponies up and hands Dicky a nice piece of change. That's how he affords those nylon shirts and handmade shoes of his. The Bird finds himself short of dough, he just swaggers over to Mama and puts the bee on her. Not like a son asking the favor of a loan, either, but like some punk kid studying to be a gangster. I don't know what it is he's got on his old lady, but she always hands out that good old folding stuff."

Julian relaxed and tipped up his beer can. After refreshing himself he added, looking stern and virtuous, "Me, nobody's ever handed me a cent in my life. Nobody's going to. Maybe that's partly why a guy like The Bird gives me a swift pain in the—pain. Always playing the big shot on Mama's cabbage, with a lousy little barkeep job that don't more than pay his room and board."

"Did you know Ruth Ann Briggs?" asked Brigit.

"No," said a tired voice from the dining room. "He never set eyes on her." Eloise stepped down from the dining room tying the sash of a quilted robe of weepy blue, once handsome but now bearing traces of many a conflict with housewifely tasks.

"Well, well, if it isn't little Miss Bright Eyes," said Julian.

Eloise gave him a cold, bleared glance. "Where's Susie?"

"Outside playing." At mention of his daughter Julian looked grave, rather important.

"Didja give her breakfast?"

"Two bowls of cornflakes and a couple of fried eggs."

"Is there any more beer?"

"Yep." Julian made no move to rise, and Eloise disappeared briefly into the kitchen, to return clutching a can of beer and a tall glass. With a muffled moan she sank into a platform rocker.

"Julian doesn't like Dick," she told Brigit, pouring beer. "So don't pay attention to anything Julian says about him." She took a dainty swallow, rested the glass on the chair's arm, looked gravely down at small rising bubbles. "Dicky's no dope. I don't blame him for making his mother fork over once in a while when he knows she's flush. She owes him something after the way she shoved him into the background when he was a kid. First with us, then military schools, places that board kids. She couldn't have married as well as she did the last couple of times if she'd been stuck home taking care of Dicky. She knows that as well as he does. That's why she's willing to do what she can for him now. And furthermore, Dick doesn't throw all his money around on expensive clothes, the way Julian makes out. I been with him shopping. He shops careful, buys the best, which lasts. Dicky has this ambition to own his own little bar someday, and he's saving up toward that. I bet he makes the grade, too. I bet he's sitting pretty a few years from now."

"With liquor licenses costing the way they do? Don't make me laugh!" cried Julian. But his face wore a reluctant fear that his wife's despised cousin might indeed attain this pinnacle. He frowned darkly at a world which supplies some men with indulgent mothers.

"Furthermore," said Eloise, "I don't think he came back here to L. A. just on account of Aunt Dot's ready cash. I think it was partly on account of Helene Crone. She was real class, to him. He was goofy about her. Other girls haven't meant anything to Dick."

"Not even Ruth Ann Briggs?" asked Brigit.

"Don't be silly. To Dicky, Ruth Ann was just my friend, a nice little kid."

"He seems to have written to her from camp, though, made a date with her."

"If he did, it was just because she happened to live on the same street as Helene Crone. It was to have a girl to go and see if Helene stood him up. To sort of bolster his ego, if you know what I mean. Because Helene didn't treat Dicky any too good during the year or so they knew each other. I think she kind of used Dicky in case nothing better came along. She was always calling off dates, or pretending she forgot them. By the time Dick was in the Army he'd found out the best way to work things with Helene was just to drop in or call her casual-like on the chance she might be home. That way, his feelings didn't get hurt so much."

"This is breaking my heart," said Julian. "But I think what Miss Estees here is trying to find out is whether your dear, sensitive cousin Dick was in town on the week end of the murder."

"Absolutely not!" Eloise relaxed into the rocker and with an unconvincing casualness began to rock. "How I know is that Aunt Dot was down in Tia Juana that week end with some friends, including Uncle Harry that she's now married to, and Dicky knew she was going to be—in Tia Juana, I mean. And whenever his mother happened to be away Dicky always stayed at my folks' house, and he didn't. Besides, I remember distinctly that it wasn't until two or three weeks later that he came down. Just a little before he shipped overseas, that was. And he hadn't even heard Ruth Ann was dead! I guess it was in the Salinas papers, but he just never happened to read any."

"Did he tell you that he made a date with her? For the night she died?"

For the first time Eloise's expression of candor slipped. Her brown eyes evaded Brigit's, and she put one palm to her forehead. "With a hang-over like the one I've got, it's hard to remember anything."

"You know what to do for a bad hang-over, don't you?" asked Julian.

Eloise looked hopeful. "No. What?"

"Drink less."

"Ah, you heel."

Julian, hard-eyed and smiling, turned to Brigit. "My wife's not so dumb as she looks. She knows that if Dicky

Bird did keep mum about a date he made with Ruth Ann, he maybe had a reason. It could of been a damned good reason, too."

"The trouble with you," Eloise said hotly to her husband, "is your folks are so tight they wouldn't hand you a plugged nickel if we were starving. Which is why you got such a grudge against Dicky. Aunt Dot may be a bag in a lot of ways, but at least she's not tight!"

Julian's face curdled with chagrin, but he elaborately ignored his wife by suddenly feigning intense interest in a large fly which was buzzing above her head. His big body moved with the stealth of an Iroquois as he set down his beer can, stood up and moved to the table on which a flyswatter lay. The fly buzzed down to the arm of Eloise's chair; Julian stalked toward it. Then, with alert and murderous fury he brought down the swatter. It missed Eloise by an inch or so. As he triumphantly brushed the fly from the chair's narrow arm, Eloise, still rigid, said stoically, "I told you and told you to buy a sprayer and not go around mashing flies all over the walls and furniture like you do!" But in her upraised eyes there was a curious submissiveness.

Julian took a wild swishing swing at nothing; the swatter whistled through the air. His face was jubilant, his good spirits were manifest. "I like swatting 'em. Sneaky little sons of bitches!"

Somehow Eloise seemed more cheerful too. "I can just see you as a kid, pulling their wings off!"

"I only pulled wings off vampire bats. Flies I kept in a bottle to feed to my pet tarantula."

"To get back to Cousin Dick," said Brigit, "did he tell you, Eloise, that he planned to see Ruth Ann if he came to town?"

Now her eyes were large with false candor. "I think he

did," she said. "In fact, now that I stop to think about it, I'm absolutely sure he did."

When the doorbell of Brigit's apartment rang at five-thirty that evening it was a shock to look into the face of Richard Carewe. He smiled, thrusting out his jaw to make himself look tougher. "I bet you didn't expect to see me so soon."

"I didn't have any opinion one way or the other. Come in."

He entered and looked about in a bored yet jaunty way. "Nice place you have here."

"I like it. Let's get down to brass tacks, because I'm expecting a dinner guest."

"I was gonna ask you to have dinner with me. I guess that's out, though."

"It is."

"Mind if I sit down?"

"Help yourself."

He selected a corner of the sofa, leaned back with an exaggerated air of ease. Brigit chose the rather imposing Renaissance chair she had bought at an auction. He laughed nervously. "You were a lot easier to talk to last night than now, sitting on that throne."

"You were in a condition last night that made anyone easy to talk to."

"You got something there. That's sort of what I'm here about." He sat straighter, leaned forward with his eyes very steady on hers. "The thing is, I got to thinking over what I told you last night and I decided I might of been wrong. It's plenty hard, remembering back to six years ago. Try it sometime if you don't believe me. But today—well, I got to thinking. Maybe I don't have any cast-iron alibi at all." He swallowed. "The more I thought it over, the more it seemed to me that I got that pass on February first that I told you I didn't get. The only thing I'm pretty sure of is that I didn't come down to L. A. On account of several reasons. For one thing, I remember that the ride I was counting on petered out; the guy decided to go up to Frisco instead. It was sometime around then that I went up there with this buddy with the car. I think it was the week end Ruth Ann Briggs was killed. Stubbs would probably remember for sure . . . but he's dead."

"Why didn't you let Ruth Ann know you weren't coming down? You knew she was expecting you."

Carewe's eyes were without expression. "Expecting me?"

Brigit felt a tingle of excitement, the feeling she always had when within the next moment a suspect might trip himself with a lie, an unnecessary evasion.

"What do you mean, expecting me?" he asked blankly.

"I mean you wrote her to that effect."

"Oh, that." Now his face was bright with understanding. "That was just this post card I wrote her to say thanks for this Christmas card she sent me. All I said, though, was I *might* get a leave that week end and *might* drop by if I did and give her this tango lesson I promised her. Or maybe *rumba*. And that's another reason why I don't think it was L. A. I spent that leave in, if I got one that week end. I mean, I'd of at least phoned the kid, and that way I'd of learned from her mother what happened to her. Get it?"

"I get it."

He sounded stiff and self-conscious when he added, "The way it was, it was a couple of weeks later when Eloise slapped me in the kisser with the bad news." Abruptly he stood up. "I don't want to keep you from fixing up for your company, so I'll take off now . . . and thanks for your time."

Brigit rose promptly.

124

". . . But I wanted to tell you I was maybe full of hops last night."

"You were full of whisky, anyway."

He smiled vaguely. "I'm sorry I can't remember better. Things were kind of rugged back then in '45. Kind of queer. I mean, we all had gangplank fever, but bad. We all kept hearing about buddies who shipped overseas being dead. It was rough all over." His eyes came back to the present, and he smiled with assurance. "Don't forget now! The Bird tried to be level with you."

"Why do they call you The Bird?"

"It's a nickname."

"That much I figured."

"It was kind of wished on me, but then I made something of it." He sensed that this did not satisfy and added, "It was my old lady. She called me Dicky Bird when I was a kid. After this canary she had once that died. I had yellow hair then, I guess was the reason."

From her doorway she watched his well-tailored shoulders recede, and then she telephoned the Adolphs. Julian answered. "Did Carewe pay Eloise a visit today?"

"Nope."

"Or telephone her, do you know?"

"Nope, and I've been here all day."

An hour later a wire from a Captain Staunton at Fort Ord stated: "Available records show that Private Richard Carewe, 39547701, received three-day pass effective from 1300, 1 February 1945." 1300 was one o'clock in the afternoon, and seven hours would have allowed time for Private Richard Carewe to reach Acacia Street and kill a girl. But the news had a secondhand quality, robbed of emphasis by Carewe's volunteering this same information, whether out of candor or cunning, whether out of his knowledge of his innocence or of his guilt.

## 11

Plevis was a young reporter and took his work seriously. When Brigit entered the Homicide Department the next morning he was sitting on one corner of Tuck's desk. Tuck was saying, "Don't talk out of the corner of your mouth, Plevis. Every reporter under twenty-five talks tough. Be different."

"I'm twenty-six," said Plevis, flushing, "and if I talked out of my——" He saw Brigit then and abandoned a striking comment. "If I talked out of my ears it would still be irrelevant. You're just trying to dodge the issue. And that makes me damned sure my hunch about that glove was one-hundred-per-cent correct."

"How did you find out about the glove?" asked Brigit conversationally as she removed her coat and hat.

"I have my pipe lines," said Plevis.

"One of the lab boys got chatty," Tuck said.

"Why not be level with me?" asked Plevis.

Tuck leaned back in his chair and appeared to consider. "O.K., Plevis. As you know, that glove is in the hands of our top expert on bloodstains."

"Yeah."

"If he finds the stain on that glove is blood—"

"Yeah?"

"—human blood—"

"Sure, sure."

"—and if this blood does *not* agglutinate with blood of a certain type—"

"Go on."

"—then we'll be absolutely certain . . . of nothing."

Plevis leaped off the desk, glaring with rage.

"All we'll know," continued Tuck calmly, "is that there is a possibility that this blood may have once flowed in the veins of a certain individual."

"What individual?" Plevis demanded.

"On the other hand," said Tuck, "and this is far more likely, the lab tests may fail to indicate anything whatsoever. Your pipe line has perhaps informed you that the bloodstain on the glove is not very new."

Plevis turned away from Tuck's desk, and Brigit could almost hear his brain clicking, straining to cook up a good lead and enough story to follow it.

"You don't have a prayer," said Tuck, also reading the reporter's mind. "But try, though. Try writing up what I just told you. Then don't show it to your editor." With morose satisfaction he watched Plevis walk out and slam the door.

"Why are you so down on Plevis?" asked Brigit.

"I'm down on all reporters right now. If it turns out that the blood could be the Briggs kid's, they'll blow it up, make it sound like a fact instead of a possibility and dig up the corpse of the Briggs case. Which will then be dropped into our laps." He stood up and walked to the window, where he stood looking down at crawling cars and hasty bipeds.

"You sound sick, or something," observed Brigit.

"It was bad enough failing once. Twice is going to be too much."

"I know how you feel. It's because she was so young."

Tuck cast her a dark-brown glance. "Have you considered the infant mortality rate in India lately?" he inquired. "Her relative youth has nothing to do with it. We failed. Missed the boat. Gummed up the works. Somehow. Will we do any better after six years?"

It was exactly twenty-four hours later that the lab expert came in person to make his report. A faint flush, which might have been the excitement engendered by an intellectual victory, showed on his thin cheeks. He spoke at some length of the procedures he had used and ended by saying, "And so, as I have made clear, the agglutinins extracted from the stain agglutinated its antiagglutinogen present in the test serum."

"No fooling?" asked Brigit.

"There is no doubt of that," said the expert briskly. "My work done, I then telephoned the girl's physician who told me, after checking his records, that the girl's blood was of the AB group. No, gentlemen—*ladies* and gentlemen—I do not hesitate to say that two facts are clear: The Briggs girl's blood was, according to her doctor, Group AB. The blood on that glove is also Group AB. Of course this does not mean that the blood on the glove *is* Miss Briggs's. However, as only five per cent of the human race belong to this group, the possibility is mathematically a stronger one than had she belonged to, say, Group O, to which forty-five per cent of us belong."

He looked brightly at their faces. "One more point. I frankly had little hope of extracting anything from so old a stain. The fact that I did indicates that the glove was very carefully preserved in a cool, dark and almost antiseptic place. I have found myself wondering why, and where. Do you know?"

"When we know that," said Tuck, "we'll probably know who killed her."

The afternoon edition of Plevis' paper showed that his pipe line had operated faithfully.

### GORY GLOVE LINKS ATTACK
### TO GIRL'S MURDER

It was learned today that a strange clue found in the home of Mrs. Eric Crone, attacked on the night of February 15, links her unknown assailant with the murder six years ago of a fifteen-year-old high-school girl named Ruth Ann Briggs, whose mysterious death puzzled Los Angeles investigators for many months.

A woman's bloodstained white glove, found in the Crone living room and evidently dropped by the attacker, was analyzed yesterday by F. Bronson Biggs, police expert on bloodstains. The blood proved to belong to the same rare group as that of the dead schoolgirl. Homicide Investigators Richard Tuck and Brigit Estees, who discovered the glove while searching the Crone living room for clues which might lead to the apprehension of the attacker, state that though it is possible that the dried blood on the glove is the Briggs girl's, this fact cannot be definitely proved. The dead girl's mother has admitted to the press that the bloodstained white glove closely resembles one of a pair given to her daughter on the Christmas preceding her death.

A résumé of the Briggs case followed, and the story ended with the suggestion that the attractive schoolgirl's killer now roamed the area of his old crime, hitting lone women on the head.

It was just four o'clock when the telephone on Brigit's desk rang. The operator announced that she had a telegram for Investigators Tuck and Estees: "If you want to know more about who attacked Ruth Briggs and Mrs. Crone, be on porch of old house northwest corner Franklin and Vine at six tonight." The operator added, "There is no signature."

"O.K. Now I want to talk to the Western Union operator who took this message."

The message had been telephoned at three-thirty from a pay station in Hollywood. The girl could remember nothing significant about the voice of the sender, except that it had sounded like a man. She had duly noted, for the office records, the fact that he had refused to give a name or address.

Before she left, Brigit typed out the message and placed it on Tuck's desk, weighting it down with her round glass paperweight inside which snow fell on a perfect red rose.

"There's an old Turkish proverb that fits you to a T," Tuck once said to Brigit. " 'If I place my head in the pestle, shall I then weep when the mortar grinds it?' " He added, "You smell trouble, you know it's trouble, but do you walk the other way? Do you hesitate, or even approach with caution? No, you decide it's a challenge. You go marching into danger like a kid trying to prove she's brave. Then I have to go marching in after you. And I don't like being brave. So next time, Brigit, *don't*."

She remembered Tuck's admonition as she stood on the hilltop intersection of Franklin and Vine, which lay directly in the path of the new freeway. By day this was an area of ragged foundations, buildings in the process of being torn down, bulldozers roaring and straining. Crushed cement walks led to empty sky where once a front door had been, raw reddish soil showed nakedly, forlorn stacks of old lumber and broken pavement waited for trucks to take them away.

In the quiet dusk the old corner house was even more

desolate than its setting. It stood on a high terrace, jacked up above the cement of its foundation, and seemed to have a slight forward tilt, like a monument pried loose from its pedestal to be carted to some unhonored resting place. A red-and-yellow sign on one porch pillar said it was for sale and would be moved to any new site chosen. Brigit had often passed such old houses being slowly trundled on great rollers along quiet streets in the early morning hours.

A more significant observation rode atop the tide of these impressions, as full of warning as a bell buoy. To anyone watching from the windows of the deserted house a person ascending the terrace steps and approaching along the wide walk would be a perfect target. Brigit's right hand was already deep in her coat pocket; her thumb checked to make sure that she had released the safety catch of her revolver. Its cold, solid weight was comforting; so was her knowledge that she was an expert shot.

When she reached the top step and stood on a level with the foundations of the uprooted house she saw that one of the narrow windows flanking the front door was broken: An acute triangle of empty blackness was gashed out of the dull dark shine on the pane. All other visible windows were intact, and the front door was closed. Now she knew what her target would be, if it came to shooting.

All this time cars swished past on the narrow sloped street below with the slow regularity of a light going on—off—on—off, long moments of darkness after each brief flash. The cars were not a great comfort because of the speed of their passing. It seemed as though they were steered by their own intricate machinery rather than by human beings.

Watching the broken window, Brigit stumbled on a chunk of wood lying across the walk. The flat nasty roar of the gun and the impact of the bullet were synonymous. She felt herself spun around by the same thrust that rocked her backward. She was firing at the broken window even before she threw herself flat on the pavement, removing her silhouette from against the twilight sky behind her. She fired again, wiggled quickly back, felt her toes drop over the top step, fired a fourth time.

Then she shoved and writhed herself down the bumpy slope of the terrace steps. As she fired once more, she felt blood running down the skin of her left arm. "Why, I've been shot!" she said with surprise.

"Hey, what's going on here?" asked a man's voice nervously. From the car, which Brigit had not heard pull to the curb behind her own, a woman called, "Ask her if that was a shot we heard. Ask her if she's hurt."

The stranger turned his head to bark at his wife, "Of course she's not hurt. She's just laying on those steps for the fun of it." Solicitously he put his hand under Brigit's left elbow to help her to her feet, murmuring, "Take it real easy, sister. . . ."

Pain jabbed down her arm to the tips of her fingers which lighted up with red electric bulbs of enormous wattage. At the same time pain stabbed up her shoulder and neck into her brain. She heard her own scream after it was out. She listened vacantly to its echo. She was standing up. Now the man was looking at the pavement at their feet. She looked too and saw the blood drops falling very fast and dark. "Hey! You've been shot!" cried the man.

"I also stuck my head in the mortar," she told him with a laugh which sounded absurd if not maniacal. "How about a lift to Georgia Street Receiving Hospital?" Because of the odd sound of her laughter she quickly lifted the flap of the purse swinging crookedly from her right shoulder and displayed her badge.

"Sure," he said quickly. "Be glad to." He called to the

132

woman peering from his car, "It's O.K., hon. She's a police-woman. We're driving her to the hospital. We better spread that beach blanket over the back seat. She's bleeding pretty bad." He hustled toward the car, saying over his shoulder apologetically, "New seat covers. Set me back forty bucks."

Brigit made it into the back seat before all the bells in the world chimed slowly and the quick black curtain came down. There was just time to remember the one unspent bullet in the gun in her pocket and to slip the safety catch home.

A doctor who looked almost old enough to go to medical school removed the bullet from Brigit's left shoulder. Then a big handsome young intern joined him to watch him work deftly with tape and gauze. "That shoulder oughta be in a plaster cast," the intern observed with assurance. The young doctor snipped gauze and said quietly, "No cast is needed, Dr. Pratt. The X rays showed all bones intact."

"Is his name really Pratt?" asked Brigit, watching the intern's wide rear wag from the room.

The thin young doctor nodded, almost concealing a smile.

And then Tuck's giant form rounded the screen between bed and door. "I got there," he observed, "using a siren all the way. I was just in time to learn that you had been driven either to the hospital or to the morgue. The pint or so of blood distributed about the pavement was not very reassuring."

"Your husband?" asked the nice young doctor.

"He might as well be," said Brigit gloomily.

With a faint smile the surgeon left them alone. Tuck stared down at Brigit with sad brown eyes.

"Well," said Brigit, "at least the Briggs case reopened with a bang!" Her laugh died under Tuck's immobile gaze. A last *ha, ha* hung on the air like a bubble, and burst.

"It was a real booby trap," Tuck said. "No one was in the house, of course. A cheap thirty-two-caliber revolver was propped in the broken front window. You obligingly tripped on the piece of two-by-four and jerked the string tied to the trigger."

In a small voice Brigit said, "Someone didn't care much whether that bullet had my number on it!"

"Or mine!" agreed Tuck.

"I understand that someone tried to kill you, my dear," said the voice of a total stranger. Around the brown screen at the foot of the bed trotted a neat, plump, elderly little man, very bald, with dark eyes, ferocious brows and a chubby, square jaw. His necktie was gay with unicorns. He smiled kindly at Brigit. "Need I add that I'm glad his aim was faulty?"

He retained his worn and bulging leather brief case as though it were permanently attached to him, but absently handed his dark Homburg to the stout intern who had followed him in and who looked faintly belligerent and very distrustful. "The last murderer I was involved with," said the little man, "was more successful. Not only did he poison the woman, he also pushed the body off a hundred-foot cliff."

"How did you know someone tried to shoot me?" demanded Brigit. She sat up; pain seared her shoulder. "And who in hell *are* you, anyway?"

"I am not in hell, strictly speaking," the little man replied. He sat down on a hard chair near the foot of the bed as though for a long chat. "Although in contrast to the atom in fission, the mere Biblical inferno becomes a childish blaze warming tepid demons, does it not?" He decided to relinquish the brief case on his lap, and bent to lean it against the legs of his chair, watching with affectionate concern to make sure it would not topple over. "As to how I know that someone tried to shoot you, a gentleman named Gufferty told me.

so when I telephoned the Homicide Department half an hour ago and asked where I might find you. As to who I am, I am not at all surprised that you haven't the slightest idea. When I last saw you, you were twelve years old."

"He *said* he was your uncle," offered the handsome intern dubiously. "He says his name's Fentwill."

"Uncle *Mordecai!*" A dozen memories from lost childhood flashed through Brigit's brain.

"I said I was her *great*-uncle," Mordecai Fentwill told the intern on whom he had turned a piercing dark gaze. "In your profession, young man, it is well to realize this: All that sets you a notch above the witch doctors of slightly more primitive cultures is a certain respect for exactitude." He eyed the Homburg in the intern's hand. "You may place my hat on the table by the door as you leave."

While the intern walked away backward Mordecai Fentwill returned his attention to Brigit. "Yes, my dear, I am your Great-uncle Mordecai. Since it will be awkward to call me 'Great-uncle Mordecai,' and since 'Professor Fentwill' is too formal for our sanguinary tie, and since 'Mordecai' is unsuitable to the forty years difference in our ages, particularly in the absence of the slightest degree of friendship between us, I am going to suggest that for the present you call me 'Uncle Mordecai.' This is the best we can do with the troublesome fact that I am your grandmother's brother on the distaff side." He beamed at Brigit fiercely. "I must say that you seem to me entirely unlike your cousin Daphne Estees, of Boston. Not only is she abstemious and very plain, but she likes to listen to Bach. Or, indeed, any contrapuntal music. And I can imagine no one shooting Daphne except by the most fortuitous accident."

In the voice of a little girl of seven or eight, Brigit introduced Tuck to her great-uncle. Mordecai Fentwill bowed while sitting, and it was then that Tuck saw in the dark

135

bottomless eyes under the pirate's eyebrows a distinct sparkle of humor. Tuck realized that Mordecai Fentwill had taken prompt charge of an awkward situation. In doing so he had also subtly established himself as a personage, without bringing forth one of the many facts which would have guaranteed to Mordecai Fentwill everyone's deference.

For Tuck knew that the little man sitting on the hard hospital chair was considered by many renowned scholars one of the great living philosophers. And as a college professor Mordecai Fentwill had made himself unforgettable to several decades of undergraduates in both England and the United States, to whom he was a Mr. Chips with the sentimentality of a diamond, a tongue that could clip tin and an almost passionate hatred of two forms of human error: emotional indulgence in prejudice and the cold use of expedience. Fentwill's many admirers included Einstein, the late George Bernard Shaw, Russell, Hutchins, Churchill, the late President Roosevelt, Sister Kenny, Eisenhower, Faulkner, the Sitwells, Albert Schweitzer, Bing Crosby, and Richard Tuck of the Los Angeles Homicide Department.

With a dashing yet faintly inexpert air, like a youth just learning to smoke, Mordecai Fentwill lighted a cigarette while offering his silver case to Brigit and Tuck. "Judging by your size, my dear, I should say that the person who shot you knew nothing of the use of firearms."

His black stare transferred itself to Tuck's face. "Sit down, Mr. Tuck, and tell me this: Did or did I not, as I was entering this room, hear you say 'booby trap?' "

"I read your book, *The Void after Freud*," said Tuck.

Mordecai Fentwill looked vaguely pleased.

"I particularly liked the chapter on 'Crime and Prejudice.' "

"Thank you. Now, to return to the matter at hand . . ."

136

# 12

$M$Y BOOK, which you have been kind enough to praise," Mordecai Fentwill said after a moment's reflection, "was published at a fortunate time. Thousands of dissatisfied believers in both the conditioning of reflexes and dianetics were moodily toying with yoghurt, wheat germ and blackstrap molasses in the hope of growing very old and looking more and more youthful while doing so. But such a purely bodily approach is never satisfying to those who enjoy the suspicion that they are complex creatures harboring interesting neuroses of which they can cure themselves by reading a book.

"*The Void after Freud* was perhaps injudiciously subtitled 'A Re-evaluation of Certain Theories Concerning the Human Will.' This subtitle alone aroused such violent reactions among critics that two of these gentlemen came to blows in a public place. The one armed with Freud's *Introduction to Psychoanalysis* sustained the greater injury, for despite his heavier weapon his aim was poor. Whereas his antagonist, lightly armed with my three-hundred-page volume, scored a direct hit. It resulted in a black eye and a battery suit, later dropped.

"My first audience consisted of persons who apparently

would have been happy to see me lynched. Certain letters printed in the *Saturday Review of Literature* rose to real fury against me. I had attempted to destroy the comforting belief that human beings are creatures of their environment and therefore cannot be held responsible for their own actions.

"On the other hand, I also stated that scientists are falsely accused of denying the existence of God because they state that the world is considerably older than was believed by an Irish archbishop of the middle seventeenth century, who wrote that the earth was created in the year 4004 B.C. My condemnation of psychology and my defense of paleontologists made it impossible for some people to understand where I stood in the intellectual scheme of things.

"Of the tales circulated about me, many were true. It is quite true that I was a student and disciple of Freud, although instead of following him into his theories concerning the not-conscious human mind, I lingered behind with hypnosis, the keyhole into the human psyche which was abandoned by Dr. Freud and which was perhaps too small a means of egress for his tremendous and imaginative genius. My youthful discoveries led me to entirely different philosophic conclusions than those of my great teacher. I came to believe the reverse of what other disciples of his were later to preach. I came to believe that channeled human thought can transcend the ordinary functions of the human body, and therefore the human environment as well. I chose to conclude that this channeled human thought which I had seen so many times in potent action is no more than the human will, that now-unpopular asset of all the ancient heroes of the race of man."

He cleared his throat. "My caution about the feats of yogi reassured many, but others seemed confused by my admission that the necessity of earning a living by teaching had not permitted me the time needed for full investigation of the matter. All I could be sure of is that under self-hypnosis men and women can stop their hearts from beating, their blood from flowing, can conquer pain, insomnia and the non-virus diseases. There is no doubt that self-hypnosis once saved my life.

"While climbing Mount Rainier alone, I fell and broke my leg, severing an artery. Unfortunately I was also partly buried under a modest landslide, and my arms were pinioned so that I could not put on a tourniquet to stop the flow of blood. Realizing that before the time when the rest of my party would join me I might well bleed to death, I induced a level of hypnotic slumber which enabled me to will my blood to cease pouring from my injured leg for the next three hours. By ill luck I was accidentally found in an hour, and in two I was lying on an operating table in the nearest hospital before three spellbound doctors who attempted to explain to one another the seven-inch gash from which no blood could be induced to flow. They had got out the usual tools for amputation when my hypnotic state fortunately ended. In considerable pain, I rather waspishly suggested that they put away the hacksaws and get out the catgut. Although none of them had a satisfactory explanation for the fact that as I reproached them blood gushed from my wound in the normal manner, they were all sure that there was a reasonable cause other than the one which I astounded and troubled them by offering."

Mordecai Fentwill smiled grimly. "I remember that one of them said the newspapers would regard me as quite the hero. I replied that the appellation was no longer a compliment to the discerning.

"The hero was once a man who faced impossible odds and overcame them by the power of his will. A Buddha by contemplation, a Beowulf with a sword. But now, in our day, 'hero' means, to millions of people, a prepossessing young man not less than six feet tall who desires to mate with an equally prepossessing woman of shorter stature.

"As for the human will as a force shaping human destiny, it is an outmoded concept which has been abandoned in favor of the behaviorist's naïve notion that our environment is invariably stronger than we and thus shapes our lives, our minds, our—forgive me the word—souls. This, of course, is a comforting belief, but then all prisoners have the same comfort—that they can do nothing whatever about limitations enforced upon them.

"Of late years there has appeared a crevice in the wall enclosing the behaviorists and their congregations. Geneticists have at last seen—and photographed—the genes which carry inherited traits from parents to child. A photograph, however blurred, carries in this day a convincingness which Da Vinci's most detailed anatomical sketch could not. And so the varied schools of psychology are fairly well agreed that we mortals are no longer mere blank slates on which environment writes with massive hand; it is accepted that we inherit from our multiple ancestors certain capacities which may vary almost as widely as the schools of psychology themselves. But the majority of psychologists and psychiatrists and psychoanalysts are firm about their major tenet: Destiny is spelled 'childhood trauma,' and is forged before we know it by forces we cannot control.

"The dismal spectacle of psychoanalysis has one virtue of which I am certain: It imposes a mental discipline whereby innumerable new synapses are formed in a brain where dormant nerve cells then may function, which frequently makes the brain's owner equal, for the first time, to necessity. But this does not occur because of what the supine patient had learned or thought he had learned of his childhood traumas. I believe the road he retraced was important because the journey forced him to call on the very power he had been schooled to believe did not exist: He *willed* the recollection of forgotten episodes. The particular scorn which many psychoanalysts, psychiatrists and psychologists reserve for the term 'the human will' is rooted in prejudice and does not obliterate the fact that it is the simplest explanation for a phenomenon they encounter every day—the mentally disturbed patient who will not co-operate with the doctor.

"Fat people often believe that what they need is a great deal of exercise and are shocked to learn that a ten-mile hike would not balance the intake of one ham sandwich. When they are told there is one sure and simple way to grow thinner—to eat less—it is amazing to find how hard this is for obesity to grasp. To get thinner by merely eating less? Too ridiculously simple! A power flowing through us which can command the blood to stop flowing, the heart to cease beating, the spine to stiffen for the hardest task? Too ridiculously simple!

"I believe my unpopularity in certain quarters rises from the fact that a modern agnostic will defend the omnipotence of 'Science' as hotly as a Christian of the Dark Ages defended God's ability to work such miracles of showmanship as making marble statues weep tears of blood on given holy days. And the heretic of today is one who raises his voice against the popular delusion that science can accomplish all the miracles, and more, once attributed to a heavenly father. Among the more 'intellectual' groups in North America, to criticize the total validity of psychoanalysis, as they understand it, is to provoke a highly emotive defensive. They have accepted wholeheartedly this current approach to understanding the human animal, and they are inclined to be dogmatic—a frequent vice of the wholehearted, for which they are to be forgiven.

"Men like to accept promises of their time, even though they suspect that fulfillment may be deferred. The promise which psychiatry holds out is redemption of past error, a promise much older than the Christian faith, the most popular promise since human society developed to the stage of creating taboos and inflicting punishment. Where the Christian faith—and other religions—make promises which will be kept in Paradise, psychiatry offers to make good here and now, as any popular faith in a highly materialistic culture must do. Complete psychoanalysis, we are informed, is costly and may take many years, but for most of us the speedier, streamlined psychotherapy treatment can bring about adjustment to life.

"Adjustment to life! What a telling phrase! Life is no longer to be regarded as a journey, a series of adventures for the buoyant, or, for the serious, a pilgrimage. Ah, no. Life, we are assured, is a prison labyrinth with all the trick doors and electric grills of a psychologist's maze for caged white rats in a laboratory. Human beings, like those rats, must, in the psychologist's eyes, 'adjust' to the torments of an elaborate, prearranged passage. Desire to escape is neurosis, because, in the laboratory maze, escape is impossible. The balked white rat who huddles and shivers and will at last move neither forward nor back is a victim of neurosis. And this white rat, psychology students are told, is a classic, simplified picture of the way in which neurotic human beings behave. The fallacy of both the experiment and the last assumption is sadly apparent, but not, apparently, to psychologists.

"How easy to arrive at a given conclusion if one creates the factors on which it is based. The psychologist is full of the belief that environment is all-powerful. He then creates a laboratory maze which is a perfect expression of that belief. When the expected comes about, when the rat collapses, he considers his belief proved. But he seems unable to look farther and see that his 'experiment' with maze and rat was in the nature of a ritual, a solemn, elaborate assertion of dogma.

"I suppose very early, sincere and transported Christians could believe during the ceremony of the Mass that the wine they reverently tasted was indeed the actual blood of their Saviour, materialized by some heavenly miracle to feed their faith. Since faith and clarity of reasoning do not always go hand in hand, I could forgive psychologists their equally prejudiced beliefs if they would not insist that it is the scientific method which they use to arrive at the suppositions they present as proved laws."

He smiled charmingly. "But I fear we have digressed a trifle. You were going to tell me, Mr. Tuck, whether or not I heard you mention a booby trap as I entered this room a few minutes ago."

The piece of twine tied to the trigger of a cheap revolver led to the anonymous telegram, which led to the newspaper story earlier in the day in which Brigit's name had been mentioned. Then Tuck and Brigit described the attack on Mrs. Crone and the murder of Ruth Ann Briggs to which it was or was not linked by the bloodstained glove. Nearly an hour passed before Mordecai Fentwill picked up his brief case and arose. "Since we have no way of proving beyond the possibility of doubt that the blood on the glove is Ruth Ann Briggs's, and in the absence of any explanation for the glove's presence in the Crones' living room, we would do well to pursue at once certain other clues demanding attention. The anonymous letter sent to Mrs. Briggs has been woefully ignored, especially in view of the remarkable fact that she received this letter *three years after the murder*."

He disappeared around the edge of the brown screen, returned in a moment wearing his black Homburg hat. It gave him a mysterious and faintly sinister appearance, like one of those international financial wizards who are known to have accumulated untold millions of dollars through years of secret transactions.

"I suggest that you, Mr. Tuck, find out exactly when the revolver was set up in the window of the old house. It probably could not have been placed there earlier than the publication of the news story mentioning your name and Brigit's, but workmen in the area may be able to limit the time further. This is not too important, because the person who set the trap will undoubtedly have provided himself with a reasonable alibi."

"Froody's working on that now," said Tuck, also rising.

"I do not know who 'Froody' might be, but I suggest that you help him. I shall confine my initial efforts to the anonymous letter which told Mrs. Briggs that her daughter's death was probably an accident. You have no idea how much that letter interests me. Persons who hide behind such signatures as 'An Unknown Friend' cause almost as much harm as those who believe that the end justifies the means."

Brigit found herself staring at Tuck, who was staring rather stupidly down at Mordecai Fentwill, who turned to Brigit and said, "You, Brigit, can try to find the identity and whereabouts of 'R.C.,' the young man mentioned in Ruth Ann's diary."

"I did. He was the cousin of the girl she met at the movies the day she died."

"Oh. You didn't mention that in your brief résumé. Fine. As you can both see, I am dividing our triple efforts among the three crimes. Although in detective stories it is a rule that a series of crimes must be committed by one villain, we are dealing with reality, which is always inartistic and aims toward no final unmasking, no last chapter. It is therefore

144

quite likely that the three crimes we are considering had each a different author: the person who killed a pretty schoolgirl six years ago, the person who struck Mrs. Crone five days ago and the person who arranged the trap for Brigit four or five hours ago."

"But I don't agree at all," said Brigit flatly. "That telegram definitely links the three crimes and also strongly suggests that one person committed them. Maybe I didn't make that telegram clear, Uncle Mordecai. It specifically said that the same person hit Mrs. Crone and killed the Briggs girl."

"You told me that."

"Well, then, it doesn't take a genius to figure the only person who could have known that. The killer."

"But why did he set that absurdly inefficient trap? Surely you both see that the person who did so had not the slightest desire to kill anyone." He regarded their blank faces brightly. "I see my point escapes you. Had the person who set the trap wished to kill one of you, would he have used so haphazard a method? The most meager intelligence, the barest knowledge of firearms, insist that an unaimed gun rarely hits the bull's-eye of a moving target. No, there was another reason for the gun in the window. But it is far too early to deal with theories. I shall not mention the rather obvious motive which had occurred to me."

"What was the name of Sherlock Holmes's brother?" asked Tuck softly.

"Mycroft," Mordecai Fentwill replied. The swift answer was followed by a sudden burning blush. A look of false innocence accented the childish outline of the little man's square and chubby jaw, but his composure returned almost at once. "You are quite right, Mr. Tuck. I do believe that I would make a very capable detective. But," he went on rather hurriedly, "we must not impose ourselves on Brigit any longer." He cast his niece a smile, a nod of farewell.

145

"Just a minute, Uncle Mordecai!" Brigit's stern voice arrested his departure. "What makes you think you'd be a good detective? What do you know about murder?"

"I understand, I believe, why it is committed. I know the extremes to which men can be driven by prejudice. We all, of course, are strongly prejudiced in favor of ourselves, but a murderer overdoes it. He believes himself worthier than his victim, even in the very act of proving otherwise by killing him!" Mordecai Fentwill's face glowed with a kind of pleasure as he presented them with this gem of human contradictoriness.

"But how about murder in self-defense?" Brigit demanded.

"All murders are in self-defense. Or rather, in defense of part of the self."

"Oh, sure, I see. The id, the ego, or the superego?" she demanded.

The look of extreme distaste on her great-uncle's face was startling. "You will forgive me if I remark that the terms you have just used are indicative neither of originality nor of the desire to think with clarity. If you wish to entangle your intellect—I am assuming you have one, a conclusion which nothing I have yet observed forces on me—if, however, you wish to tangle your thinking processes with hackneyed and generally misunderstood remnants of bargain-counter psychology, kindly save such repartee for those with a similar faith in labels."

Somewhat crushed, Brigit saw that Tuck was wearing his dimpled grin, which suddenly faded as Uncle Mordecai's deep, dark eyes rested coldly on his face.

Speaking somewhat to them, but also to an absent audience remembered in his mind, Mordecai Fentwill said, "At my age there are many ideas in which one does not believe any longer, and some in which one has never believed.

146

Among the latter, in my case, is the notion that on Allhallow Eve witches ride on broomsticks to a festival of corpses which arise from their graves for the occasion. I never believed that, even as a small child, and I feel safe in saying that I never shall. As a young man, as I have told you, I was a student of Sigmund Freud. I have always been a stanch admirer of his genius. However, I have never believed that the human mind is divided into three parts called the id, the ego and the superego. Sigmund's mind may well have been, but he was an extraordinary individual, and what was true of him could hardly be generally applied."

Brigit spoke with helpless annoyance. "Well, how do *you* think the human mind is divided?"

"Against itself."

Brigit pounced with triumph. "Self-preservation fighting the death wish!"

Her uncle smiled with disdain that was not unkind. "I prefer to say the True struggling against the False."

"It sounds like a parlor game."

Now he looked like a gentle old scholar. "No, my dear, it is not a game. It is a running fight. We are all seriously involved from cradle to coffin. Our flattering prejudices are by their nature at odds with the implacable truth. I wish I could say that truth always triumphs. But there are escapes from its authority. Suicide. Insanity. And murder, of course."

"I don't get you."

With something like gusto Mordecai Fentwill said, "As a pastime I have analyzed some two hundred modern murders. I have found these axioms to be true. A killer seeks the peace of being entirely wrong instead of nearly so. Whatever a murderer may *seem* to have killed, he was really seeking to destroy that unendurably truthful part of himself with which the rest could not live. You might say that murder is a symbolic suicide, since actual suicide cannot be partial and is always fatal. I believe, therefore, that in the nature of the victim is to be found the chief clue to the nature of the killer. Because the corpse symbolized, for a time, that part of himself from which the murderer sought escape."

He drew his watch from his vest pocket, looked at it with amazement and glanced at Tuck with an expression which stated that consideration of Brigit as well as good manners demanded their prompt departure. Then he looked down at Brigit almost fondly. "Good night, my dear. You may count on my help to the limit of my ability, which is not inconsiderable." He then preceded Tuck toward the door of the room, but paused to peer at Brigit around the bulk of the tall detective. "I shall be in Los Angeles for the balance of the present semester. I am delivering a series of lectures at the University of Southern California. I would have called on you much sooner were it not for the fact that consanguinity has inflicted some of the most boring hours I have ever spent."

Modest old guy, Brigit thought, after the two men had gone and a nurse had given her a sedative. In the hospital-smelling darkness she became lost in speculation which soon found itself in a maze. R.C. was Richard Carewe, was Eloise's cousin. A long-ago voice suddenly said, "The wind that night made me feel kind of zippy, like anything could happen, right out of the blue. . . ." And out of the blue a white glove with bloodied fingers wafted down like a falling leaf to lie, palm up, on Brigit's lap. But she was reading an anonymous telegram and didn't pay it much attention until the glove stirred, filled out with someone's living hand. Terrified, she looked up at a face in a black domino mask: The tawny mustache was Eric Crone's, the red hair belonged to Dayleen Burke, the broad white smile was that of the high-

148

school boy named Desmond Grover. With a girlish laugh like Helene's the mouth spoke in Mrs. Crone's precise and ladylike voice: "The Bird's not a bad guy when you get to know him!"

If a prophet is without honor in his own country, he is even less revered in his family. To Brigit, Mordecai Fentwill was her late Aunt Rosie's eccentric husband whose remarks at family dinners were now legend, and who had sent her a copy of the *Phaedo* on her twelfth birthday along with a card which said that no one should reach that advanced age without reading of the trial and death of Socrates. And so when Brigit learned from Richard Tuck that he had promptly turned over to Uncle Mordecai the letter and diary which Mr. Briggs had brought to the Homicide Department, as well as all the records of the Briggs case, she told Tuck that he had acted like a plain, unvarnished sap.

But exactly twenty hours after the bullet entered Brigit's shoulder Mordecai Fentwill telephoned Brigit, and after inquiring how she was feeling added, "By the way, my dear, I believe I know who wrote that anonymous letter. Could you and Mr. Tuck have a Martini with me at my flat near the university at five this evening?"

Brigit hung up the telephone and found herself full of the elated notion that the small spry old gentleman whose interference she had decried would now magically unravel the knots with which she and her partner had been fumbling.

The pain of her heavily taped shoulder vanished, the doctor's instructions to rest quietly at home for another day or so were forgotten, and she replaced the grim white sling on her arm with a gay red polka-dot scarf.

# 13

"ALL CHILDREN wish they could fly," said Mordecai Fentwill to Brigit and Tuck. "Adults learn not to wish to fly, but they do not learn not to wish. All of us have succumbed in fantasy to childish transcendence of the earthy present."

He sipped from a Martini glass held with the level care long bestowed on cups at faculty teas. His modest apartment, furnished like a thousand of its kind in durable brocades and false mahogany, was without a single personal possession that might erase past transients from the atmosphere. Brigit wondered why, unlike all other old people she had ever known, her uncle clung to no mementos out of his lost past.

"What struck me most forcibly about the anonymous letter," he continued, his dark eyes alert, "was that the person who wrote it *wished* to believe that the Briggs girl could have died as the result of an accident like the one described. But why should anyone wish to believe that murder had not been murder?"

Brigit sensed that the question was rhetorical, but nonetheless started to answer. "Well, it could be because——"

Her uncle silenced her with the pained polite surprise of a professor confronting interruption from a student at his lecture. "The most obvious conclusion is that the writer of the letter suspected who had committed that murder but did not want to believe it. Probably the hope was that time in its passage would deny the troubling doubts.

"And time produced . . . a windy night which must have insistently recalled the night on which the Briggs girl died, and also a flying palm branch which obligingly struck the writer as the anonymous letter describes. A mind nagged by a distasteful suspicion wishfully flew to a pleasanter conclusion and gulped it gratefully. To wit: The same kind of accident could well have struck down Ruth Ann Briggs! Improvisation of the means whereby her body could have got to the canyon followed swiftly. In brief, a wishful fantasy was enacted. In the grip of it the mind so full of its own imaginings was moved to put them down in black and white, to share them with the dead girl's parents. I think that this impulse was less generosity than an unrecognized desire to endow the fantasy with an audience, on the fallacious but very common conviction that if more people believe a lie, it becomes more true."

"In plain words," said Brigit, "whoever wrote the letter is wacky."

Mordecai Fentwill shook his head. "If by that you mean insane, no. Had the writer fully believed in the absolute truth of the accident theory, then I admit we would be dealing with delusion, a major element of several known forms of psychosis. But the writer of the letter never stated the accident theory as true—only as possible. This shows an active knowledge of the difference between fact and fancy, which is one of the differences between sanity and madness. But sanity has its gradations. The writer of the letter is certainly capable of clinging to the comfort of illusions with more strength than the majority of us possess."

" 'Neurotic' is the word for that," said Brigit.

"'Neurotic' is the word for almost anything of late," said her uncle. With an insulting smile he added, "In the days of Lombroso, when facial characteristics were supposed to indicate criminal tendencies, any fool could tell a pickpocket by the shape of his ears. Now he can recognize a neurotic without even the ears to judge by." His piercing gaze abandoned Brigit and seemed to turn inward. In an instant he continued: "To return to the next natural step in my speculations, it seemed to me that a suspicion haunting enough to have given birth to the anonymous letter was attached to someone known to the writer. And this would explain why the writer had not confided the reason for that suspicion to the police. It is hard to inform on someone one knows, for if one is wrong, the opportunities for retaliation are often considerable."

He thoughtfully dipped his small beaked nose into his glass. "Like a bird," Brigit said to herself. "A small, fierce bird. A ferocious robin."

"Since this is the United States," continued Mordecai Fentwill, "and since the letter showed a certain literacy, it seemed to me unlikely that it had been written by anyone who received his basic education in the last fifteen years, during which the type of education described as 'Progressive' has been busily producing college students seventy-five per cent of whom cannot write a declarative sentence. I need not dwell on the fact that the most obvious persons to have entertained the suspicion which I saw as the primary reason for the anonymous letter are the parents of the youthful suspects, Manuel Reyes, Desmond Grover, Dayleen Burke and the recently discovered Richard Carewe.

"I eliminated the family of the Mexican boy at once. Since your interview with Manuel states that he was of the first generation of his family to be born in the United States, it seemed to me unlikely that an older member of the family, suspecting the boy, could have written the letter. So it proved.

"I found the parents of Desmond Grover to be eminently sensible people, as those in possession of considerable wealth are so apt to be. After young Desmond had been questioned by the police his father had quietly engaged the services of one of the best criminal lawyers in the city, a fact he freely admitted to me. The mother told me that since Desmond had known Ruth Ann, if but slightly, they had sent a spray of pink rosebuds and lilies of the valley to the funeral, this choice of blooms having been related to the girl's youth and innocence, recollection of which brought a look of appropriate sadness to Mrs. Grover's large face. I was forced to the conclusion that persons capable of such conventional expressions of sympathy as well-chosen funeral sprays do not tend to write anonymous, comforting letters. Nor do I believe that people so realistic as to hire a criminal attorney at the mere possibility of future jeopardy are also so unrealistic as to harbor secret suspicions and wishful fantasies after the danger is past. I abandoned them both as incapable of writing the letter whose author I sought."

"I've seen the Grover mansion," said Brigit. "How did you crash the gate?"

Mordecai Fentwill blinked as though slightly surprised. "I rang the doorbell and presented my card."

"But after you got in, how did you explain your visit?" asked Tuck.

"Why, I said that certain aspects of the Briggs girl's murder interested me. The Grovers then interrupted each other in explaining that although their son had been in adolescence a trifle high-spirited, he would not have harmed the lowliest of God's creatures. I pointed out that the lowliest of God's creatures do not arouse our wrath as human beings do, which is the reason why several murderers have been noted for their kindness to dogs. This did not deter Mrs. Grover from a narrative concerning a pet rabbit whose death had caused Desmond such grief that they bought the child a Shetland pony."

"All this you got away with, without so much as a deputy sheriff's badge!" marveled Brigit, feeling a surge of respect for her great-uncle.

"I have learned that in the United States people are as a rule most amiable about answering questions, once you have relieved them of their fear that you are trying to sell them something they do not desire," said Mordecai Fentwill. "I will pass over the parents of Dayleen Burke Pflugel very briefly. Within ten minutes they had committed, between them, nine grammatical errors of a glaring nature, as well as incidental malapropisms and mispronunciations. Neither of them could have written our anonymous letter.

"The last of my most obvious questionees was the mother of Richard Carewe, a Mrs. Harry Schneider. She was just stepping out of the door of her apartment as I reached it. She was on her way to Las Vegas, Nevada, and perhaps her excitement over this holiday accounted for the fact that at first she had not the slightest recollection of anyone named Ruth Ann Briggs. When I reminded her that this had been the name of the victim of the murder on Acacia Street she became grimly suspicious and informed me that her son had been at that time in the Army fighting in defense of his country, and that Fort Ord was four hundred miles from Los Angeles. All the time she spoke so vehemently her brazen hair seemed to blaze, and her long red fingernails plucked at the clasp of her large purse, opening it and snapping it viciously shut again." Mordecai Fentwill reflected a moment. "She was a very terrible woman. Terrible with that shallow, frustrated prettiness which seems at last to enclose those American women whose reading staples since childhood have been love stories where the heroines are rewarded with bliss and wealth because they possess an anatomy different from the male." Mordecai paused, remembering Mrs. Schneider with a look of wry and sorrowful humor. "She did not write the letter.

"With the elimination of the parents of Richard Carewe —I did not mention that his father has not been heard from in more than twenty years—I came to the end of my small group of initial questionees. Unless my emotional and intellectual reasons for exonerating them were in one instance wrong, and this I did not believe, someone else had entertained suspicion of one of the four young people, or doubts had been entertained concerning a person not suspected by the police.

"Before exploring that new byway I asked myself if I had overlooked anyone who might have been deeply troubled by suspicion of one of the main known suspects. An answer so obvious leaped into my mind that I wondered why I had wasted half a day with the people I had seen. Helene Crone, according to the records of the Briggs case, had known and liked Desmond Grover in high school. I saw it as quite possible that some action or comment of his had aroused suspicions, just or not, in her girlish heart. After two and a half years at college Helene could conceivably have learned enough of written English to produce the letter. It was with a sense of certainty that I went to the Crones' home to talk to her.

"Her mother opened the door and told me Helene was out. She then said that my name struck her as very familiar. Seeing in the hall bookcase a copy of my book, I told her why. She most effusively invited me to have tea with her, believing me an Englishman and believing that all Englishmen like tea.

"We spoke of literature. It was as we talked that Mrs.

Crone's manner of speech struck me. I suddenly realized that I was hearing the forced style of the anonymous letter as it would sound spoken aloud. And when I transferred the conversation to the Briggs girl's unsolved murder, mention of it plainly troubled Mrs. Crone. I described the anonymous letter, drawing it from my pocket as I spoke. The look of discomfort and surprise on her face seemed confirmation of my guess. But how could I force her to admit authorship? Especially since it would mean admittedly that she had suspected either her husband or her daughter of being the person who killed Ruth Ann Briggs."

"Wow!" said Tuck. "Helene?"

"Eric Crone?" said Brigit. "Oh, no!"

Mordecai Fentwill went to a desk on which Brigit noticed for the first time a large loose-leaf notebook with a cover of brown leather. "I made shorthand notes immediately after leaving Mrs. Crone, and as my memory for the spoken word is excellent, you may take the following dialogue to be accurate.

"QUESTION: 'To know who wrote this most interesting letter, Mrs. Crone, would be to eliminate a number of misleading possibilities which at present confuse my thinking and so prevent my arriving at a belated solution of the mystery surrounding Miss Briggs's death.'

"ANSWER: 'I may seem stupid, Dr. Fentwill, but I do not see what you mean.'

"Q: 'Here, read the letter, Mrs. Crone. [Pause of several minutes while Mrs. Crone complied.] Now, Mrs. Crone, does it not strike you that the writer of the letter must have suspected someone of the crime?'

"A: 'It does rather strike one like that.'

"Q: 'Since there is nothing at all shameful about entertaining suspicions, even if they later prove unfounded, I have wondered why the writer of the letter chose to remain anonymous.'

"A: 'That seems quite natural. Three years had gone by since the poor girl's death, and the parents might have thought it odd that someone should write them such a note at that late hour.'

"Q: 'There must have been some basis for the suspicion which gave rise to the wishful theory of accident. Does it not seem to you, Mrs. Crone, that the writer would have done better to let the police determine whether those doubts had foundation?'

"A: 'But to do so might have been to jeopardize the safety of an innocent person, Dr. Fentwill!'

"Q: 'I do not believe I will surprise you when I say I believe that you wrote this letter, Mrs. Crone.'

"A (after a brief pause): 'Surely you realize that even if I had, I would not wish to make a statement which would harm a possibly innocent person now any more than then.'

"Q: 'But if I were to tell you that I already know whom you suspected, could acknowledgment of authorship possibly do any harm?'

"A: 'There is little use in concealing the truth any longer. Your insight, Dr. Fentwill, is amazing. Yes, I did once suspect my son-in-law of that dreadful crime.'

"Q: 'Your son-in-law, Mrs. Crone?'

"A: 'Perhaps I should have said, the young man who later became my son-in-law. My daughter Helene was married a little over a year ago. It was a lovely wedding, in St. James Episcopal Church. We had over 200 at the reception. By then, of course, I had come to realize how wrong I had been in my suspicion of Desmond.' "

There was a moment of silence while Tuck and Brigit absorbed the fact that Helene was now Mrs. Desmond

157

Grover. Brigit was nagged by the feeling that Helene's flight from her husband on the night Mrs. Crone had been attacked was in some way connected with the several trains of events in which they were all labyrinthed.

"Did Mrs. Crone have any reasons for suspecting Desmond Grover besides the ones we had?" asked Tuck.

"Only the fact that early in 1948 Dayleen Burke paid Mrs. Crone a visit to warn her that Desmond Grover was mentally unbalanced. Motive: jealousy. In the society section of the previous day's paper there had been a photograph of Helene and Desmond, taken while smiling at each other at a college function. But there is another reason for Mrs. Crone's uneasy doubts, of which she is unaware. As Mrs. Crone made delicately clear to me, blue blood flows in Desmond Grover's veins from numerous family oil wells. This fact, coupled with all the rest, would have made any vague suspicions the good mother felt about so eligible a suitor additionally tormenting."

"How did she explain not signing the letter?"

"Very believably," said Mordecai. "She did not know the Briggses very well and was shy about expressing herself on so delicate a topic in person. And then when she copied her first draft of the letter it occurred to her that they would undoubtedly hurry across the street to question her about her theory, so on impulse she decided to remain unknown to them. And I now await your questions with interest."

"What questions are there to ask?" demanded Brigit. "You went over that letter like Sherman through Georgia. It's too bad it's such an incidental clue."

"I have a question," Tuck said. "When did Mrs. Crone stop suspecting Desmond Grover?"

"An excellent point. Her troubling doubts had abated by the time he married her daughter. Time and her accident theory account for this in part, and wishful thinking also did

158

its work. So perhaps you should have phrased your question thus: When did she begin again to suspect her son-in-law of having murdered Ruth Ann Briggs?"

"Did she say she did?" Brigit asked.

"Surely it is strongly implied, my dear. Otherwise, would she have so freely confessed to those earlier doubts of him?" He added: "We are fortunate in having a convenient way of checking the plausibility of Mrs. Crone's uneasiness about Desmond Grover. If there is any sound basis for it, Mrs. Desmond Grover must surely entertain suspicions of a much stronger nature."

"Which is why Helene telephoned her father to come and get her out of there!" Brigit exclaimed.

"Unless, of course, Desmond Grover criticized Helene's cooking, took another woman to dinner, became grossly intoxicated in public, lost a large sum of money by betting on the wrong horse, insulted her best friend's taste in clothes, called Helene's mother a simpering hag, wiped his hands on the guest towel after repairing the carburetor of the car, or told Helene he no longer loved her," said Mordecai Fentwill. "I am having a chat with her at ten tomorrow morning to see if I can possibly plumb the troubled depths of her young soul."

"If you plumb it as well as you plumbed the mama," Brigit said, "Helene Grover's married life is going to be as secret as a true-confession story."

Mordecai gave Brigit an odd look. "I see you have missed the point, my dear," he said. "So I shall give you this hint. When there is only one person's unsupported statement of a given matter, there are always but two alternatives: The person has either told the truth or is lying. From the first Mrs. Crone has made exactly two statements for which we have other witnesses. One is that she entertained members of the Third Thursday Club in her home on the night of

February 1, 1945. The other is that her daughter and Desmond Grover were married a little over a year ago."

"You mean that she may be protecting someone by admitting things that aren't true?" Tuck said.

"I do."

"But that brings us back to the place we started from! Whom would she protect except Eric Crone or Helene?" Brigit said.

"Herself," said Mordecai Fentwill.

Brigit's mind felt as blank as her voice sounded. "But there were all those women who said Mrs. Crone was at home in her living room when Ruth Ann was killed!"

"You misunderstand. What I mean is that Mrs. Crone could easily consider herself to be in danger from the person she suspects, should she reveal what she knows. If that is the case, she believes Desmond Grover to be innocent, not guilty, which is why she desperately drew our attention to him. Like the trap at the old house, her sole purpose was to confuse the issue. That is, if I am correct in my conviction that someone entered an abandoned house in the concealing twilight with a revolver and a length of twine on his person, arranged them as we know, and departed believing that the Briggs murder and the attack on Mrs. Crone had been inextricably linked. Whether the gun went off or whether you merely found it propped in that window—waiting."

# PART FOUR

*The Colonel's Daughter*

# 14

Helene's in the garden taking a sun bath," said Mrs. Crone. In her long quilted house coat splashed with small pallid flowers, she contrived to look more convalescent than was suggested by the fact that she had been dusting the living room when Mordecai Fentwill rang the front bell. She led him to the back porch saying, "I told her it was too early in the year, although the sun is unusually warm today, isn't it? And so good for the nerves."

Framed by the dim screen of the back door, Helene lay on one of the ubiquitous redwood chaise longues which Californians seem to consider even more necessary than barbecue pits. She wore brief blue denim shorts and a white cotton shirt tied just above the diaphragm. As she stood up like a polite schoolgirl the innocent candor of her bare midriff reminded Mordecai of the long half century between their ages, of the perhaps unbridgeable chasm between her attitudes and his own. He liked her round young face in spite of the hurt and sullen eyes; a few gold hairs from her lost childhood sparked her brown hair.

Mrs. Crone introduced them and added, "Dr. Fentwill's hobby is amateur criminal investigation, and he is quite interested in our unsolved neighborhood murder." She turned to Mordecai and presented him with the false and perfect smile common to receiving lines. "But you didn't tell me why."

"Brigit Estees is a relative of whom I am fond. She was shot in the shoulder two nights ago. Circumstances suggested that the person who did this may have killed Ruth Ann Briggs."

Mrs. Crone's face became grotesque in its look of amazement. Helene looked puzzled, but undisturbed. "Was it serious?" Mrs. Crone asked.

"No." He smiled at her twice as politely as she had just smiled at him, saw that her thin face seemed blanched in the sunlight. "I will be ignoring the customary procedure unless I speak with your daughter alone."

Mrs. Crone's eyes grew swiftly thoughtful. Then she resumed the game of smiling. "She already knows you questioned me, although of course I did not go into details." Now her dark eyes were asking him to say nothing of her doubts of Desmond Grover.

Mordecai turned to scan Helene's rather blank young face. "Among the more decent police investigators, of whom there are a number, data given during informal interviews usually remain a private matter between questioner and questionee, unless, of course, the matter discussed is relevant when the case comes to trial."

"I know that," said Helene with casual superiority, "because of my father's profession."

"Which reminds me to call the cleaners to see if they've found his brown trousers yet," said Mrs. Crone prosaically. She moved so swiftly and quickly toward the back door that she seemed to float above the grass.

Between the door and driveway was a large poinsettia plant holding up flat red blooms as big as plates. "What a splendid bush!" said Mordecai Fentwill, sitting on a collapsible chair of canvas and white-enameled metal.

"Let's not beat around it." Helene lighted a cigarette in a tough, practical manner. Then she belatedly remembered her manners and offered her guest one, in a confused, almost childlike way. "What do you want to ask me, Mr. Fentwill? If it's about Ruth Ann Briggs, I'm afraid I don't know much that will help you."

"But you do know why you telephoned your father to come out to your home on the night your mother was attacked," said Mordecai.

"It had nothing to do with Ruth Ann Briggs. Or with the attack on my mother," she said flatly.

"It might be best if you told me the nature of this trouble between you and your husband."

Her eyes evaded his and she stared at a big purple iris growing against the high fence; in the next-door driveway someone was washing a car, whistling over the splash of water. "It began about six months ago," she said suddenly. "That's when Desmond and I had our first real row." Her eyes met Mordecai's and one corner of her mouth smiled. "It was over that damned Glam-mask."

"I beg your pardon?"

She sat up very straight and made a wide, theatric gesture. "Glam-mask, for the skin like damask! Lovely women for thousands of years have known the secrets of *natural* aids to beauty, but today's women jeopardize their most priceless asset, a beautiful skin, with harsh chemical products!"

"Indeed?" asked Mordecai politely.

"A Glam-mask a day helps keep age lines away," Helene continued, her eyes bright with wicked humor. "So Glam-mask *your* skin *now!* Smooth the clean-smelling pink paste on face and neck, let it dry, gently wash off with cool water. Feel your skin come alive! You are ready to look the world in the eye with your best face forward!"

"This all seems somewhat irrelevant," complained Mordecai calmly.

"Oh, but it isn't! You see, Glam-mask was my husband's brain child. And do you know what it's made of? Oatmeal! Just plain powdered oatmeal is the basis. It costs nine cents to produce a two-dollar kit of the stuff. Or maybe it's nineteen. And that's what we had our first big row about. The social and ethical aspects of producing and selling Glam-mask. I said the whole thing stank, was just another way of bilking the public by getting around the Pure Food and Drug Act. But he said oatmeal is good for the skin and if he didn't bilk the public someone else would because people are suckers by nature, especially women. Oh, we had a diller of a battle! He knew I was right. He knew I was absolutely moral and sound and that he was a toad and a heel. As I pointed out, it wasn't as if we needed the money, either. We didn't speak for a week. And that was when Miss White stepped into the picture."

"Miss White?"

Now Helene looked brooding, bitter. "It's the old story. If a wife doesn't butter up her husband, some other woman will. I don't know who she is or where he met her, but I know she feels she has enough of a hold on him to telephone his home and make dates. And to——" Her voice stopped abruptly. "On the evening I left him he went to a bar called the Blue Grotto for a rendezvous with this deep-voiced siren. I was also there, roughly disguised as a matron in my mother's clothes. For some reason Miss White didn't show up. That, plus some things my mother said, made me feel silly. I returned to my happy home by taxicab, prepared to be adult and reasonable. But——" She suddenly turned her head away. "I don't want to talk about it!"

"You found proof that your worst fears were true. In anger, and perhaps revulsion, you telephoned your father,

166

asking him to come and take you away from there, which he did." Mordecai made his voice stern. "Or else you are rowing me rapidly up Salt Creek where you intend to leave me stranded with left-handed oars."

She stared at him, startled, then managed a smile. "Do you imagine you're talking slang?" she asked.

"You are astute enough to realize that since I am interested in finding the truth about Miss Briggs's murder, I am also aware that your husband was once one of the persons under suspicion of having killed her. You know that there could be a very glaring reason why you found you could no longer live in the same house with your husband. A reason having nothing whatever to do with either his invention of Glam-mask or his infatuation with Miss White. She is extremely unreal to me, incidentally. Against your vivid description of your husband's gift to American womanhood, she appears as an insubstantial wraith surrounding a husky voice."

"Not husky, harsh. Deep and harsh. O.K. Little as I happen to cherish my husband, I don't want you to go away from here with the idea that I left him because I think he committed murder. I'll make it brief. When I got home, at about eight o'clock, I found our car in the driveway. The house was brightly lighted. I went in ready for a showdown, because of a note I'd left saying I was going to stay with my parents for a while. I'd left the note on the mantel, which is where we always leave them. I found it on the coffee table. So he'd read it. I called him and got no answer. I went to our bedroom. The door was closed and locked. I knocked and called, but he didn't answer. I listened. I was sure he was in there. I couldn't hear anything, but that room had the feel of not being empty. I went around to the patio and looked in the window. It was dark, but I could see him lying on the bed. I could make out his leopardskin bathrobe, his light

167

hair. I yelled his name. I beat on the screen. He didn't move. He didn't stir. By now my eyes were used to the darkness. I could see he was breathing. There was no sign of anything wrong. Then the truth hit me. He was faking. He was pretending to be asleep. Because there was someone in that room with him. In the closet. Miss White. There hadn't been time for her to get away. So this was all he could do." Tears abruptly filled her brown eyes.

"You seem somewhat obsessed by this Miss White."

"What other explanation is there? He couldn't have been so drunk he didn't hear me pounding the door and yelling his name. It takes time to drink yourself into that kind of coma, and I saw him perfectly sober at six-thirty. And why did he lock the door? Both doors? The one to the hall and the one to the bathroom? What explanation is there, except that he read my note and very promptly telephoned Miss White to tell her the coast was clear." Her voice shook. "It made me sick! It made me furious!"

"The sanctity of your home had been besmirched," said Mordecai gravely.

"You can sing that! I took off like a rabbit. I walked down the hill to the canyon and phoned Dad. And that-a is that-a."

Mordecai rose. "Thank you, my dear, for your candor. I would like to say there is nothing so deceiving as appearances, and not solely when their purpose is to deceive." He started toward the driveway, then turned. "I am going to have a talk with your husband. Is there any message you want me to convey?"

"Yes, but it would embarrass you."

Mordecai had started down the driveway when he heard the back door close softly. "Do you think it was wise to discuss such personal matters with a stranger?" asked Mrs.

Crone's faint clear voice. "And out here in the back yard where our neighbors can hear?"

"Maybe it wasn't wise, but it was a big relief."

Mordecai paused, and then retraced his steps to the poinsettia bush. He could give no specific reason for eavesdropping and was surprised to find that his intention bore with it no sense of shame.

"I've never told you much about my father, have I, Helene?" asked Mrs. Crone in a soft voice which he could hardly hear. Peeping through the bush, he saw Mrs. Crone seated in the chair he had occupied. She looked pensive. Her question was so irrelevant that it interested him at once.

"No, not much," Helene said. "Why?"

Mrs. Crone looked toward the fence, then murmured, "I believe it right that you should know the story my mother told me when I was eighteen. I was engaged then to a handsome, rather wild young man. I found he was involved with rumrunners. I didn't know what to do. He was a criminal. What I really wanted was to forgive him and marry him. I believed myself much in love. But my mother was wise. She told me that there is no horror comparable to that of a wife forced to protect a worthless husband from his just deserts."

Helene observed, "That phrase always misleads me. It sounds like something good and means the reverse."

"And then," said Clare Crone, her low voice full of conscious drama, "my mother told me the truth about my father."

"Was he a rumrunner too?" Helene asked with mild interest.

"How could he have been, in 1907?" demanded Clare Crone sharply.

"What happened in 1907?"

"Please don't keep interrupting. I'm telling you something very important."

169

"I'm listening."

"My father, judging from photographs, was a very handsome man. He was also a weak and foolish one. When I was born he was a lieutenant at a large Army post in the South. At this post there was a young girl, a colonel's daughter, who had for some time been a subject of scandal. She was, to put it bluntly, a nymphomaniac."

"That isn't so awfully blunt, Mother, but go on."

"When I was a baby she came home one evening and weepingly told her father that a young sergeant had tried to seduce her. But although the court-martial made it plain to many that the boy was innocent, the colonel had him broken utterly. The example of the sergeant was a failure, for at one time or another every good-looking officer on the post was known to have conducted a flirtation with the colonel's daughter. My father was one of these.

"When I was two years old the colonel's daughter was found dead one night in the woods near the camp. She had been shot through the head, and the bullet had come from an Army revolver."

"Don't tell me your father shot her?" Helene was sitting bolt upright, and her voice showed her shock.

Inexorably Mrs. Crone proceeded without reply. "Half a dozen young men, my father among them, were closely questioned. It was never determined which one of them had killed the girl, although the motive was plain. She had been spurned, and had threatened her escort with the same treatment the sergeant got. In fear and anger he had ended her life.

"There was some disgrace, of course, but it was spread among many. In time the affair was forgotten. But after my father had been transferred to another camp, my mother quietly divorced him. I was five then, and it was rather a shock to me, although Mother and I went to live with her parents who were well-off, established people. My life was in many ways happier than it would have been on some Army post.

"My mother told me the real reason for the divorce to help me make the proper decision about my engagement to a scoundrel. She told me that my father had not been with her on the night of the murder, as he had stated. She had backed him up. She did not know where he had really been. But she knew that at the time of the murder one of his two Army revolvers disappeared. She found it months later when she was digging a flower bed in our garden. One bullet had been fired."

"God!" said Helene bleakly.

"Of course the act of burying the gun could have come from my father's sense of guilt at having had anything to do with the girl, and his fear of being unjustly suspected. He told my mother he had fired the gun at one of the rats which infested the camp, and this may have been true. But my mother could never be sure. She could never know whether or not she was married to a murderer. She bore this for three long years. She told me that if he had not been transferred to another camp, she would have hung on for years more. Because, of course, if she had left him while they were still at the place where the colonel's daughter had been killed, too many people might have guessed the reason. And she wished to protect me against any future remarks about the old scandal, about my father's character."

There was a pause. In a different tone, casual instead of prim, Mrs. Crone said, "You are more fortunate than my mother was. You have no child to protect."

"Hey! Just a minute! You seem to think that I think . . ."

"There is nothing to keep you from doing what my mother

171

did as soon as she could. Sometimes suspicions have a way of remaining unsolved. Such doubts are agonizing in the extreme."

"My God!" gasped Helene. "You think Desmond killed Ruth Ann Briggs!"

"Don't talk so loud! What I think is unimportant. I don't have to spend the rest of my life with him."

There was a silence. In a thin voice Helene said, "He didn't hit you on the head anyway. He had other fish to fry that night!"

"Please don't be vulgar. I know this is hard for you, but you must not beg the issue."

Mordecai peered through the stalks of the poinsettia bush in time to see Mrs. Crone lean slowly toward her daughter. The flowery robe fell open to reveal a pale breastbone. "Be truthful with me, dear! Do you believe Desmond could have killed poor Ruth Ann?"

Helene stared at her mother. "No! I don't believe it! I don't believe it at all!"

Mrs. Crone stood up. As Mordecai backed out of sight she said, "There are reasons why I have had certain doubts of him."

"What reasons?"

Mrs. Crone's voice was austere. "Reasons which I have fully confided to no one. And which I shall now forget. They are meaningless, if you have been honest with me."

"I have, Mother!" Helene sounded like a child, a child about to cry.

And Mordecai Fentwill walked toward the cement glare of the sidewalk knowing that once again he had been privileged to see how the present can be shaped by the past. Not precisely like it, nor patterned by simple and conscious motives, but forever forming itself out of old events in the mind that remembers them. The bloodied glove was an Army revolver buried long ago in a garden. Innocent or guilty, the father of Clare Crone still cast a long shadow. Innocent or guilty, the husband of Clare Crone walked in it, for Ruth Ann Briggs was the colonel's daughter, the girlish huzzy who toyed with married men until one killed her. Desmond Grover? Innocent or guilty, he was the only reply the anxious present could logically make to the powerful and persuasive voice of the past.

By her silence Mrs. Crone may have fully recreated what happened in 1907. Once more, a dead girl. Once more, only suspicion to rest on those who could have killed her, and then to fade, leaving the murderer free, again.

The Grovers' house, two miles to the west, clung to the brink of a canyon. It was a low and angular redwood dwelling, its uncompromising lines set off by luxuriant tropical plants that made Mordecai Fentwill think of night clubs.

The long, deep-green Cadillac convertible parked before the door told him that Desmond Grover was at home, and he heard chimes sound inside with full expectance that the door would be thrown open by a young man in a leopardskin bathrobe. But the ring remained unanswered for several minutes. He tried again. Again only silence greeted him. A car roared past, bound for a still higher level on the hill, and the quiet it left behind seemed suddenly unpleasant. Remembering Mrs. Macabee, he smiled a little as he walked to the big front window and peered in between severe curtains which were not quite drawn.

On the long, low sofa lay a blond young man wearing gray slacks and an open white shirt. The foot in view was bare; a heelless leather slipper lay on the floor near it. One arm dangled to lie along the floor, palm curled upward. Then Mordecai saw something that made him step back, shocked,

173

looking about him for a way to get into the silent house. On the green rug, near the limp arm, a cigarette had burned a long black trench in the nap. Uneasy smoke still unraveled from the last quarter inch of white paper.

"It's not possible!" he said aloud as he hurried around to the back door. He meant that it was not possible that he, like Mrs. Macabee, should peer into a front window to encounter what looked like death.

The kitchen door was locked, but, on circling one wing of the building, he entered a central patio overlooking the canyon below. He hurried across flagstone, past outdoor furniture, into the big dim living room. Through almost-drawn curtains at the west of the house a finger of sunlight pointed to the man on the sofa. The warm touch of brilliant light on his cheek did not disturb him. But when Mordecai laid one hand on the flat chest, his palm felt the faint beat of the heart. He saw then that the man's pallor was not the pallor of death, and knew the kind of sleep which gripped Desmond Grover.

Stirred by vitality, the face would be a handsome one. But now all its weakness was revealed. Serene, unashamed, the sleeper continued to achieve his ugly miracle. For him there was no time, no wife, no house above his head, no yesterday or tomorrow. For the moment his every desire had been fulfilled and would always be.

Mordecai raised one of Desmond Grover's eyelids, saw the hugely expanded pupil. In a dark-red leather box on the coffee table were a set of platinum shirt studs, three pairs of cuff links, a tarnished swimming medal, seven red capsules filled with a white powder, and a hypodermic syringe.

And now he knew who Miss White was. Another fact was doubly sure: Desmond Grover had not struck Mrs. Crone on the head. For by Helene's testimony he had been lying on that night as he lay now, untroubled by such trivia as a wife or a mother-in-law.

Later that day a troubling thought intruded as Mordecai Fentwill spoke to his class about the disastrous effect on European culture of the loss of Aristotle's writings: The killer of Ruth Ann Briggs had been a user of marijuana, and it is well known that addiction to this drug often leads to the use of more dangerous ones, such as cocaine.

# 15

THE CRONES' HOME presented to Tuck, Brigit and Mordecai a perfect picture of after-dinner felicity. Mrs. Crone was clearing the table, and Mr. Crone had evidently been reading the evening paper by the cheery fire. When he opened the door and saw who his visitors were he looked mildly surprised. Mrs. Crone gave them a brief, pleasant greeting and apologized for continuing with her task. But as she moved toward the kitchen with her laden tray her slender back seemed watchful.

Tuck looked as sadly solemn as a Saint Bernard when he asked, "Eric, why didn't you tell us about the blood in your car?"

"Blood? What blood?" Eric Crone spoke conversationally, looking from face to face.

Mordecai Fentwill answered him. "The blood your wife got on her glove."

"*Her* glove?" Eric Crone was frowning slightly. "I'm afraid I don't know what you are talking about." He half turned toward his wife who stood by the dining-room table with a plate in each hand. "What is all this, Clare? Do you understand what these folks are driving at?"

Before she could reply Mordecai said to her quietly, "I do not believe that the glove was Ruth Ann Briggs's."

"What do you mean? Helene gave her a pair like that for Christmas! Mrs. Briggs has confirmed this!" Mrs. Crone swept into the room.

"Your daughter's gift to Ruth Ann was a fortunate coincidence, of which you have taken full advantage. But I believe that it is far more likely the glove is yours, Mrs. Crone." Mordecai took it from his coat pocket and held it out. "Will you put it on, Mrs. Crone?"

"I will do nothing of the kind." She spoke in an equable tone which was almost pleasant or at least held a kind of pleasure in refusing the request.

"If you avoid so simple a method of demonstrating that the glove does not fit, we shall have to assume that it does," said Mordecai Fentwill as pleasantly. He continued to extend the glove; two of the bloodstained fingers had been cut off.

Tuck said, "I think it will simplify things if you try on that glove for size, Mrs. Crone. We would rather not be forced to hold you for questioning."

"As an accessory after the fact," Brigit added as Mrs. Crone remained silent.

Woodenly and yet suddenly, as though obeying the quick thrust of a strong compulsion, Clare Crone, standing very straight, held out her right arm. With neat dexterity Mordecai Fentwill slipped the glove over her hand, smoothed it, patted the cuff. Then, holding Mrs. Crone's wrist delicately between thumb and forefinger as though the hand in the glove was disassociated from the rest of her, he swept the watching faces with a stern glance in which there glimmered a faint, impersonal triumph.

Moving with one impulse, they all stepped forward, a human semicircle whose three pairs of eyes were soldered to the white glove on the rigid hand of Mrs. Crone. The two protruding naked fingers had nails lacquered a refined red;

177

they were like something stripped, revealed, like bone jutting through naked flesh.

"The glove," said Mordecai Fentwill, "fits. I have no doubt that expert microscopic examination will reveal more subtle proofs of ownership." He looked levelly into Mrs. Crone's eyes. "Why did you and your husband remain silent about the blood on this glove?"

"My husband knew nothing about it. He's as innocent as a babe unborn." Mrs. Crone stripped off the glove with restrained violence and tossed it, inside out, to the floor.

"There is nothing particularly innocent about a babe unborn," said Mordecai, watching her hard, trapped eyes. "A babe unborn, as I am sure you realize, exists in a realm where only the most limited actions are possible, and it is to our actions that the labels 'guilt' or 'innocence' are attached."

"Oh, shut up!" cried Clare Crone, and stepped sideways to collapse onto a hard chair by the doorway. She bent her head forward, one flat hand shielding her face, and began to sob flatly and regularly. With a closed look Eric Crone went to her side and began to pat her sharp shoulder mechanically. "There, there, old girl."

"Don't call me 'old girl!'" Clare commanded in a muffled voice. Without looking up she fumbled in the deep pocket of her pale-blue dress for a handkerchief.

"The presence of the glove lent credibility to your wife's story of a prowler," Mordecai Fentwill said, looking up at Eric Crone. "But now we know to whom the glove belonged and must ask ourselves whether a prowler ever existed, or whether there is another explanation for the fact that Mrs. Crone was found unconscious on her hearthrug."

"I naturally didn't want to air purely private matters," began Eric Crone in a vague, remote voice.

"Then don't!" Clare raised her thin face sharply. Her

178

recent tears had left surprisingly little mark. Except that the tip of her nose was pink, and the neat, sharp outlines of her lipstick a trifle blurred, she looked very resolute and in control of herself and the situation.

"I'm afraid I haven't much choice," Eric said with a faint smile. He certainly did not look like a man in fear of an indictment for murder. Brigit saw that Mordecai Fentwill was staring at Crone with peculiar intentness, like a scientist looking at a caged animal which has been inoculated with the germs of a rare disease and may at any moment display the first alarming symptoms.

Clare stood up and went to his side. "I can explain things very simply," she said with utter sincerity.

"You will forgive me, Mrs. Crone," said Mordecai, "if I remark that you have shown far too much glib inventiveness for me to invite you to becloud the issue at this crucial point. That the glove is yours you do not dare deny. That the blood on the glove is Ruth Ann Briggs's is a very strong possibility. When did the blood get on the glove? The records show that you used your car to go shopping two hours after Ruth Ann's body was found. I think that you probed into the crevice at the back of the seat for moisture which would prove what the condition of the leather indicated, that your husband had carelessly left the car open to the rain the night before. You found more than you had bargained for. You found proof that the car had been the scene of the neighborhood crime that night. You got blood on the fingers of your glove."

Eric Crone stood beside his wife, wearing the dazed half-smile of one who does not get the point of a joke. Mordecai Fentwill said to him, "I am afraid that the blood made your wife's mind dwell on the fact that you had used the car, and the fact that she did not know where you had been."

"You're wrong," Clare flashed back. "I never had the

slightest doubt of Eric! You know whom I wondered about!"

"Just a minute," said Eric's heavy, firm voice. "I'd like to get a word in here. I never saw that damned glove until Tuck showed it to us that night last week! If what Mr. Fentwill here is saying is true, I have no more idea than any of you do why my wife didn't show me that bloody glove six years ago!"

"You mean you *had* no idea why she chose to conceal it. You *have* some idea now, have you not, that she suspected you of murder?"

"That's hard to believe," Eric said. He turned smoothly to his wife. "Did you, Clare?"

Although her face was pinched, her voice was slick with angry contempt. "Certainly not! Nor will I for another moment put up with these wild and unfounded accusations! I insist on explaining this matter!"

"Because you are about to accuse someone of murder, Mrs. Crone," said Mordecai Fentwill, "I insist on clearing up any doubts in my colleagues' minds concerning the attack on you." He turned briskly toward Tuck and Brigit. "I ask you to remember that there is only Mrs. Crone's word that the attack occurred at half past nine. Mrs. Crone's integrity has been shown to be open to slight doubt. If the attack had occurred an hour earlier than she said, a convenient and murderous prowler, who left no trace but Mrs. Crone's glove, is eliminated. The attacker, we see, could have been Mr. Crone. And the cause of his anger lies on the floor before our feet."

After a pause Tuck bent his huge bulk to pick up the crumpled glove. He avoided Eric Crone's eyes.

"The nature of the Crones' argument I do not pretend to know," Mordecai went on. "But I am certain that we found this glove on the floor because, at the peak of their angry discussion, Mrs. Crone retrieved it from its long hiding place and confronted her husband with what she believed was proof of his past crime."

"But she didn't," Eric said sharply.

Only briefly taken aback, Mordecai Fentwill said, "She intended to, then. You lost your temper and hit her before she could do so."

"I didn't hit her!" Eric said. A flush mantled his big face and made him look like a schoolboy unjustly accused of having cheated on an exam. "I just shoved her aside and left the house fast. I didn't know she fell and hit her head. I didn't know she had a bad heart, either. And I didn't know anything about any damned glove!" He turned on his wife. "Clare, for God's sake straighten this out. Why did you keep mum about the blood on the glove? Why did you hide the damned thing in deep freeze all these years?"

Mordecai seized on the words. "An excellent phrase, 'deep freeze'! Before Mrs. Crone directs her suspicions to someone other than her husband, I wish you all to consider this fact: Mrs. Crone saved the glove!"

Clare tensed slightly, then stepped still closer to her husband and slipped her arm through his.

"Which," said Mordecai, "was a remarkable thing to do! She saved it. She preserved that glove. In the fullest sense of the word, she preserved that glove against the day when it might prove useful."

Rather slowly Eric Crone disengaged his arm and walked to the sofa. He sank down heavily on its center cushion. "I suggest we all sit down," he said somewhat dully. Self-consciously Tuck and Brigit took the two chairs flanking the small crackle of the fire. Mrs. Crone and Mordecai Fentwill remained standing.

Mordecai, looking from one face to another, said, "For six years Mrs. Crone's lips remained shut. She went through all the little routines of her days as before. No one guessed that there were very troubling suspicions rooted in her mind, to appear in ugly dreams, to dart out forked tongues at her in those strange moments when anxieties we believe deeply buried become vividly alive."

Now Mrs. Crone's face wore a less armed expression, as though, in a strange place, she was hearing music heard many times before. Not, perhaps, pleasant music, but imbued with the disarming quality of the familiar. Then her face hardened. "The glove may be one of mine. But I did not find it the day after the murder, as Mr. Fentwill insists. I found it months later, wedged down in the bend of the car seat. I didn't show it to my husband because he might have leaped to conclusions. Helene was very much in love with Desmond. He had been questioned and cleared of suspicion. I believed him innocent. I liked Desmond. But my husband did not."

"I don't get this Desmond stuff," said Brigit. "He wasn't driving your car the night she was killed. Your husband was."

"That car was parked at the foot of this street for nearly two hours! And Desmond had a key to it. Helene's key. A few nights before the murder they used my car to go to a dance. Desmond drove, and he forgot to return the key to Helene. I know this because he brought it to me a week after the murder." Her face was very white, and sweat made tiny beads on her forehead.

A quiet, shaken young voice spoke from the front hall. "Why are you telling them this?" Helene walked in slowly. She looked very young in a short, fleecy white coat. Her pumps had absurd little bows on them. She stopped a few feet from her mother, frowning. "Sure, Desmond had a key to your car when Ruth Ann was killed! But what does that prove? Are you trying to say he could have killed that girl? That our car was the murder car?"

Mrs. Crone's face showed sorrow. "I am afraid it was, Helene."

Helene looked wildly about at their watching faces. "But how do you know it was the murder car?"

Clare answered quickly, "I found a glove with blood on it in our car, dear. I kept this to myself as long as I could. For Desmond's sake. And for yours."

Helene clapped her hand to her forehead. "No! This I can't believe!" But she did, for she stared at her mother with horror. Her voice was angry. "Why did you do such a thing? Don't you realize how much worse it is for him to have it pried out of you *now?*"

"I did what seemed best for all concerned," Clare replied.

As Helene retreated numbly to the arm of the sofa and perched there without seeming to know she had done so, Mordecai said to Mrs. Crone, "But you still haven't explained why you *kept* the glove. If your only desire was to protect a person you then thought innocent, would it not have been wiser to burn the glove to ashes?"

"I intended to show it to my husband when I felt the time was right. I put it away, and then I simply forgot it."

"It must have been in your mind when you wrote that letter to Mrs. Briggs," Mordecai said.

"I suppose it was. Why I didn't look for it and toss it away I simply can't tell you at this late date! I came across it quite by chance last week. I tucked it into my pocket, intending to throw it into the trash. Before I could do so, my husband and I had a very bitter argument, as you know. After my heart attack, when I came to on the sofa, I found that the glove had fallen out of the pocket of my skirt when I fell. I admit that I told a white lie. Two, if you wish. To

183

keep from discussing the glove—or the very private matter we have been forced to humiliate ourselves by laying bare tonight."

"What private matter?" demanded Helene. She looked down at her father. He summoned a wry smile. "I seem to have pushed your mother aside rather roughly, a grossness she thought it best to conceal." He looked down at one of his big hands. "I'm very sorry for my connivance in this hush-hush campaign."

"You mean *you* knocked her down and hit her with the poker?" Helene was on her feet, and her face was horrified.

*"No!"* roared Eric, surging up from the sofa. "No poker! She just made that up! Along with the prowler! Pure fiction, both of 'em. To save her face. See?" He sat down again.

Clare spoke with a cool dignity. "Your way of putting things is not gallant, Eric. Surely it is understandable if a woman tries to prevent scandal." She appealed to all of them with mute and suffering eyes. "I hope you will excuse me now." Like an injured queen she moved with a high head to the hall. They all watched her. At the foot of the stairs she paused with one hand on the newel post. "I regret that so much soiled linen has been laundered publicly," she told them with a ghastly smile, and then went up to the privacy of her room.

Eric Crone sat like a waxwork of himself. But when Helene turned sharply toward the front hall, he stood up woodenly. "Where are you going?"

"Home."

Eric nodded once. "I thought so."

She came a step toward him. "I'm grateful for your help, Dad. But this is no time to walk out on him." Her face took on a bleak curiosity. "I know you've never liked him much, but you don't think he killed her, do you?"

Eric's big body seemed to grow firmer as he went to his

184

daughter's side and slipped an arm around her waist. "I can say this much with no hesitation whatever. I don't believe that his having a key to the car means a thing. Your mother attaches too much significance to that. Because if I left my key in the ignition that night, anyone on earth could have got in and driven the car to the canyon. Anyone on earth! Or, at least, anyone who happened to pass along Acacia Street between eight and half past nine!"

He turned resolutely to Tuck, Brigit and Mordecai in turn. He seemed aware that his daughter's face was looking up at him. "If the car I drove that night was used by the killer, there's a far more obvious explanation than the assumption that young Grover decided to go for a joy ride in it. I didn't drop my keys in the Grotto, as I thought. I left them in the ignition. It was the killer who dropped them in the bar, later. Psychologically this theory is very sound. I happened to dislike that car of my wife's. I considered it pretentious and unnecessary. More than once I used to catch myself leaving the keys in the dash. As an invitation, you see, to a thief. I secretly wanted to lose the damned car. It's a pure example of Freudian error."

"Or at least of a very usual error," said Mordecai Fentwill. "But why did the murderer take the keys with him?"

"Why, Freudian error again!" Eric had dropped his arm from his daughter's waist to take a step toward Mordecai. He had the shrewd look of a clever investigator. "It's common knowledge that criminals are constantly leaving clues that lead to their arrest, or retaining evidence that damns them. On the unconscious level their sense of guilt operates against their safety, makes them do the very things which lead to their arrest. Criminals aren't 100-per-cent bad. They have a conscience, like the rest of us. They're strongly dual personalities."

"Like the rest of us," Mordecai added. "It's a pity you

185

can't force yourself to recall exactly what you did with the keys. Your theory has points which interest me."

Eric smiled jauntily. "I may remember yet," he said. He turned to his daughter. "I'll drive you home, if you're sure you want to go."

"I'm sure. But I don't think you ought to leave Mother, now that we know how weak her heart is. She's much more upset than she's letting us know." Whatever shock she had felt on learning of the clash between her parents, her face impassively ignored the possibility that their concern for each other was any the less.

"I should be .pleased to drive you home, Mrs. Grover," Mordecai said, "if Mr. Tuck and my niece will taxi us to the café where I left my car."

They both nodded, and after a moment's hesitation Helene said, "I'll take you up on that."

As they all moved to the door Eric Crone spoke to his daughter with a forced joviality. "Your loyalty does you credit, Helene, although I can't say this is the best time to pick up a shaky marriage and start juggling the same old problems along with this new one."

"Shaky or not, it's still a marriage, and I'm stuck with it."

"I didn't expect you to change your mind. We're alike in some ways. Stubborn as government mules."

"And neither of us gets along too well with our spouses, at times." Helene's voice was deliberately light.

Her father's smile was embarrassed. In trying to ignore the presence of the strangers he made them seem all the more there. "Don't take this row of your mother's and mine too seriously. It's the first in twenty-five years of marriage— a record few could equal."

"But what was the row *about?*" With the egoism of

186

youth Helene could ignore the three outsiders quite genu-
inely.

"Oh, money," said Eric Crone. "Expenses. The taxes on
the house. The new car your mother wants to buy."

# 16

For a few minutes it was silent inside the big police sedan. But suddenly Helene Grover's light voice spoke with nervous speed and yet a certain precision which showed that her thoughts were marshaled.

"It was silly of Mother to keep quiet about the glove, but I don't see that finding it makes a great deal of difference. After all, from the first it was plain that a car like ours had gone up Acacia Street toward the canyon a few minutes after Ruth Ann got off the streetcar. And the same kind of car was seen leaving the canyon at a little past nine. If Mother had found the glove then instead of later and hadn't kept quiet about it, you'd have known the murderer used our car. And Dad would have realized that he left his keys in the dash. I think the killer got in intending to steal the car and sell it. Then Ruth Ann came along, recognized the car, saw someone in it and stopped to talk because she thought it was me or one of my parents. The killer hit her to quiet her, and then drove her to the canyon!"

"What did he hit her with?" asked Mordecai Fentwill conversationally.

"With . . . well, a wrench or something."

"You've pointed out one of the main snags in this case,"

188

said Mordecai. "What was the murder weapon? People don't carry wrenches in their pockets, my dear. Nor are they as a rule left lying close at hand on the car seat. And this is equally true of any other object heavy enough to have smashed a girl's head at one blow. As long as we assumed that the killer drove his own car we could assume the presence of just such a weapon as a wrench which he reached for as soon as Ruth Ann Briggs appeared a menace to his safety. But when we start thinking in terms of a killer who used someone else's automobile we run headlong into the question, 'What was the weapon?' "

"Unless the killer was a criminal type who carried a lead pipe or something like that," said Helene.

"That the killer was a criminal type is proved by his having murdered a young girl," said Mordecai. "If you mean that in addition to being a car thief and murderer the killer was also a footpad with a blackjack in his pocket, I find that my mind rebels."

"I don't go for this car-thief angle," said Brigit. "If he got into the Crones' car planning to steal it, why didn't he drive away in it after the murder instead of parking it where he found it? I don't think the killer ever planned to steal that car."

"Then why did he get into it in the first place?" asked Helene.

"Maybe to wait there for you," Tuck said. "But another pretty girl came along. The keys were in the dash. He offered her a ride. He ran a risk bringing the car back. But there was a bigger risk, as he saw it, in driving off in it. All he could do was leave it as he found it, open in the rain, and hope for luck."

"A theory which means that the killer was no stranger to either the Crones or to Ruth Ann Briggs," said Mordecai.

"Because my mother found the glove in the car, does

that mean the car was used to murder the girl in?" Helene's voice was shrill. "Maybe someone put the glove there to make you people believe just that!"

"If that was the desire, he hid the glove rather well," said Mordecai. After a pause he added, "In fact, he must have hidden it with extreme care, since it shows not the slightest sign of soil or wrinkling."

Tuck pulled up behind Mordecai's car and turned to look at Helene Grover over his huge shoulder. "I don't get any satisfaction out of arresting the wrong person," he said. "Neither does Miss Estees. Mr. Fentwill's integrity is terrific. Your husband convinced us that he had no motive for killing Ruth Ann Briggs six years ago. It's certain one hasn't developed since." His words reassured Helene. She smiled pallidly and thanked him for the ride.

Mordecai Fentwill's MG coupé offered Helene something trivial to talk about after the evening's tension. "It just doesn't seem right for a professor of philosophy to drive this little bug," she said after she got in beside him.

"One of the obligations too many professors avoid is offering students a touch of color about which they can make jokes," said Mordecai. "This car serves the purpose nicely. Also I can park it within two or three blocks of my destination. I may one day be crushed by a Cadillac, but I shall perish with my nerves unfrayed."

He disliked himself for putting a period after her laughter. "I know who Miss White is," he said.

She slowly stiffened. Her head turned toward him. A street lamp threw its brief cold light on her face. "Who?" she breathed.

"A narcotics peddler. Your husband did not go to the Blue Grotto to exchange amorous comments, but to exchange a sum of money for a supply of cocaine."

"Co . . ." She was unable to complete the word. Her shock was real.

"That is why he locked the bedroom door. And why he did not hear your voice or your knocking. The body on the bed was there, but the man was gone. I hope his journeys have not been frequent."

Her voice was strange and hard. "How do you know this?"

"I saw him lying as you saw him. But it was by daylight, and his trouble was very plain." He pulled to a stop before the angular redwood house. She turned her head toward the front door but made no move.

"Now you know that your rival is merely one of the most dangerous drugs on earth," said Mordecai. "Perhaps you also know how few men escape unaided from her fatal charms."

Helene opened the car door and got out.

"I believe I shall wait for you," said Mordecai. "Loyalty, like so many attitudes we consider virtuous, can destroy the possessor if wrongly applied. There is a great moral difference between aiding a man one believes innocent and aiding a man one believes guilty. You are about to discover whether your husband, in your eyes, falls into the latter category. You are also about to discover whether you are one of those persons who prefer to live with doubt rather than suffer seeing their suspicions put to the test of impartial investigation."

"I understand you, Dr. Fentwill," she said with a remote and very young dignity.

"Don't call me 'Doctor,' my dear. It makes me feel that I should be removing gallstones instead of thrusting my elderly presence along the cool trail I find myself following."

He watched her walk with quick loud steps to the front door. As she fumbled in her purse for a key the door opened.

Desmond Grover stood motionless in an oblong of light, and then abruptly put his arms around his wife. He seemed to cling to her slender body like a man afraid of drowning.

They went into their house together, and the door closed quietly after them.

After Mordecai's little car drove off, Brigit and Tuck sat side by side in silence for a moment. Then Tuck said, "Whether Jenkins will remember much after six years is anyone's guess. But he's Eric Crone's only witness, as far as I can see."

The fat proprietor of the Blue Grotto was not behind the bar. Only The Bird was there, polishing a glass in a superior manner. Now televised wrestlers menaced, tangled and broke apart on a square screen at the counter's far end. But the half-hidden blue lights still provided atmosphere for the life-size mermaid, and the rough brown plaster walls still contrived to look like the Tunnel of Love.

On seeing Brigit The Bird looked very surprised.

"We want to talk to Mr. Jenkins," Tuck said. "Do you know where we can find him?"

"Sure. He's home. He lives near here. Want me to give him a ring?"

"Please. Tell him it's important."

The Bird went to the telephone booth in the rear corridor where two doors were marked "Mermaids" and "Mermen." The explanatory words "Ladies" and "Gents" had been added below. He spoke briefly, and returned to his place behind the long bar to fill an order for two bourbons and soda. As he measured out the liquor he nodded meaningfully at Tuck and Brigit, indicating that Jenkins was on his way. They moved to the rear booth and in a moment he followed and stood looking down at them. "Is this guy the B. F., by any chance?" he asked Brigit with a tense smile.

"The B. F.?"

"Boy friend," said The Bird.

"Oh. No, he's just the E. P."

"E. P.?"

"Eternal Partner," said Brigit.

"You mean that in a business way?" asked The Bird.

"Strictly."

"Oh. Well, then, how about you and me having dinner my next night off? Some good joint, like Perino's."

"The Bird goes for big broads," Brigit explained to Tuck.

The Bird looked uncomfortable. "Listen, maybe I got out of line the other night; only don't hold it against me. After all, a guy spends six nights a week mixing drinks for other people, and on his night off . . . well, what do you expect?" Duty called him then in the form of a foggy voice desirous of whisky.

"So that's Richard Carewe," mused Tuck.

"That's Richard Carewe."

Tuck watched the bartender give a highball a quick, tinkling stir, then his brief interest vanished. He looked solemnly at Brigit. "Mrs. Crone has done a lot of lying, but we mustn't let that confuse us. I think she's passing the buck to her son-in-law, but that mustn't confuse us either. Here's how it shapes up to me: If she really believes her husband's guilty, he may all the same be innocent. Because she seems to be trying to distract us by throwing her daughter's husband to the lions, that doesn't mean Grover couldn't be guilty. It's an open question with both of them, but neither of them may be our man."

"I agree. But I'd like to make this point: If Eric Crone were anyone else but a juvenile investigator . . ."

"Assistant D. A.," Tuck corrected.

"O.K. But if he were just Joe Blow, on the basis of the new evidence we'd at least hold him for questioning and spend a good long day sweating out a lot of answers. As it is, we get embarrassed and wind up helping Uncle Mordecai drive Helene home."

"Agreed," said Tuck.

"I mean," said Brigit, "the fact that Desmond Grover had a key to that car and the possibility that Eric Crone left the key in it are both alternatives. The main fact is that the bloody glove was found in Eric's car, and he was driving it."

"You folks wanted to talk to me?" asked a meat-fed voice.

The proprietor of the Blue Grotto had grown no thinner in six years. His eyes had the anxious bulge of a fat man verging on apoplexy; he had evidently hastened.

"Sit down, Mr. Jenkins," Tuck said. Jenkins obliged, wedging his belly around the curve of the semicircular table. The padding of his gray suit sat stiffly on his melted shoulders, but he achieved a vague air of honesty.

"All we want to know is this, Mr. Jenkins: Can you recall whether Mr. Crone visited this bar on the evening of February 1, 1945?"

"You mean the night that little girl was killed?"

"We do."

Mr. Jenkins mopped his crown and forehead lavishly. "I got a confession to make. I want to make it now so you'll unnerstand I'm a man who's usually honest. It's like this. A couple of nights after that girl was killed, a lady—very refined type, said she was Mrs. Crone—came into this bar asking me if her husband was in the night you're asking about. I told her no. I told her a lie, see, because Mr. Crone was a steady client of mine, and from remarks of his I'd got the idea his wife was some sort of teetotaler. On the spur of the moment, I tried to do him a favor, see?"

"I see," said Tuck.

194

"Normally I'm as honest as the day is long," announced Mr. Jenkins, glaring as though someone had implied otherwise. "And the honest truth is, Mr. Crone *was* in my bar here that night."

Neither Tuck nor Brigit spoke, waiting for him to go on. A cautious look suddenly congealed on Mr. Jenkins' expansive face. "What's the point of this?" he asked.

Tuck could, on occasion, be as verbosely uninformative as a statesman. "The truth of the matter is, Mr. Jenkins," he said, lowering his voice and glancing around for spies or underworld characters, "that we're closing in on the Briggs killer. Certain people have talked, certain new evidence has come up, and our problem now is to work out a close timetable. Your café here is one of the elements involved. We want to find when everyone who was here that night entered and left, if possible. Mr. Crone, too, as a matter of routine."

Mr. Jenkins looked enormously enlightened. "Sure. Sure." He leaned toward them, important and confidential. "I can back anything Mr. Crone says. He was in here for, oh, about half an hour. He got here at nine o'clock. He left about nine-thirty."

"You looked at the clock?" asked Brigit.

"Yes. When my singer came in, a few minutes after Mr. Crone did. She was due at eight-thirty. I wanted to see how late she was. After Mr. Crone left at nine-thirty, he came back again to look for his keys. I helped him look, but they didn't turn up and he hadda phone the auto club to send out a locksmith. 'Not a word of this to my wife,' he kept saying."

"But you're sure he didn't get here until nine?"

"Absolutely positive."

# 17

Helene Grover opened the front door and walked quickly to Mordecai Fentwill. "Will you come in, Mr. Fentwill? I want you to hear what my husband has to say."

Desmond Grover's fair hair, cut very short, had been bleached by sun to a butter-yellow, with which his tan contrasted handsomely. He moved with an almost feline grace and had fine-fingered hands. His very broad smile showed amazingly white teeth, framed by pale lips. His eyes, of greenish-gray, seemed intelligent, and their glance was very direct, as though, Mordecai thought, he had heard that shifty-eyed people were dishonest and was determined to make the right impression.

He said, as they shook hands, "I'm not hooked. I've been, well, sort of showing off by tinkering around with potential hell and dynamite. 'Chippying' is the technical term. Of course, I'm fully aware that an otherwise normal person who engages in a dangerous activity with insufficient reason is like a kid trying to get even with the world by hurting himself so everyone will be sorry." Desmond Grover glanced at his wife.

"I take your somewhat tortuous explanation to mean that

you succumbed to the lure of cocaine because of recent disaffection between you and Mrs. Grover," Mordecai said.

"You couldn't put it more clearly."

"*You* could have put it more clearly. What makes you so convinced that you are not hooked?"

"I don't use it often," Desmond said shortly. He took a turn down the room and back, his hands thrust deep in his trousers pockets. "There are a few things I want to put you straight on, Mr. Fentwill. First, I never smoked marijuana. This damfool cocaine business is very recent and has no logical connection with the case you're interested in. Secondly, although I do recall having had in my possession a key to the Crones' convertible at the time Ruth Ann was killed, I certainly would not have considered that this gave me the privilege of using the car without their permission. Hell, I didn't even know the car was parked at the foot of Acacia Street! And thirdly, there is no Miss White." He looked at Helene. "It's Mr. White. As I've told Helene, I let her believe it was a woman calling me just to be ornery. The second time White called, Helene got pretty flip about it, said it was either a man with a high voice or a woman with a low voice. I said, purely to devil her, 'Oh, it must be Miss White.' "

"And Mr. White is a drug peddler."

"Yes. And that's all I know about him. That, and a telephone number. A woman always answers. She sounds like a secretary. I'm pretty sure that it's one of these services where they take phone calls for a small monthly sum. Because White's never there, and the dame who answers always says the same thing in exactly the same way: She repeats my name and number and says, 'Thank you, Mr. Grover. I will inform Mr. White that you have called. He will telephone you as soon as possible.' "

"You've never seen Mr. White?"

"No, I never have. It happened like this: About six months ago Helene and I had a row about a cosmetic I wanted to manufacture. She pulled a lot of high-flown ethics and social consciousness on me. I wound up going down to a low joint to get the taste out of my mouth. I got myself pie-eyed, and all at once I was chinning with a good-looking guy who said he was a musician. He talked up an occasional jolt of cocaine for the blues and offered me a cap to try out. He may have been working for White. I don't know. I bought the cap for five bucks, not intending to use it, but just to keep from looking like a sissy. I could see that in his part of the world the stuff was regarded as casually as we regard whisky. This fellow also gave me, gratis, Mr. White's telephone number. A couple of weeks later when I was pretty low I found this cap in my wallet and decided to try it out. I thought of it in the nature of an experiment. I went out and bought a hypodermic syringe and melted the cap in a spoon, with a match, the way the musician said he did. In a few months I didn't need too much of an excuse to justify an occasional shot in the arm. But I knew I could stop whenever I wanted to." He sobered abruptly. "Well, I've stopped. Never again. Mr. White has lost him a customer."

"There's only one thing to do," said Helene decisively. "You're going to turn him in. You're going to telephone the Narcotics Squad and give them Mr. White's phone number."

"Hey, now, wait a minute!" said Desmond. "After all . . ."

"There is no 'after all.' You're on one side or the other. You're on this White's side, if you protect him. I'm not having any of that. You should hear my father on these characters, how they sell dope to kids!"

"I have."

"But not so often as I have. I think this is the right way

198

to work it: First make an appointment with White. Then phone the Narcotics Squad and give them the time and place. They'll do the rest."

Desmond Grover frowned. "I find myself strangely averse to winding up dead one night. What'll White get? Three months? And then come out of poky looking for my blood!"

"Do you suppose any intelligent officer leaves a helpful citizen out on a limb like that?"

"What if he can't help it? What if White guesses the truth? Hell, what if I get jailed, too?"

"That," said Helene, "is a chance we have to take. But so long as you continue to protect White, you can't convince me that you're a reformed character!"

After a short pause Desmond said, "You're a hard woman." But he was smiling.

He telephoned the number through which those desiring to could reach Mr. White, and then returned and began to pace the floor. "As far as the Briggs case goes," he said, "I can see that in the pride and folly of youth I made a grave mistake. I should have told those investigators about Dayleen Burke. But I was damned if I'd crawl to that big-busted cow for an alibi."

"Ah," said Mordecai.

"I told the police that I was just wandering along Hollywood Boulevard for a couple of hours before I hit the Grotto at nine-thirty. And that was the truth, but not all of it. From eight o'clock until about a quarter to nine I was sitting on the sofa in Dayleen Burke's living room. I'd have told them that, except that on Monday, two days after Ruth Ann was killed, Dayleen waggled up to me at lunch hour and said that in case the police asked me where I was on Friday night it wouldn't be smart to say I was at her place, because she'd deny it. Her cheap malice sickened me, and when I was questioned I kept my mouth shut."

"Her vindictiveness seems extreme. Do you know the cause?" Mordecai asked.

"Sure I know the cause! Five minutes after I came into the house her mother coyly left to call on a neighbor, she said. Then Dayleen, in a satin robe and damned little else, entered from the bathroom where she'd been fixing her hair. It was a bright new horrible color, hanging in glamorous abandon around her shoulders. It didn't take me long to realize that I was supposed to make passionate love to her. She just expected that of men, I guess. I was fresh from a high-minded prep school. I felt inadequate and embarrassed. I talked about Plato. When I left she was a victim of mixed emotions. She was seething, and also bewildered. It was funny, at the time." He added, "Now, it's not so funny."

"You say you left her house at a quarter to nine?"

"About that."

"Where did she live?"

"On Las Palmas, a block from the boulevard. Not far from Hollywood High."

"And quite a distance from Acacia Street."

"About a fifteen-minute walk normally. But I stopped in to have a couple of drinks at a little bar and didn't reach the Grotto for about a half hour."

"How did she happen to go to the Grotto too? Coincidence?"

"Hell, no! I said I was going there. I said I had to meet a date."

When the hall telephone rang Desmond Grover was first to rise. He did so slowly, a trifle dramatically. Mordecai accompanied him to the telephone. Mordecai asked, "Do you have an extension?"

Helene nodded. "In the bedroom."

"Keep very quiet," Desmond warned them, his hand on the instrument. "These guys are dangerous."

"White speaking," said the faint voice at the other end of the line.

"Hello, White. This is Grover."

"How's tricks, Grover?"

"So-so. Say, I could use another half dozen. When can you deliver?"

"Kind of soon, isn't it?"

Desmond Grover was briefly thrown off stride. "Is it? Well, I've had some real mad troubles lately. . . ."

"Skip it. You can always rely on me." Now Mr. White's voice was faintly smug, like the voice of a businessman who sees a well-earned profit taking shape. "I can deliver tomorrow, same place, same time."

"Roger."

"But the price is gonna be a little higher. This item is scarce just now. It'll be seventy-five for the half dozen."

"That's not too rough."

"I try to be fair with my steady clients. Well, so long for now."

"Say, White. Just one thing. I don't want to get too deeply involved in this, you know. What's your opinion on this delivery tomorrow?"

"You're not running any risk."

"I just wanted your personal opinion. You know more about it than I do."

"I just sell the stuff, Grover. I don't use it."

"Oh. Well, so long," said Desmond.

"Take care of yourself," said Mr. White.

"You can see why I thought it was a woman," said Helene, as she and Mordecai returned to the living room. "There's something peculiar about that voice. It doesn't sound exactly like a man, does it?"

Mordecai Fentwill pondered briefly. "It sounds to me like a voice which has been crudely disguised. By some such trick as speaking through a handkerchief stretched tight across the telephone's mouthpiece. But why Mr. White would go to this trouble, I don't know. The method he uses to deliver his product is designed to prevent his ever meeting a client. The disguised voice seems redundant. Where, in the Blue Grotto Café, will you find the six capsules of cocaine you have ordered, Mr. Grover?"

"In the third booth from the door, under the inner edge of the leather seat pad. I leave the money in the same place."

"Mr. White seems a trusting soul. I should think that a gentleman engaged in his profession would be inclined to collect before delivering the goods."

"We did it like that the first two times, but it was awkward because I had to make two trips to the Grotto—one to leave the money, and another, an hour later, to pick up the package of caps. The third time I talked to him he said I'd find the caps on my first trip and to leave the money in the same place." Desmond grinned. "I guess he'd had time to check my references, find out I'm a fairly solid citizen."

"So now, Solid Citizen, you phone the Narcotics Squad," said Helene.

He did. "They said they'd be out here the first thing in the morning." He looked pleased with himself in a dazed way, like a rich man who has been talked into donating money to a worthy cause.

"And now," said Helene, "I think it would be a good idea to have a little talk with Dayleen."

"I don't know where to find her."

"I do." Helene opened the telephone directory. "She lives in Los Angeles, and her name is now Pflugel."

Desmond Grover laughed. "I know I'm on a spot. I know

202

this isn't funny, but—Pflugel! What a fate for a Grade-B glamour girl!"

Eric Crone seemed pleased when he saw Brigit and Tuck standing side by side on his doorstep. "A couple of ideas have occurred to me. Come on in and have a drink." When Brigit and Tuck declined the drink he looked somewhat hurt. "I was having a short one. I needed it!" As they sat down on the long sofa, he picked up his glass and leaned back in an armchair facing them. His coat was off, his necktie loosened. "First, I think you ought to know about the andiron."

"Andiron?" Brigit and Tuck spoke in duet.

He smiled. "That's right. You can't figure out what an andiron could have to do with this mess, can you?" He leaned forward, his elbows on his knees, the tall glass clasped loosely in his big hands. "On the night Ruth Ann died, my wife sent me down to a repair shop on the boulevard to get one of those andirons fixed. The front part came loose from the iron rod that holds the logs." He glanced toward the brick hearth; backed by the black maw of the fireplace, two andirons with round brass balls at the top stood out boldly. "The Fix-it Shop was closed, as I'd told her it probably would be. So the two halves of the unmended andiron were on the front seat of that convertible I drove. They were there all the time I was in the Blue Grotto. And they're plenty heavy. I think this fact is pretty important, in view of what's come up tonight."

"So do I," Tuck agreed.

"I mean," Eric said, leaning back in his chair and regarding them alertly, "if a stranger used that car and killed the girl in it, the important question is what weapon was used. It's not likely that anyone would have on him something heavy enough to knock in a skull with one blow. Well, a weapon was present, all right. Two of them, in fact. The two halves of that damned andiron." He glowered at the fireplace as though the andiron and that alone had caused the death of Ruth Ann Briggs.

"How is it," Tuck asked slowly, "that you didn't let us in on this at the time?"

Eric Crone straightened abruptly in his chair, his narrow eyes wider. "I think that's perfectly plain, Tuck. I hadn't the slightest notion then that my car had been anywhere else but where I left it. I believed I had lost the keys in the Blue Grotto. And that's where Mr. Jenkins found them. What reason did I have to guess that my car had been borrowed and that a murder had been committed in it? You didn't have any such notion, either, at that time."

"I seem to remember your telling us that you dried off the leather upholstery while the locksmith was making you a new key," Brigit said. "It seems funny that no blood turned up then."

"It didn't, though. The blood that got on that glove must have trickled 'way down into the crack at the bend of the seat while the weight of the girl's body was holding the cushion down. Then, when her body was removed, the cushion sprang up, closing the opening of the crevice so tightly that the rain couldn't get in at it." He jumped up. "Like this." He illustrated with the seat of his chair. "Of course, there might have been a trace of blood left somewhere on the seat, but in the dark I wouldn't have seen it, and I threw the newspapers I dried it with into the incinerator when I got home." He looked at them steadily. "A perfectly natural thing to do."

"Sure," said Tuck. "Sure."

Eric Crone stood up and freshened his drink from a pint bottle of whisky on the open secretary. "Hindsight is tricky," he said, "and as a rule I never trust it. But there's something I remember which gives me one more reason to think that my car was used by the killer while I was in the Grotto. Here it is, for what it's worth: When I came out of the bar and saw that car standing there shiny with rain-drops, my first thought wasn't that I'd left it open in the rain. My first thought was 'I didn't leave that top down!' But then I found that my keys were missing, and that took my attention. That, and my rather strong desire to keep my wife in the dark about what had happened to her precious car. Looking back, though, I'm of the strong opinion that the top of the car was closed when I drove away from the house, and that if it hadn't been, I would have closed it. Remember the wind that night?"

"You said you were in the Blue Grotto for about an hour and a half," said Tuck.

"Yes, about that."

"But Jenkins told us tonight that you were there for only half an hour, from nine until about half past."

"What?" Eric Crone's big ruddy face was amazement itself. Then he closed his eyes, put his hand to his forehead, drew his open palm slowly down his face, his alert eyes frozen with thought. His voice had lost its assurance as he said, "It's hard to remember things after six years. It seemed to me I'd been in the Grotto all evening. But that could be because I went there so often. It was my regular hangout when my wife entertained her clubwomen. Let me think a minute. February 1, 1945 . . ." After a long pause he gave a short nod and said without enthusiasm, "One eve-ning around that time I visited a friend before I went to the Grotto. She happened to live in the apartment building upstairs. Whether she'll remember this or not, I wouldn't know."

Tuck stood up. "Get in touch with her, if you can, Crone.

We'll give you a ring tomorrow and see what luck you've had."

Eric's voice was friendly and unbelieving as he said, "You can't possibly think that I killed that girl!"

Tuck said, "I'll tell you what I think. I think your wife was lying when she told us she found the glove several months after the crime. I also think she lied when she said she concealed it to protect Desmond Grover. I think she got blood on her glove the day after the crime, just as Mr. Fentwill outlined it. And I think it was you she suspected all along."

Looking very directly into Tuck's eyes, Eric Crone said quietly, "I think you're right. But that doesn't mean that her suspicions were founded on anything stronger than a vivid imagination. Like a lot of women Clare reads too many books. She's lived too far from the harsher aspects of reality all of her life. I don't mind telling you I was shocked when I realized what she had been able to suspect me of. But I can't say, after thinking it over, that I'm much surprised. It was a kind of story she made up, to excite herself with. It was a way of symbolically dramatizing a certain hidden hatred she has of men in general, gross, sensual creatures that we are!"

He laughed shakily. "But still, I may wind up being indicted for murder. I can see that all too plainly. Never underestimate the power of a woman!" His face went blank. "Or, at least, of a woman like the one I'm married to."

# PART FIVE

*The Last Victim*

# 18

CLARE CRONE drew back into the shadow of the upper hall when the two homicide officers emerged from the living room into the foyer below. Their good nights sounded falsely calm. She wondered why a woman would become a detective, would choose to soil and harden herself by continual contact with crime and depravity. In Miss Estees' case, though, the reason was plain. Her size barred her from leading a normal life, and perhaps she got a certain warped pleasure out of tracking down killers, whose guilt enabled her to prize her own honesty, whose capture allowed her to feel that she possessed a clever brain. What a grotesque pair they made, she and her enormous partner, Tuck!

Clare edged silently forward to peer down over the balustrade, and saw her husband standing at the open front door, his back to her, one hand raised in farewell. In shirt sleeves his shoulders showed that his muscles were turning into fat. His raised arm dropped to his side, and he shut the door. He turned and she glimpsed his face. The bitter anger she had felt at the things he had just said of her returned. But it was less strong now, weakened by her prudence in directing her dislike toward the red-haired woman detective. In a moment she could smile in the darkness at her own cunning; this was no time for anger.

"All right, Clare. You can come down now. They're gone."

Her husband's words shocked her. Not only the words, but the almost absent-minded way in which he spoke them. How had he known that she had been listening? How did he dare to take this for granted?

"I know you're there," he called more loudly. "Go into your room if you want. But I know you're there."

She straightened, gathering dignity, and lifted the skirt of her long wine-red velvet robe. As she started down the staircase, one hand resting lightly on the banister, she held in her mind the memory of an oil painting of a British noblewoman who had held her velvet skirt in one hand while the other rested on a newel post.

"How could you speak of me like that?" she asked, allowing her hurt to show in her voice.

"Oh, knock it off, Clare." Coarsely casual, he turned his back to her and paced into the living room, his head lowered doggedly, his hands thrust into his trousers pockets. She stood in the doorway watching him walk the length of the room, turn, walk back toward her as though in his own invisible footprints.

She took a step forward, narrowing the distance between them. "They have no proof," she said.

He halted abruptly, raised a broad, incredulous face. "No proof? My God, what do you call proof, Clare? They know the car I drove was without much doubt the murder car, don't they? They know I wasn't in the Blue Grotto during the time the girl was killed! I'm the one who has to worry about digging up proof! It's up to me to prove that I couldn't have been in that canyon between eight and nine, that I was somewhere else!"

She took another step toward him. "Eric. I want you to

tell me the truth." Her voice was little more than a whisper, and she raised it to add, "The truth, whatever it is."

"The truth!" His broad smile held no humor, and his eyes were as cold and hard as obsidian. "Would you know the truth if you heard it, Clare?" He came toward her slowly, still smiling. "Would a mind like yours recognize the plain and simple *truth?*" As he reached her, his smile perished. Very slowly his hands reached out and grasped her arms just above the elbows. "You tell *me* the truth, Clare. I've got to know where I stand. When did you really find that glove? It was your glove, wasn't it?"

"Yes." Something about the strong pressure of his big hands on her slender arms canceled her will to evade, erased her cleverness. His wide, familiar face staring down into hers was the only reality she had to consider just now. There was a certain luxury in knowing for the first time in her life that she was able to fear her husband. "Yes, it was my glove, Eric. Helene did give Ruth Ann a pair just like it, though."

"It was your glove," he said tonelessly. "Go on."

"Dr. Fentwill was right. I got blood on it. The day after the murder." She felt her face wry as she spoke the simple truth at last, and tried to straighten her mouth.

But he wasn't looking at her. He was looking to one side. At the fireplace, she realized. At the andirons. His hands relaxed their pressure and his arms dropped to his sides. He stood there stupidly for a moment and then went past her to the hall. She turned and watched him, followed him as far as the living-room doorway. He opened the door of the hall closet and came out putting on his camel's-hair overcoat.

"You forgot to put on the coat to your suit! Don't go out like that, Eric! It looks so peculiar."

He draped the overcoat across the bottom of the stair rail. It slid to the floor and lay there like something dead.

She pivoted mechanically to watch as he took his suit coat from the back of the straight chair facing the secretary and put it on.

"Where are you going?" she asked.

He walked past her to the hall without replying. As he bent and picked up the fallen overcoat he said, "To the Blue Grotto."

"Eric! Don't be a fool! This isn't something you can escape by drinking!"

He settled the overcoat about his shoulders, watching her. She realized that one of her cold hands was grasping the other in an immemorial gesture of female anguish. She forced them to relax, let go, fall to her sides.

"You underestimate me, Clare," he said as he tied the coat's thick belt. "I'm going to try to find Lily Tripoly."

"Lily Tripoly?" The false-sounding, euphonious name was echoed prettily in her light voice an instant after his deep one had spoken it. "Who is Lily Tripoly?"

"The woman I told those detectives from Homicide about. Weren't you listening? The woman I said I was with from eight to nine o'clock on the night of February 1, 1945. Jenkins might know where I can find her."

"Jenkins?"

"The fat man who owns the Blue Grotto. She sang there for two years. Maybe he knows where she is now. I've got to find her. I've got to find her fast."

"And did you . . . were you . . . will she remember, after all these years?"

"I hope so," he said quietly.

After her husband had gone Clare Crone stood in the center of the hall, her cold fingers flattened against her drawn cheeks. But soon she shook her head angrily. Why do I torture myself with doubt? she asked herself. Why do I let myself suffer so?

She walked to the gilt-framed mirror above the console table and looked at her reflection. She smiled at it. "You foolish woman," she said aloud. But even as she spoke her shadowy thoughts dissolved into the huge clear image of her husband's revolver. She turned and rushed to the hall closet, felt frantically along the shelf above the long coat rod. When her hand touched the cold round metal of the revolver barrel she could not, for an instant, believe it. "You foolish, foolish woman!" she said again, gaily. She shut the closet door, snapped off the hall light, hurried into the living room. Then she went to the fireplace, pushed aside the metal screen and laid two fresh eucalyptus logs on the charred wood. She lighted a match, turned on the gas jet, ignited it. As the false tongues of blue flame spurted up she saw her distorted face in the round brass ball of the andiron. She shifted her face away from the heat, turned the gas jet down and stood up, holding her hands out to the blaze. As the logs caught with a crackle, the diamonds of her engagement and wedding rings sparkled, and she recalled, for some reason, that diamonds are carbon and will burn to ash in the twinkle of an eye.

"Hello, is this Dayleen?" asked Desmond Grover. He spoke urbanely and wore the expectant look of a young gallant telephoning to make a late date. But Mordecai Fentwill noted that the hand which penciled doodles on the telephone pad was so tense the knuckles stood out whitely.

"Yeah, who's this?" The faint quack of Dayleen's voice at the other end of the wire was just audible. As Helene bent closer to the telephone her eyes met Mordecai's with a blank absence of expression.

"This is Desmond Grover, Dayleen. Do you remember me?"

"Yeah, I remember you, all right. I figured I might be

hearing from you, the way the papers are full of the Briggs case these days." Dayleen's voice wore its malice frankly. "You need an alibi, isn't that the deal, *Mister* Grover?"

"I could use one." He kept his voice light, but his handsome face was hard and wary. He glanced up at Mordecai and then stared down at the telephone pad. His hand had drawn two circles, side by side. He joined them with parallel lines that turned them into a dumbbell.

"You bet you could use one!" said Dayleen's voice, as hard as Desmond's face. "You wouldn't be coming to me unless you were out on a limb, but good! And maybe I can't remember what'll get you off that limb. There's some things a person forgets on purpose, and one of them's being treated like dirt. *If* I go to all the trouble of remembering where you were the night Ruth Ann was killed, it's worth something. Good, hard cash. A coupla hundred iron men."

Desmond glanced up at Mordecai, pantomimed humorous disdain. "Suppose I come to your place so we can talk this over. I'll bring along my checkbook."

"I don't wanna talk it over at my place. My husband's due home any minute, and what he don't know won't hurt him."

"Any place you say, Dayleen," Desmond said with exaggerated courtesy.

"My, how polite we're getting! Lemme think a second. . . . Listen: Remember the Blue Grotto? I'll meet you there in half an hour. And don't forget that checkbook!"

As Desmond put down the receiver Helene said, "A bought alibi isn't worth much."

He stood up, grinning, and chucked her under the chin. "It's better than none at all." He added, "And Mr. Fentwill here can see that there's been no collusion."

Mordecai followed the Grovers' long green Cadillac down

214

the hill to the canyon, but lost it in the traffic of Sunset Boulevard. When he reached the Blue Grotto Helene and Desmond Grover were seated in the front booth with a large, plump young woman whose auburn hair was arranged on top of her head in a big round bun. Her tight dress was richly shot with threads of gold, and she wore an expression of great satisfaction. She moved inward on the bench to make room for Mordecai and remarked in stilted and formal tones, "So charmed to meet you, Mr. Fentwill." She adjusted a large gold earring. "I just been admiring Helene's stole. Don't you think it's a darling stole, Mr. Fentwill?"

He saw that Dayleen was eying the long fur scarf which Helene wore draped around the shoulders of her brown suit. It occurred to him that both women had dressed up for the occasion; earlier in the evening, he recalled, Helene had worn a white sport coat. But before he could reply, a harassed blond waitress appeared and asked, "What'll you folks have?"

"A straight bourbon for me," Dayleen said, and added, "with water on the side."

"Mr. Fentwill?" asked Grover, very much the host.

"Nothing, thank you." Mordecai surveyed the place in which he found himself. Pale faces floated like fish in the dim light. At the long bar a row of people sat with their eyes glued to a television screen, absorbing the stale miniature gyrations of a woman who sang of love. And then he saw the life-sized mermaid hanging in swimming pose from the ceiling over the bar. He pointed. "Is that regarded as decorative, or does it serve some unimaginable function?"

"It's a mermaid," said Dayleen.

"Of that I am aware."

"This place is called the Blue Grotto, get it? It's supposed to be all under the water, see?" She pointed a fat finger at the lamp on their table. "That's an abalone shell." She dimpled at him. "You haven't been around much, have you, Gran'pa?"

"I think," said Desmond Grover quickly, "that the best way to work it is this: Dayleen can write a brief statement and sign it, and then perhaps Mr. Fentwill also would sign it, as witness."

"I don't go for this writing stuff," said Dayleen.

Desmond took out a checkbook and unscrewed his fountain pen. The waitress appeared with their drinks, and he asked her for a piece of paper. Looking as though he had requested the Hope diamond, she departed saying she'd see what she could do. Desmond's pen scratched as he made out a check.

"I still feel that a bought statement isn't worth a great deal," said Helene, looking at Dayleen with quiet dislike.

"Say, what kind of dope do you think I am, anyway?" Dayleen demanded. "Do you think I'd put my neck in a sling handing this guy a fake alibi for a few hundred bucks?" She smiled wisely, shook her head. "Unh-unh! That kinda thing costs *dough*." She added, "Not that I'd do it, even for fifty grand."

"And this small token of gratitude is hardly that," said Desmond, smiling at Helene and handing the check to Dayleen in such a way that his three companions could see it was for the sum of two hundred dollars.

"I changed my mind," said Dayleen suddenly. She took the check and tore it up. The waitress arrived with a piece of paper. "I decided," said Dayleen, picking up her glass of whisky and taking a dainty sip, "that taking that check makes me look cheap. Also, there's my husband Ray. For a car salesman he's got some funny ideas of honesty. So I'll tell you what. I saw this mink stole on sale at May Company for exactly two hundred bucks. Or it's practically mink, anyways. You can buy it and have it sent out to me—wrapped as a gift. As soon as I get it I'll write out that statement for you." She dimpled. "On my best initialed notepaper." She tossed off the rest of her whisky. "I could use another shot of this stuff."

"But why can't you take the money and buy the stole yourself?" asked Desmond, containing his irritation quite well.

"It makes me look cheap, is why," said Dayleen. They watched her stroll to the door, exuding unawareness of the men who briefly eyed her.

A newsboy with a sheaf of papers under one arm came in the door, went at once to the booth behind theirs. "Paper?" asked the newsboy. "Sure, Jimmy," said a man's heavy voice. The boy pocketed a coin and went to the bar with his wares. The voice in the next booth read aloud: " 'Briggs Diary Found! A diary written by Ruth Ann Briggs, high-school girl found brutally slain in a Hollywood canyon six years ago, is being examined by the police and may provide valuable information concerning her murder, investigators assert.' And so on, and so on, and so on." Eric Crone's face appeared around the side of the brown seat; Desmond and Helene twisted to look up at him. He was smiling under his mustache, but his eyes were cold. "Tomorrow the headline will probably be 'Murder Car Found!' The fact that the car was driven by a respected juvenile investigator who worked on the Briggs case into the bargain will make the reporters happy as larks! What they can do with that by wording it neatly!" .

"Dad! What are you doing here?" asked Helene.

Mordecai Fentwill caught the strong smell of whisky on Crone's breath as he replied, "I'm looking for a woman named Lily Tripoly. She used to sing here six years ago. I hope her memory is good!"

Helene's eyes widened, looking up into her father's face, and Mordecai knew the possibility which was struggling to the surface of her brain, held down by the massed forces of loyalty and love, terror and bewilderment.

But her voice sounded light, trivial, as she said, "Join us for a nightcap, Dad?"

When Mordecai went home he looked back and saw them huddled over a yellow telephone directory, lighted by the glow which fell from the lamp of abalone shell. No stranger glancing at the trio would guess that on two of them had fallen the deepening shadow of suspicion of murder.

# 19

As CLARE CRONE poured hot cocoa into a small thermos jug, the cuckoo in the living room burst out to cry the hour of one in the morning. The abrupt noise startled her; a trickle of the brown liquid ran down the side of the thermos and made a small pool on the immaculate white top of the stove. She wiped it off with the dishcloth. Eric always hated the sound of that cuckoo clock, she thought. The last three times it was repaired I paid the bills out of my private allowance. Why is it that men cannot understand the small perfections that make the difference between a truly charming home and an ordinary one? A cuckoo clock that does not run is in the same category as those pathetic imitation antiques that some women scatter about in the belief that they will be taken for family heirlooms.

She corked and capped the thermos, put it on the small tray holding a cup and saucer, snapped off the kitchen light and carried the tray upstairs. As she ascended she realized that the everyday tenor of her thoughts, like the unnecessary telephone conversation with the president of the Third Thursday Club which had consumed an hour of the evening, was really a quietly desperate effort to assert the power of their normal existence over the sudden and absurdly dramatic danger of scandal which threatened it. And recognizing the trick she had played on her dormant fears, she admitted their presence.

Had her husband found the singer whose testimony would clear away the cloud of suspicion which was closing in around him? And if he found her, would she be willing to help him? Would her recollections of a night six years in the past be clear and definite enough to persuade two Homicide detectives that someone else, not Eric, must have driven the murder car to the canyon?

Clare Crone's next thought was obscure at first, then became clearer, like a figure stalking toward her out of thick mist. Was Lily Tripoly more than a desperate hope of her husband's, the hope that a careless, amiable girl with whom he had once been intimate might be willing to aid him, for old time's sake, with a "white lie"?

She set the tray holding the thermos of cocoa down on the table beside her husband's bed, folded down the white candlewick spread, turned back a neat triangle of sheet over the top blanket and suddenly recalled her husband as a young bridegroom in absurd blue-striped pajamas still showing sharp new creases. She felt again the tender amusement which his big boyish figure had evoked in her a quarter of a century before. She smiled at that girlish self, so sure that she could subtly dominate that large and clumsy male, so aware that it was her job to direct and refine the pattern of their shared life. Grimly she acknowledged that the struggle had been stern and ceaseless and was not finished yet. To combat his warm and slovenly notions of marriage, as well suited to cave dwellers as to members of a cultured and civilized society, she had forced on herself an exaggeration of her natural feminine delicacy, almost to the point of caricature. Eric was a man who enjoyed the simple, animal pleasures of life far more than the uplifting ones, and she had early seen that she would have to make the former a reward after his having achieved the latter. It was at the opera that he had met the District Attorney who later took such an interest in his career.

Then Clare Crone remembered the shocking discovery that her husband was having an affair with a divorcee, and the greater shock she had felt when he told her she was a cold wife, apparently believing that this justified his behavior. She could recall vividly her sense of trapped terror. How could she have explained to him that what he saw as coldness was merely self-discipline? That would have been to lay bare her strategy.

As she left his bedroom she looked back at the thermos of cocoa, the cup and saucer beside it. He would not notice that she had used her best china, but he would appreciate the cocoa. He said a hot drink at bedtime helped him get to sleep, although the truth was that he simply liked sweets in any form.

In the bathroom between their rooms she took a quarter-grain phenobarbital. Somehow she began to feel better about the absurd events of the past week. The immediate future looked less ominous. And all past doubts of her husband seemed fantastic. She wondered if they were somehow related to her discovery, only a few months before the Briggs girl's death, of his infidelity. She wondered if her utter inability to show him the bloodstained glove could have been related in some way to the silence concerning her real nature which necessity and pride had forced upon her.

She fell asleep imagining, as she did not infrequently, a future moment of triumph: Eric, dazed by his good fortune, was again elected to a high-salaried public office, a dark horse winning out against the forces of political corruption. And then she, wise and smiling, revealed her true self in a gown by Adrian. He knew at last that she was not a woman of ice, but a woman of intellect who had forged of herself a better helpmate than those warm little wives who are devoid of ambition and whose husbands rise in the world by fluke, if at all.

"I owe it all to you, Clare," said Eric's dream voice, humbly.

And then her mother's calm voice said, once more, "But Clare, you can't marry a common *policeman!*"

It was still dark when the shrilling of a bell awakened her. She thought for an instant that the alarm had rung, but then she saw that it was only five o'clock. With the panicky feeling that something was very wrong she thrust her arms into her robe, closed it as she hurried down the stairs. Two men, bearing a long wheeled stretcher between them, were on the porch.

"Yes? What is it?"

"The ambulance, ma'am. For your husband."

The man's face blurred before her, and she stepped to one side on an unsteady floor. "Wait here," she commanded and ran up the stairs, rushed into her husband's room.

She recoiled from the ghastly pallor of his face.

His eyes were open and he stared at her out of huge black pupils. Laboring for breath, he sat up and heavily swung his legs over the side of the bed. His hand fumbled to his forehead, and he picked up a tall glass of water from the bedside table and drank it greedily. "Eric! What's wrong?" she cried, moving toward him.

He spoke in a wheezy whisper. "I called you but you didn't hear me. So I phoned Dr. Ferris myself."

"But what's wrong?"

He stood up and reached for his bathrobe. "That's what I want to know," he whispered. His eyes, she noticed, avoided her.

It was just nine o'clock in the morning when Tuck telephoned Eric Crone's office to learn what luck he'd had in locating the witness he had told them of the night before, and to offer help if it seemed necessary. "Mr. Crone will not be in today," said the voice of his secretary. "Mrs. Crone called just a few minutes ago. She didn't mention what was wrong, but I imagine it's this intestinal flu that's going around. He's been looking sort of under the weather for several days now."

The Crones' telephone was answered by a warm, doubtful Negroid voice. "No, Mr. Crone, he isn't home. Neither is Mrs. Crone. I'm their girl. I come twice a week, and I don't know anything about nothing. Mrs. Crone, she phoned me to my house at seven this morning and said the back door was unlocked and just to come on in and go to work."

"Do you have any idea where they are?"

"Well, yes, I got an *idea*. I got an idea they're down to the hospital."

"The same one where Mrs. Crone was?" asked Brigit. "The Good Sam?"

"No, ma'am. The Good Sam*aritan.*"

Half an hour later a nurse led Tuck and Brigit to a waiting room furnished in wicker, cretonne and pallid morning sunlight. Mrs. Crone was alone, seated bolt upright on a hard settee. She wore a housedress, tan oxfords and a black fur coat. To call her appearance distraught would be an understatement. She looked like the only survivor of a disaster involving a hundred mangled bodies. When she saw Tuck and Brigit in the doorway her eyes took on the moist, tormented glare of a frightened animal. She spoke shakily. "He's going to die. I don't want to talk to anyone."

"Now, now," said the nurse, hurrying forward to draw a paper cup of water at the cooler and then presenting it to Mrs. Crone. "You mustn't talk like that. Your husband's a strong, healthy man, and we're doing everything for him we can."

Mrs. Crone looked down into the paper cup and drank the water mechanically. "Thank you. You can go now, nurse."

The nurse took the empty cup from her nerveless hand and rustled away.

"What's happened, Mrs. Crone?" asked Brigit. "What's wrong with your husband?"

Mrs. Crone changed before their eyes. In one moment, by a strong effort, she composed herself. With an easy, calm gesture she drew her coat around her, concealing her housedress, and by tucking her crossed feet well under the wicker settee she hid the unsuitable tan oxfords. She opened her purse, held up a mirror, quickly combed her hair so it lay in its usual smooth dark waves. With a cool, steady hand she painted her mouth red.

"Forgive my bad manners," she said as she quietly closed her purse. "I suddenly realized how frightful I looked. It's so wrong to give in to morbid fears, isn't it? What happened is this. My husband made a dreadful mistake. Late last night he went to the medicine chest for some Vitamin $B_1$. They're small white pills he takes when he's been drinking too much. And instead he took several digitalis pills. You probably know that digitalis is a poison. Dr. Ferris prescribed it for me after my second heart attack. The digitalis was in exactly the same kind of bottle as Eric's Vitamin $B_1$, and the pills are the same size. Fortunately Eric realized almost at once that something was wrong and telephoned Dr. Ferris."

"Did I hear my name mentioned?" Dr. Ferris asked. While his pewter-gray eyes queried the presence of Tuck and Brigit he went to the side of the wicker settee, patted Mrs. Crone's shoulder. His voice was cheerful. "Well, Mrs. Crone, you two certainly have a talent for narrow escapes.

But the worst is over, the crisis is past. Your husband is going to be all right."

The wicker sofa creaked as Mrs. Crone, her eyes closed, fell sideways toward the flowered-cretonne seat. The doctor bent quickly and caught her around the shoulders with one arm. "Nurse!" he called.

"I'm perfectly all right," said Clare Crone slowly and distinctly as a starched uniform crackled briskly to her side.

"Just the same you're going to lie down awhile," said the doctor. Mrs. Crone rose obediently and departed on the sustaining white arm, and Dr. Ferris handed Brigit and Tuck one crisp nod apiece. "Good news affects some people like that," he confided. "And then there's that heart of hers, you know."

Tuck's long arm stopped him. The little doctor looked highly offended at the familiarity. "I'm sorry, Doctor, but there are a few questions we have to ask you about Mr. Crone. We'll be as brief as possible."

The doctor smiled with faint incredulity. "You surely realize that medical ethics do not permit me to discuss my patient's condition with anyone except members of his own family."

"Murder makes exceptions to a good many rules," Tuck told him tolerantly.

The doctor turned slowly so that he was facing them. "Do you mean to say that there's been an attempt on Mr. Crone's life?"

Tuck said, "Mr. Crone's a key figure in a murder case. In addition to the initial and highly successful murder there has been an unsuccessful and very peculiar attempt to shoot Miss Estees, here." The doctor looked rather suspiciously up at Brigit's healthy face, but Tuck continued, "And now Mr. Crone, who also investigated this murder for a time, is rushed to the hospital full of a toxic substance. His wife told us he took digitalis by accident late last night. It is now ten o'clock. Yet you just announced to her that the crisis is over. That sounds like a very large dose of digitalis."

Dr. Ferris caught himself absently nodding his agreement, and frowned.

Then Tuck smiled down at him.

Brigit knew from experience the effect on witnesses of Tuck's big kind smile. Like sudden sunrise on a crag of rock, it cast a reflected glow on the dourest face. The doctor's frown disappeared, although his face retained a troubled look.

"Mr. Crone telephoned me at half past four this morning. He was having distress in breathing, and the sound of his voice also indicated considerable respiratory embarrassment. He briefly described his other symptoms—intense thirst, severe headache, a constricted feeling around the heart—all of which had appeared about an hour and a half before and had increased rapidly in severity. He asked me to send an ambulance at once. When I offered to first pay a house call to see if hospitalization was necessary he told me, rather brusquely, that he knew he was a very sick man, that there was no time to waste.

"I reached his house a minute or two after the ambulance. The attendants were helping him down the stairs. His pupils were enormously dilated and his pallor was extreme. After the ambulance left I saw that Mrs. Crone was in a state bordering on shock, and I merely told her that her husband was very ill, that I was not yet certain of the cause. It was seeing her that reminded me of the digitalis I had prescribed for her a year ago. Headache and dilated pupils frequently accompany digitalis poisoning. I asked Mrs. Crone if any of the digitalis pills were still in the medicine chest, and she replied that she believed so. I found only two in the container and asked if that was all that had been left after her

226

medication was changed. She did not know how many had been left.

"It is unfortunate that people have a way of retaining the unused balance of drugs and medicines, even though many lose much of their effectiveness with time, while others become dangerous. When I noticed that Mr. Crone's Vitamin $B_1$ pills were in a bottle identical with the one containing the digitalis I thought I had discovered the cause of his symptoms. He knew the Vitamin $B_1$ pills to be very mild, and might easily have taken as many as four or five over the period of an hour or so. And four or five digitalis could possibly have brought on the headache and dilated pupils, although the thirst, pallor and respiratory embarrassment are not characteristic.

"Mrs. Crone rode with me to the hospital, and I learned from her that her husband had evidently been drinking heavily the night before. This could have accounted for his thirst, and made an error like selecting the wrong bottle from the medicine chest all the more likely. But . . ." The doctor debated with himself for a moment. "I have ordered a complete laboratory analysis of stomach contents," he said briskly. "In seven or eight hours I should be able to give you a more conclusive picture."

"I don't suppose it would be possible for us to talk to Mr. Crone," Tuck said.

Dr. Ferris looked grim. "It is not possible for anyone to talk to him. He has been in a state of mild delirium ever since he reached the hospital. Delirium, I may add, is not as a rule produced by an overdose of digitalis."

"But at least he knew whether he'd gone to the medicine chest for vitamin pills!" said Brigit.

"When I asked him that," said Dr. Ferris, "he said that he was tired of hunting. He asked me to make his bed because he wanted to lie down. And when I pointed out that he was already in bed he said that they swelled up and died."

"Who?" asked Brigit.

"His dogs. Only I happen to know that the Crones don't have any dogs. No pets of any kind, not even a canary." He looked at his watch and showed dismay. "Call me between five and six this evening and I'll be glad to tell you the results of the laboratory analysis," he said as he hurried away.

# 20

IN HIS SMALL dim office tucked away in the depths of the Philosophy Building, Mordecai Fentwill listened without comment. Brigit let Tuck do the talking because she was still troubled by Dr. Ferris' last few remarks. When Tuck's voice stopped she said, "You didn't tell Uncle Mordecai about the delirium."

"Yes, I did."

"I mean, what Eric Crone said." She looked at her great-uncle and almost forgot what she had meant to tell him. The old man's eyes looked as black as coal, seemed to crackle with excitement. But his voice was curiously placid. "Yes, my dear?"

"It rang some kind of a bell with me, what Eric Crone said to Dr. Ferris when he was delirious, or supposed to be. About hunting. That he was tired of hunting and wanted to go to bed. And then the dogs. They swelled up and died."

" 'O where hae ye been, Lord Randal, my son? O where hae ye been, my handsome young man?' " quoted Mordecai Fentwill. "An English ballad. Rather old. Very good, too. Suggestive. It tells about a young man who was poisoned by a woman. His sweetheart, or possibly his wife. As for the dogs, the mother asks where they are and he replies, 'O

They swelled and they died; mother, make my bed soon;
For I'm weary wi' hunting, and fain wald lie doun.' "

"That's it!" Brigit shouted. "That's what Eric Crone
was doing. Quoting 'Lord Randal.' Only Dr. Ferris thought
he was delirious."

"I'm very certain that the doctor based his recognition
of delirium on something more solid than a poor literary
background. But as you say, Brigit, the allusion is interesting. More important just now is the problem of finding Lily
Tripoly."

"Who?" Tuck asked.

"The woman Eric Crone was trying to find last night.
The singer who used to entertain in the Blue Grotto," said
Mordecai. "If you will wait until I induce Doctor Eames
to take my one-o'clock class, I will join you."

"Yep," said Jenkins, "Mr. Crone came in last night about
eleven. He wanted to know if I had any idea where Lily
Tripoly is. I told him the name of the talent bureau I hired
her from six years ago. He was in the phone booth quite
awhile, calling different numbers. Must of made maybe
thirty calls. Ran me out of nickels for a while."

"And did he find Lily Tripoly?" asked Mordecai.

"Yep. It took him until nearly closing time. He mentioned
that she's singing at the Jungle, out on Sunset Strip." Jenkins lowered his voice confidentially. "I hope Mr. Crone
isn't in any sort of trouble. He's been a steady customer of
mine for a good many years." With the air of a character
witness he added, "The kind of customer a bar likes to
have. Orders the best whisky, never asks for credit and
behaves like a gent no matter how many he's had."

"He had more than a few last night, I understand," said
Tuck.

Jenkins nodded and said stoutly, "But except that he

had to walk out kind of careful, no one would have guessed it."

The cheerful voice of the woman who took telephone reservations for tables in the Jungle told Brigit that the night club did not open until six, although the headwaiter usually arrived at about five-thirty. She was able to give them his telephone number. In a suave, pleasant and unconcerned voice he told them several somewhat disturbing things. "Yes, Miss Tripoly did get a telephone call last night. Very late. While she was singing her final number. A man. I asked his name. It was an odd one. Crone. The first name, as I remember, was Eric. Or maybe Earl. But something like that. He said he was an old friend of hers. I happened to overhear the last of their conversation. She was making an appointment to meet him. I don't know where or when."

"Do you know whether she went home last night?" Brigit asked.

"I assume so. Is there anything wrong?"

"We hope not. We've been to her house, and it doesn't look as though she was there last night."

"She has a sister she visits sometimes. Lives out in the Valley somewhere. I don't know her name or address. Miss Tripoly's crazy over her nephew and niece—kids about three or four years old. But I don't think she'd pay them a visit at three in the morning. It was two-thirty by the time she changed her costume and left the club." His voice became less casual. "There's one thing I do remember, though. When she left the club this morning a car parked at the curb started up just as she swung out of the parking lot. It went in the same direction she did—north, toward the hills. I didn't think of it at the time, but now that I look back, that car could have been following her."

"What kind of car was it?"

"I really don't remember. I gave it only a casual look while I was starting my engine." He added, "Will you give me a ring when you find her? I'm a little worried. If for any reason she isn't going to be able to sing tonight, we'll have to find a substitute, you know."

When they telephoned Lily Tripoly their only reward was to hear a bell ring nine times in an empty house. On the chance that one of her neighbors might know where the singer had gone, they drove to her Laurel Canyon home. The canyon wound tortuously through Hollywood Hills into the San Fernando Valley and was populated by eccentrics of the artistic sort and people who like canyons. Lily Tripoly's house was of the rustic variety, half hidden among eucalyptus trees and native verdure.

The garage was empty. The brass knocker fell hollowly against an unopened door. At the back door stood two quarts of milk.

Clare Crone opened the door of her husband's room and tiptoed in. The shades were drawn, but he was not asleep. He was propped against pillows, looking at her. She was relieved to see that his pupils were no longer so enormously dilated. Some of his natural color had returned, too.

"You look much better," she said. "How are you feeling?"

"Much better."

"Do you want the shades closed like this? Isn't it a little gloomy?"

"Matches my mood. Rests my eyes."

She went to the bureau, set down the suitcase. "I brought you some clothes. The doctor said you'll be well enough to leave by tomorrow." She picked up the empty vase. As she went to the bathroom to fill it she added, "And I've brought a few flowers from the garden. Some roses and some irises."

"That was nice of you."

She filled the vase, brought it to the bedside table and began arranging the flowers. "I'm glad I took the doctor's advice and went home and changed my clothes. I was a dreadful sight this morning. But I was so worried I didn't know what I was putting on."

"That was natural," he said.

"So after I knew you were out of danger I decided to present a somewhat more cheerful picture when you saw me." She stepped back to scan the flowers. "There! Don't they look nice?"

He turned his head obediently. "Very nice, Clare."

She drew a chair up to the bed, sat down and reached for his hand. He let it rest on hers passively. "Do you want to talk about it, Eric? Or will it upset you?"

"What is there to talk about?"

"I agree. What? It was the sort of accident that happens every day. You were tired and on top of that had had too much to drink. You simply reached into the medicine chest for your vitamin pills and got the digitalis by mistake. The bottles were exactly alike and the tablets are quite similar." Her voice was firm and bright, and she pressed his hand reassuringly.

"Only I didn't go to the medicine chest for any vitamin pills," he said. "And so I couldn't have taken the digitalis by accident."

Even though she had half expected to hear him say this, the reality was shocking. She made her voice calm, soothing. "You should have had more faith in me, dear. You must have realized, in your heart of hearts, that I would never have let you down. You should have trusted me a little more." He was looking at her oddly, she was aware. But she continued: "I was afraid, from the moment you left the house looking for her, that this Lily Tripoly person would not prove very co-operative. Whatever you may have been to her then, you are nothing to her now. And from what I am able to understand of them, such women are not very tender about past attachments."

He was smiling tightly. "You're going a little fast for me, but I think I get the gist of it. You believe I went looking for Lily because I have no alibi and hoped she would lie for me and provide one. Is that it?"

"Putting it very baldly, yes, Eric."

"And then, realizing that I was going to be arrested for murder, I took a dose of digitalis to escape from facing the music, and then got cold feet. Is that it?"

"But you admit yourself that you didn't take the digitalis by accident! What other construction is there?"

"Now get this, Clare. Listen to me carefully and get it. I didn't take any digitalis at all, Clare. By accident or otherwise. None. None at all."

The cold firm voice numbed her brain. "If we don't co-operate with each other . . ." she began.

"I've been lying here thinking," he cut in, looking up at the ceiling. "The digitalis is merely an assumption of the doctor's. So far no chemical test's been made of what they pumped out of me. If it should turn out that the good doctor is right about the digitalis, then there's only one answer that I can see." His eyes turned and met hers. "You gave me the digitalis, Clare. You put it in the cocoa I drank."

The room spun slowly. Clare Crone opened her eyes to find herself collapsed against the back of the chair, pulled into a heap by gravity. His voice went on, low, but with an undertone of shaken nerves: "I keep trying to remember if the cocoa tasted bitter, or strange in any way. It was strong, the way I like it. It wasn't sweet enough, but you never make

234

it sweet enough. But was it bitter? I keep trying to remember."

She made her brain form a question, which she spoke carefully, not looking at her husband's face. "Why would I do such a thing?"

"Because you believe that I'm guilty of murder. Because you preferred the dignity of widowhood to the role you saw facing you, the role of wife of the accused."

If he had shown anger, she could have replied with rage. But his strange quietness robbed her of this outlet for the sick, crushed feelings which squirmed in the pit of her stomach. She stood up, wondering if she were going to vomit. "I swear to you, Eric, that I—" she felt her chin tremble like a child's; her voice was little and feeble and shaken— "that I didn't—" her throat ached suddenly, and the tears sprang to her eyes and seared them—"do what you say." She felt her stiff face crack apart like cement in an earthquake. "I . . . I . . . I love you, Eric." As the tears slid down her twisted cheeks and the first sob tore past the tightness in her throat, she turned and ran from the room.

She had to stop outside the door because her wet eyes bleared and distorted the long corridor. Having no handkerchief, she tried to wipe the tears away with the back of her hand. Then she turned to the wall, her face hidden in the curve of her bent arm, and let her sobs come out. Inside her head a voice was saying, "I love him. I really love him." The voice was full of wonder, and a faint surprise.

It was half past four when Brigit, Tuck and Mordecai Fentwill asked the nurse at the desk the way to Eric Crone's room. She consulted a chart. "He's in room 606. Straight down the corridor, turn to your left, and it's the second door to your right."

235

Brigit was the first to enter Eric Crone's room. But she stopped abruptly. The bed was empty, a white hospital gown lay in a heap on the floor, and on the chair a man's open suitcase gaped at her. "Why, he's gone!" she cried.

At first the nurse did not believe it. Hurrying along the corridor beside them, she said they must have got into the wrong room. Then, standing in room 606 she stared at the empty bed, looked up sharply at the number on the open door, glanced at the open suitcase. "He *is* gone!" she said. They followed as she bustled out, trailing comments: "Well, I never . . . just walked out of here like . . . what will his doctor . . ."

Mordecai's loud firm voice arrested her. "Madam. Control this flow of inconclusiveness! When did he leave?"

"Why, it couldn't be more than a few minutes ago! His wife paid him a visit and she left at four, so he was certainly there then." She added grimly, "He must have used the other stairs. He didn't get past *me*."

"We are really very fortunate," said Mordecai as they rode down in the elevator. "We know why he left and where he has gone and it is even possible that we may arrive there before him. He must have taken a cab, for I somehow do not believe that his wife and he are capable of having planned this together. That means that unless he had the great good fortune to find a taxi waiting before the building, he suffered the delay of telephoning for one. Does this black sedan of yours have a siren, Mr. Tuck? Are you, like uniformed police officers, permitted to exceed the usual speed limit?"

"Main floor," said the elevator attendant, half turning to give Mordecai Fentwill a strange look of which the old man was utterly unaware.

"You're way ahead of us, Uncle Mordecai," said Brigit

236

as they pushed their way through the great entrance door into the golden glare of late afternoon sunlight. She looked up at Tuck's face and saw that it looked as baffled as she felt.

"Hurry!" commanded Mordecai Fentwill. "And while we drive rapidly to the west I shall clarify my comments." He added courteously, "I fear that surprise has made me express myself clumsily, for I am sure that what I have attempted to say is as apparent to you as to me." He concentrated then on haste, his little legs taking two steps to Tuck's one. He was breathless when he hurled himself into the back seat of the black sedan and leaned against the wide cushion with a certain dignity not in the least damaged by the fact that his black Homburg was crooked on his bald dome. "On the speed of your driving depends the solution of this damnable series of crimes," he gasped out to Tuck. The sedan shot forward toward the lowering sun.

In a moment Mordecai spoke in a more natural voice. "We know that Eric Crone telephoned Lily Tripoly last night and made an appointment with her. Since it was two-thirty before she left the night club, it seems unlikely that the appointment was for such a late hour. So he must have arranged to meet her some time today."

"But where?" demanded Brigit. "And when?"

"The answer to that becomes obvious when we consider the circumstances attending this reunion. That Eric Crone had not been in contact with the singer for many years is abundantly clear. Yet he wished to ask a favor of her—that she repeat to the police a story which would exonerate him of guilt. Therefore he would have deferred to her preference, to a great extent, as to the place and time of their appointment. Since she must arise late, it would not be in the morning. Had she suggested that he meet her at her place of work, the appointment must have been made for some hour after

237

six when the Jungle opens its doors. But for such a meeting it would not have been necessary for Mr. Crone to hasten from his hospital bed at four in the afternoon. Cut over to the Hollywood Freeway here, Mr. Tuck. Your speed in this traffic leaves much to be desired."

Mordecai leaned back in the seat again. "As to where they were to meet, I believe Miss Tripoly's own home is the logical answer. What other place provides the privacy necessary for so delicate a discussion?"

Tuck turned into the ramp leading up to the wide freeway which rose fresh and new above the clutter of old buildings, the frustrating mesh of narrow streets. The speedometer needle trembled at the figure seventy, and Mordecai Fentwill automatically held onto the brim of his hat in the quiet air. The wind of their speed roared past them like a river.

"It is entirely on Lily Tripoly's evidence that the solutions we seek depend," said Mordecai Fentwill. Brigit turned to look at her great-uncle. A small man, a figure more of the past than the present, he sat there holding firmly to a hat which did not need to be held, and yet he inspired her unquestioning belief. Tuck, she saw, his eyes glued to the road, had turned his head a trifle, his ear alert for the old man's words.

"We face three general possibilities," said Mordecai. "One: Lily Tripoly's statement will convincingly show us that Eric Crone could not have been the person who drove Ruth Ann Briggs to the canyon where she died. Two: Lily Tripoly's statement will fail to clear Mr. Crone of possible guilt. Three: Lily Tripoly will make no statement, because she is dead." He paused a moment, and then added bleakly, "And if she is dead, the truth about the Briggs murder will never be known. It will elude us as the murderer has eluded discovery these many years. Once again events will have demonstrated that justice, occurring on the small scale

238

which most men can understand, comes about only rarely, an exception among the many instances where good is not rewarded, nor evil confounded."

"But why the rush?" asked Tuck.

"If Miss Tripoly is still alive, her life may be in danger. And it is best that we reach her before Mr. Crone does. For if he is given an opportunity to prompt her memory, we shall deal with one more uncertainty—that her story was not the impartial truth."

"The way I see it, though, the mess is narrowing down," said Tuck. "If Crone tried to kill himself, it means he's guilty. The story he told about having a witness, this Lily Tripoly, was a stall. On the other hand, if someone tried to kill him, it was to make us believe that he committed suicide rather than face the music. It was a bad method, incidentally, because very few men kill themselves with poison. That's a typical female trick."

"Statistics prove nothing about individual instances," Mordecai remarked. "Enough digitalis at hand, I am quite able to believe that Mr. Crone would use it to end his life, even though, in doing so, he became one man in a hundred, thousand or million." He waited for a moment and then asked, "Is that *all* you have to say?"

"That covers our only alternatives, doesn't it?" Tuck sounded somewhat aggrieved.

"It covers the main two," agreed Mordecai. "Let us now consider the motive for the Briggs murder. We have assumed, because of the three quarters of an hour which elapsed between the moment when she got off the streetcar and the moment when she died, and because no meeting could have been premeditated, that she was struck in a sudden rage, for reasons unknown. To try to find the most likely reasons, we have only Ruth Ann's character to judge from. Of her we know, first, that she was not a girl to indulge in a casual flirtation in a canyon. Second, her attitudes were rigid, to judge from what she felt about the smoking of marijuana, as expressed both to Manuel Reyes and in the diary she intended no one to see. We can believe that she meant it when she said she would never shield the user of this drug, and would not shield herself from such a person's dislike by using secrecy in informing the proper authorities about him. And I believe we may assume that this same forthrightness would apply to any other criminal, illegal or indecent act of which she had knowledge.

"But the killer apparently did not know this. The killer, I firmly believe, made the mistake of assuming that Ruth Ann was one of the young women in a hectic time who made up the easygoing crowd. Because he did not drive her home. He drove her to the canyon.

"Upon being rebuffed, the killer suffered a shock. The pretty lipsticked schoolgirl revealed her horror, terror, disgust, anger, loathing, or whatever term applies to his unknown behavior. Her reaction must have stung the more fiercely in that it revealed to the killer his own deviation from decency, to say nothing of his clumsy error in choosing her as the target for his attentions.

"But that is not enough. For to have aroused the fear and anger which backed the blow that killed her, Ruth Ann Briggs must have, in some way, represented a menace to the killer. I submit that it would have been in character for her to let him know that she would not remain silent about what had happened that night in the canyon. I believe that the killer must have struck her as she was angrily leaving him to walk to her home, and while he was filled with two emotions: the ego-sting of her rejection and the much stronger fear of exposure.

"But here we run into a rather ugly snag. The medical evidence showed that, aside from the blow on the head, no

240

other physical violence was done her. And merely to attempt to embrace a pretty girl in seclusion does not normally carry with it such odium as would drive a sane person to sudden murder. But before we leap to the conclusion of insanity, there are these possibilities:

"One. The killer, being a particular individual and not the very general male I have sketched, was peculiarly averse to having the world know that he had made amorous advances to a girl of fifteen. An older man, such as Eric Crone, fits nicely into the category; Desmond Grover and Richard Carewe certainly do not.

"Two. It was not an attempt at love-making which the killer did not want anyone to know about, but something else. Enter the green cigarette case containing marijuana. If it was the killer's, could Ruth Ann have discovered what it contained? Or could she perhaps have recognized, from description in the auditorium lecture at her high school or perhaps from some past experience, the peculiarly distinctive, tealike odor of the drug on the killer's breath? Quite possible. But the serious objection here is what any user of marijuana would know: A mere accusation without proof carries no legal weight whatever, and could scarcely doom him to exposure in the newspapers or to arrest.

"Three: The violent state of mind which ended in murder was caused by both the above factors, to which we will add a somewhat unsound personality that magnified the importance of the exposure he feared, perhaps because of a temporarily manic state induced by the drug found near the corpse.

"The fourth possibility is, of course, that nothing I have just said was the actual truth, and the girl was destroyed because of something unknown to us, by someone also unknown."

"I must say that at this stage of the game the case against

Eric Crone seems the most plausible," Tuck said. "Especially when the front seat of his car seems to have been the scene of the crime."

"Oh, I agree with the first part of your comment," said Mordecai. "But the fact that his car seems to have been used to drive the girl to the canyon strikes me as being rather in his favor. From the first it has struck me that were he the killer, he would have used more caution about removing all signs of blood."

"Still," said Tuck, "killers have been careless before."

"Quite true."

Brigit frowned. "What bothers me is the suicide theory. I don't go for it. If Crone is guilty, I think he wanted to toss us the well-known red herring by making us believe that someone—the actual killer of Ruth Ann, of course—tried to do him in in a way that would damn him as an attempted suicide."

"Rather devious," said Mordecai. "But not implausible, granting him the artistry actually to swallow a lethal substance rather than fake the symptoms."

"But then there's that trap in the old house," said Brigit. "Do you still think the only reason for it was to make us fall for the idea implied in the telegram? That the killer of Ruth Ann and the attacker of Mrs. Crone were the same person?"

"I find no other explanation."

"But then doesn't that kind of eliminate Crone? I mean, he knew darned well that he knocked his wife down. If he killed Ruth Ann, why send us a telegram linking two violent acts he knew he was responsible for?"

"You seem to forget Mrs. Crone's lack of candor. She created a mysterious prowler to explain the presence of the glove. Crone seemed to me to be telling the truth when he said he had never seen that glove before the night it was found on the hearthrug. Could not Mrs. Crone have taken him in with the prowler story as well as us? In which case, to create a scapegoat, he seized on the fortuitous existence of a housebreaker with violent tendencies."

The big car wheeled onto a ramp which led off the speedway. To the west a late sun glared ominously in a hazy sky. "We'll be there in another five minutes," said Tuck.

When the black sedan pulled to a stop before Lily Tripoly's house it seemed still deserted in the early false twilight of the canyon. But a moment after the knocker fell the door was opened by a small brunette who wore black velvet trousers and a Chinese jacket of saffron yellow. "Miss Tripoly?" asked Tuck.

The smile of welcome slipped from her face as she eyed the three of them. "That's right. But who are you?"

When Tuck showed her his badge she eyed it without expression, opened the door wider. As they filed past her she said blankly, "You know, this is weird. I've been wondering all day if I should call the police. Last night someone tried to kill me."

Standing against the closed door, she smiled into their staring faces. "I know it sounds crazy, but I actually think somebody's out for my hide. It's the only way I can explain the mad thing that happened."

# 21

L<small>ILY</small> T<small>RIPOLY</small> had a faintly improbable look. Her subtly exaggerated make-up screamed her difference from the majority of women; her big dark eyes sparkled as though they had been trained to do so; her upswept mop of curls dangled with a precise carelessness from the back of her otherwise sleek head; and her smile was so extremely merry that it made her seem sad, as clowns do. She curled up in one corner of her low modern sofa in a room of big surfaces and clear colors and subtle lighting effects. Smoking a cigarette which she held in a contrived and slightly unusual way, she told them of her narrow escape from death.

"Right after I left the Jungle, the club where I work, I noticed a car that seemed to be following me. I mean, at two-thirty in the morning there aren't too many cars out, and so the way this one kept a little way behind me, it was noticeable. And when I turned in at the canyon and a minute later it did too, I thought, What goes on here? I pulled into the garage, and as I came out I saw a car stop in front of the place next door. I mean, through all the trees and bushes and stuff I saw its headlights go out. And in a second I heard leaves crackling, but very softly, like someone coming toward my house on tiptoe. There were no lights on anywhere around, only there was a kind of mist in the air and it kept it from being pitch-dark, some way. I mean, you could see the shapes of things, the bushes and trees and even the porch steps. I was just going to start toward them, from where I was standing in the driveway, when I noticed the big bush on the other side of the lawn. The branches nearest the house, they moved a little, as if someone was standing just behind them, waiting. On the steps I'd have my back to the bush, and whoever was there could rush out and . . . well, anyway, I didn't like the setup one little bit. In fact, I don't mind saying Lily was scared silly.

"More people warn me about living alone like I do, and I always laugh at them. But last night I sure wished there was someone in this house. To make a long story shorter, I eased back into the garage, started up my car and backed down that driveway, but fast! Then I headed out to the Valley where my kid sister lives. Believe it or not, in a couple of minutes this car was on my tail again! I broke every speed law there is, winding out of the canyon. In the Valley, I shot through a couple of boulevard stops and ignored a red light. For once in my life I wanted a cop to roar up beside me and yell, 'Move over to the curb!' So did one?" She paused, beaming broadly. "Yep. Just after I was sure I'd lost the car that was tailing me, and slowed down and took a deep breath, up comes this motorcycle cop, sore as a boil. I told him about the car behind me, but I don't think he believed a word of it. And I got a nice, fat ticket for doing sixty in a twenty-five-mile zone. But that's one fine I'll be glad to pay."

"So you spent the night at your sister's?" Tuck prompted.

"That's right. And most of today. She's got two of the cutest kids you ever laid eyes on. I don't pretend I know a lot about kids, but those two are smart beyond average. Why, at lunch today—it was their lunch and my breakfast —Lily-Ann said to me . . ."

"We will dispense with your niece's bon mot," said Mordecai. "You have, have you not, an appointment with Eric Crone?"

Her dark eyes snapped at him. Her smile was strained. "Is it your business who I have a date with? Which reminds me to inquire what you three dicks are doing in my parlor by Sloane's?"

"We want you to tell us where Eric Crone was between eight and nine on the night of February 1, 1945. We would greatly appreciate hearing your statement now," Tuck said.

Lily Tripoly sat up, planted her fists on her lips. Her wide-eyed, charmingly comic face became as shrewd as a banker's. "Say, what is this? Have you got the idea I was his girl friend or something? What makes you think I know what he was doing on some night or other in 1945?" She made the year in question sound as remote as 1066. "Why, in 1945 I was singing week ends, for beans, in the Blue Grotto! A little neighborhood pub! I hadn't even signed with Goldstein yet! Why, in 1945 the war was still on! Wasn't it? And I'm supposed to remember where a mere acquaintance of mine was some night in 1945."

"The night a girl named Ruth Ann Briggs was killed," Tuck reminded her quietly. "The night you found blood on a white piano. Do you remember the night we're talking about, now?"

Lily Tripoly sank back onto the sofa. "I sure do. She was fifteen years old. I must have known Eric Crone about two or three months by then."

The door knocker sounded. Lily Tripoly stood up. "That's him." She looked at her watch as she crossed the room. She opened the door. "Hello! You're late."

"Hello, Lily. It's been a long time, hasn't it?" He came into the room smiling down at the singer, and Brigit saw that to some women he might be quite attractive. When he raised his eyes and saw the three of them he became motionless; his expression did not change.

Lily Tripoly circled him to look up into his face. "My God, Eric, you look terrible! Sit down! Can I fix you a drink?"

He smiled down at her, shook his head rather stiffly, sank into the nearest corner of the low sofa. Lily Tripoly's eyes had taken in the situation; recognizing that she had the center of the stage, she strolled to the grand piano and arranged herself against it in a tough and jaunty pose.

"Actresses and singers having the reputation of so many alley cats, I would like to go on record with an explanation of my relations with Mr. Crone. I have a kid sister who I was then attempting to raise, our parents being dead. She was fifteen, and she thought she was in love with a no-good, two-bit, ex-juvenile-delinquent type fellow. I told her he was poison, but she didn't pay any attention. Mr. Crone used to drop in at the Blue Grotto, where I was entertaining then, and when I found out he didn't regard me as having loose morals because I sang for my supper, I sometimes would join him at his table between numbers. I finally told him about this Romeo my kid sister was sneaking out with, and that's when I found out Mr. Crone worked in Juvenile Division. He said the boy's name sounded familiar. So one night he came up to my apartment with a folder full of information about this laddie. He showed Genevieve how her Romeo had been arrested for various crimes five times before he was eighteen, how he'd been sent to a reform school and how, if he followed the usual pattern, he'd wind up paying a long visit to San Quentin. At first Genevieve would hardly listen because Romeo looked like Humphrey Bogart, but she finally realized the truth and began to bawl. She broke the date she'd made with him and never saw him again. And the night this happened was the first of February 1945. The night of the Briggs murder. Mr. Crone rang our bell at eight sharp and stayed an hour." Lily Tripoly went to the long slab of coffee table, picked up a cigarette, lighted it. Blowing out smoke, she grinned around the room. "In other words, at the very time you smart detectives thought Eric was maybe busy killing one fifteen-year-old girl, he was sweating blood trying to help another kid that age!"

For a moment no one moved. Eric sat slumped on the sofa, staring down at his hands lying curled on his lap. He looked like an aging, exhausted athlete. Mordecai Fentwill sat very erect in a modern chair whose every curve was shaped to invite the relaxed human spine. His eyes, Brigit noticed, stared straight ahead as though at a rather frightful object which was invisible to the rest of them. He said, "I believe that the only animal which actually sweats blood is the hippopotamus."

Then everyone laughed and moved: Eric got out his pipe and began to fill it; Lily patted his shoulder; Tuck sat down; Mordecai stood up. "You went nowhere last night, Mr. Crone, but to the Blue Grotto?"

"Nowhere."

Mordecai extracted his watch from his vest and looked at it. "Mr. Tuck, I believe it would be well to telephone Dr. Ferris to find whether the laboratory has discovered the poison with which the murderer attempted to kill Mr. Crone." Mordecai ignored Lily Tripoly's comic surprise; she led Tuck to the telephone. "When I left the Blue Grotto last night, Mr. Crone," continued Mordecai, "you had, I recall, accepted your daughter's invitation to join them for a round of drinks. Did you leave the table at any time?"

"Yes, to get some change to phone with."

"And did your daughter leave the table then as well?"

"Yes, she went to the powder room, I remember."

"Had you ordered your drinks?"

"Yes. They were on the table when I came back."

"And were your drinks alike or different?"

"Mine was a double brandy-and-soda. Helene had a Daiquiri. And Desmond ordered bourbon with water on the side."

"So the poisoner was undeterred by the possibility that someone else at the table might drink the fatal potion by error."

"But here's the big difficulty," said Brigit. "That is, if I'm right in gathering that this meeting last night was accidental." Both her uncle and Eric Crone nodded. "Then that means that Desmond Grover just happened to have some kind of poison in his pocket. Is that very likely?"

Eric Crone was frowning. "There's another thing. I don't have much fondness for my son-in-law, I admit. But I find it hard to believe he's insane."

"Between insanity and the cunning born of desperation there is a wide margin," said Mordecai, his ear plainly intent on the mumble of Tuck's voice in another room. "You were poisoned impulsively, Mr. Crone. Like a loaded, hair-trigger gun, the killer dealt out death at a touch, and the aim was imperfect. But what bold, if warped, reasoning lay behind the scheme? Why was more care not taken to insure the death of Miss Tripoly? If we assume that the killer had the inspiration to attempt to create a scapegoat of you, the death of your witness as well was certainly imperative."

Tuck loomed into the room behind the vivid figure of Lily Tripoly. "Crone wasn't poisoned with digitalis," he said. "The poison used was cocaine. Taken orally, it can kill within a few hours. The fatal dose is highly variable. The amount used was probably small."

Brigit was somewhat surprised to see that her uncle was standing with his eyes shut. When he opened them they were bleak. "It is my duty to inform you," he said in an emotionless voice, "that yesterday afternoon at two o'clock Desmond Grover had in his possession seven capsules of cocaine, although they were at that time in a leather case containing shirt studs and a badge for athletic prowess."

"And a hypodermic syringe?" asked Eric Crone in a hard, peculiar tone.

"Yes."

"A junky," said Crone flatly.

With the blond, cocksure face of the high-school boy as vivid in her mind as though she had seen it yesterday, Brigit Estees demolished the thin slice of silence just as it crumbled into small sounds of shock and surprise. "Well, what are we waiting for? A voluntary confession signed by a notary public?"

"I believe," said Mordecai Fentwill, still speaking in an emotionless voice, "that since it is nearly six o'clock, we shall find Mr. Grover at the Blue Grotto Café, in the third booth from the door. I feel that I should add that he is there for the purpose of co-operation with the local narcotics authorities."

"That's mighty white of him," said Tuck. "But we're still going to hold him for questioning."

Desmond Grover's face, looking up from the dim depth of booth three, showed no surprise or fear when Tuck quietly told him that his presence at headquarters was greatly desired. "I had an appointment at six-fifteen," he said, looking at his watch. "I'm meeting someone outside in the parking lot. It won't take long. Any objection to that?"

Tuck said there was no objection to that, and he and

Brigit watched him speak briefly with a short, stocky young man waiting by Grover's car.

By the time it occurred to Brigit to be surprised that her uncle should have known where they would find him, Desmond Grover was seated between them on the front seat of the black sedan, a light sweat shining on his forehead, and his face still wearing the extravagant surprise which had flooded it when he learned of the attempt on his father-in-law's life. Mordecai Fentwill was not present to explain his ubiquity. He had chosen, for some reason, to remain behind in the Blue Grotto; Brigit had looked back to see him gazing up at the mermaid with quiet horror.

# 22

Beer, Pop?"

Mordecai looked up at the young bartender who stood before the booth wearing a faint smile below a narrow mustache.

"It is not my custom to drink beer before dinner, and I never drink pop at any time."

"I wasn't asking if you wanted pop. I was calling you Pop, get it?"

"I am not your Pop," said Mordecai. "One of the boons for which I shall remember to thank our Creator. Do you know how to make a Martini which does not taste of cheap vermouth and the pits of unripe olives?"

The oval face with the tragic eyebrows and the fop's mustache showed puzzlement and a faintly foiled look, and Mordecai realized that he had not reacted as old men should —grateful for any bone of friendliness, glad for a little "kidding."

"I turn out the best Martini money can buy!" asserted the bartender in a bored tone.

"Turn me out one, then," Mordecai commanded.

Sitting alone in the booth with the small-stemmed glass diamond-clear on the glossy brown table bearing its indecipherable legend of nicks and scars, Mordecai found himself feeling old and lonely. The illusion gripped him that he was not any more a part of the flow of life, but only joined it briefly, as a withered leaf may ride the main current for a while, then be shunted into a side pool where its motion is stilled.

He shook his head impatiently. "It's this grotesque cavern," he told himself, and mordantly observed once more the ugly and unplayful fakery of the rugged brown plaster walls, the wooden flesh-toned torso of the mermaid, hanging by obvious wires from the ceiling. Her golden hair, he noted with fresh horror, was real hair, a flowing and slightly shopworn wig. The body, arms and head belonged to a store-window dummy. The fishlike tail was made of a green metallic fabric, lumpily stuffed, an afterthought. She was a drunken dullard's dream of the Lorelei.

Mordecai found himself frowning, not at the mermaid, but at an elusive and nagging thought which he caught with a swift pounce. Why was he so uneasy and dissatisfied with the turn events had taken? Why did it seem to him that Desmond Grover had been the intended scapegoat all along, not Eric Crone at all?

Suddenly reminded of the subsidiary train of events in which he had become involved, Mordecai raised his head and searched the long bar alertly to see if he could determine which of the Blue Grotto's patrons might be the narcotics investigators whom Grover had so reluctantly telephoned the night before. He found one of them easily, because he had left the bar only a minute after Grover did, undoubtedly to meet him in the parking lot and learn whether the cocaine had been delivered as usual. Now he sat reading the evening paper on the high stool at the front corner of the bar. He was young and bulky, with the dogged profile of a small-business man competing against big corporations who could undersell him most of the time but had not yet broken his spirit. The older man in the gray suit who sat next to him might have been the manager of a branch bank; he poured beer from the bottle before him with a precise motion and thinned lips, as though he did not often so indulge himself and faintly disapproved of his present behavior.

Mordecai stood up suddenly. At home were the records of the Briggs case which Tuck had entrusted to him, and his own notations as well. He wanted very much to go over them all with scrupulous care. He was sure that the complexity of events new and old concealed some small fact which his mind had noted and then had all but forgotten; like a fossil bone, it must be found and studied.

Out on the cold sidewalk he remembered that his car was parked across the city at the university, but he was able to hail a passing cab at the corner of Acacia Street. As it sped him away he glanced back at the sullen trees into whose shadows a dead girl had walked so many years before; their branches were perfectly still and gave the impression that the trees were waiting. . . .

Brigit telephoned Dayleen Pflugel at eight o'clock. An hour had been spent in extracting from Desmond Grover details of all sorts: the clothes the redhead was wearing, what had been said, the kind of furniture in Dayleen's living room, how it was arranged, whether or not there was a clock in plain sight and what kind of a clock it was. It was plain that Grover had visited her home; that this had not necessarily been on the night of the murder was also obvious.

As when they had first tried to telephone Lily Tripoly, a bell rang imperiously in an empty house. This happened thirteen times. Dayleen's neighbor Eloise Adolph had no idea where she might be. "I haven't seen her since last night. She dropped in real late, on her way home from some place. She was all set up about something, real pleased with herself. She went up to her house around one in the morning, and I haven't set eyes on her since."

Grover's first uneasiness had slowly turned into a smiling semiassurance. But when at eleven o'clock Brigit put down the telephone and said to Tuck, "I wonder if anything's happened to her?" Grover looked suddenly afraid.

It was half past seven when Mordecai turned on his green-shaded student lamp and spread open on his desk the Manila folder lettered, "BRIGGS, Ruth Ann." Within a few minutes he found the fossil he had left the Blue Grotto to rediscover. "Of course!" he said, and leaned back in his chair.

As vividly as though it stood there on his desk he could see a clear green plastic case the size of a package of cigarettes. A lid at one end divided and sprang open at the touch of a thumb, and there showed through one slick side a red target lettered in bold black, "LUCKY STRIKE."

The invisible thumbprint on the cellophane was centered neatly on the target and pointed toward the bottom of the package. From the folder before him Mordecai selected an enlarged photograph of that print and looked with fascination at the black maze of loops and arches around a central whorl.

He spoke aloud, as he sometimes did when he was alone. "The print on the package of cigarettes found near the body did not match Desmond Grover's. The record states that clearly. But it is not the thumbprint of the person who sold the cigarettes, nor of any of the persons who might have casually handled the package. That thumbprint belongs to the last person who held that pack of Lucky Strikes. Because of the green plastic case. The thumbprint has to belong to whoever slipped the cigarette package into it."

As vividly as he had visioned the green plastic case Mordecai now saw a pair of hands performing that unremarkable act, the right thumb holding the package firm, slipping it into the narrow opening at the top of the green container. No need for caution. The owner of the green case had not then known that it would be lost a few feet from a dead girl's body.

The convolved maze of the killer's thumbprint seemed suddenly a crude symbol for another maze, for the pattern of events which, seen without distortion or prejudice, would show themselves to have arisen from one mind, one creature, the killer.

It was nearly midnight when Dayleen Pflugel clicked breezily into the Homicide Department. She was somewhat drunk and exuded with the fumes of alcohol a blowzy good nature. She wore, Brigit noticed, a stole of brown fur of which she seemed very proud. It looked new.

With many digressions she told her story. Although she occasionally had difficulty in recalling certain minute points which Desmond Grover had remembered under questioning, her version of the three quarters of an hour matched his with unusual accuracy. As to the fact that his one visit to her home had occurred on the night of the murder, she was adamant. Nor did she waver on the hour. "He got there at eight and stayed till quarter to nine and maybe a few minutes longer. And it was February 1, 1945. That's flat and final."

When she left the inner office Grover stood up to open the outer door for her. He had evidently been able to judge what her testimony was, for as she passed him, adjusting the fall of her fur stole, he said, "Thank you, Dayleen."

Her big grin was triumphant and her eyes were wise. "It was a pleasure."

# 23

THEORETICALLY SPEAKING," Mordecai Fentwill told himself, "one other person besides Desmond Grover had the physical opportunity to put poison in Eric Crone's brandy-and-soda. Helene Grover was also at the table. But the notion that she would kill her father is a fantastic one. Parricide is uncommon, and surely her average, pleasantly pretty face cannot conceal so striking a degree of cold, unfeeling cruelty, nor a mind so twisted."

And when he attempted to postulate a hypothetical reason for her to have furiously struck down the Briggs girl, his mind balked. More believable was the impossible notion that the shadowy figure of the boy mentioned in Ruth Ann's diary had lurked in the Blue Grotto the night before, had seized some unknown moment of opportunity to draw suspicion away from himself.

Never having seen Richard Carewe, Mordecai could only picture him from Brigit's brief description: a vague, besotted and stupid young man in golfing attire, practicing putts without any ball. He went to the desk and drew out one of the dossiers he himself had made for each possible suspect. Carewe's was the briefest of all. Only one side of a five-by-seven file card was filled. The last notation read: "Occupation, bartender."

An odd possibility struck Mordecai, and he telephoned the Homicide Department to ask Tuck or Brigit whether, by any remote chance, Richard Carewe tended the bar of the Blue Grotto. But they had gone. Nor had either yet arrived at his home.

His heart pumping in an oddly disturbed manner, Mordecai took his watch from his vest and looked at it. It showed the hour to be a quarter before one in the morning. He remembered that Los Angeles bars closed by official edict at two.

As he drove across the late city he told himself that his quest was as ridiculous as the notion which had prompted it. That Richard Carewe might be the bartender who had called him "Pop" was not outside the pale of possibility. But, because cocaine had been the poison used, to add to this mere possibility the notion that the bartender might also be "Mr. White" represented a type of thinking which Mordecai Fentwill deplored—visceral thinking, prompted not by the powers of logic, but by the same loose, warm emotional hunches that savages employ to explain a troubling universe, assigning mystic powers to oddly shaped stones, trees of unusual age or persons born feet first.

As he neared the Blue Grotto and saw in the darkness ahead the blue neon of the sign above its door, he severely reminded himself that events conceal meanings, that to read merely the surface story of a chain of actions is to overlook their real import. To presume that Carewe was Mr. White was actually to presume a meaningless accident: that the main stream of events, those which surrounded and sprang from the Briggs girl's murder, had been joined fortuitously by a side stream, the point of union being the moment when Desmond Grover was given a capsule of cocaine and Mr. White's telephone number by a stranger.

Although, thought Mordecai, it would perhaps be only

fair to add Helene Grover's reaction to the discovery that her husband had been using drugs, her insistence that he turn Mr. White over to the police. "How different she is from her mother!" he told himself as he pulled to the blank area of curb near the Blue Grotto.

He entered the dark cave, resolutely putting behind him all thoughts about the savagery of hunches. Looking up once more at the face of the young bartender, he ordered a Courvoisier cognac which he did not want. He told himself that if this man were Carewe, and should prove to be also a peddler of narcotics, then perhaps after all the pattern this revealed was not without meaning. Between a sudden act of violence which results in murder and the ugly business of selling a stuff which brings death more slowly there is no moral difference.

The bartender set on the table a small bubble of glass, the dark brandy pooled richly in the bottom. "This imported stuff's a buck a shot," he told Mordecai, not without satisfaction.

"The best, like the worst, always costs dearly, Mr. Carewe."

His hand on a five-dollar bill, the bartender looked at once wary and vaguely pleased. "How did you know my name?"

Mordecai looked down into the round glass. "I guessed it," he said.

When he raised his eyes he saw the stubborn-looking young narcotics investigator sitting near the rear of the long bar, engaged in what seemed a drunken argument about baseball scores. His presence could mean only that Mr. White had not been apprehended. The detective was still waiting for the drug peddler to collect the money hidden under the seat cushion of booth three. Mordecai leaned back against the seat of booth two and also waited.

As the hands of the clock neared two, only a handful of

patrons lingered within the Blue Grotto. The man and woman in the first booth abandoned a long discussion over a woman named Bella in whom the man disclaimed even slight interest and who, according to the woman, was losing her figure. The puffy man brooding at the foot of the bar roused from his daze and looked about with bleared angry eyes. A young couple who had been laughing went hand in hand to the door. The gentleman with whom the narcotics officer had dissected baseball scores rather gratefully beat an exit. And with an unsteady gait the young detective walked to the men's room.

Carewe, polishing a glass, watched him for a moment and then turned toward the puffy gentleman to say, "Sorry, sir, but we're closing now." He looked at Mordecai. "We're closing up, Pop." Mordecai rose obediently.

Now the bar's last customers made a dark clot at the door. Carewe watched them move slowly out into the early-morning street. Then his head turned toward the door of the men's room. He added the glass he had polished to the row gleaming like ice against a long mirror, then strode to the rear end of the bar and ducked under a flap in the counter.

As Carewe rapped on the door of the men's room Mordecai quickly wrapped the empty liqueur glass in his handkerchief, sat down and slid quietly under the table of booth two. His knees under his chin, his head bent forward below the brim of his black hat, he tucked the glass bearing Carewe's thumbprint, he hoped, into his overcoat pocket. As he hid his hands in the sleeves of his dark overcoat he recalled that he had fortunately put on dark socks that morning.

In a moment the blue lights went out. The feet of the narcotics officer blundered to the door, followed by the shiny shoes of Richard Carewe. The door closed, and there was a loud click as the bartender locked it. Except for the concealed lights behind the bar and the reflected glare of the long mirror, the Grotto was dark, the cramped space below the table of Mordecai's booth as black as his hat. He risked raising his head. The legs of Richard Carewe passed, taking long strides. They stopped at the third booth from the door. Mordecai heard a leathery creak as the seat cushion was raised, a padded thump as it dropped back into place. In the silence he heard the soft rustle of bills being counted. Then Richard Carewe began to whistle.

His next actions startled Mordecai. After stuffing the folded bills into his trousers pocket the bartender snatched a newspaper left on the bar and spread it open halfway down the counter's length. Then he mounted one of the tall chairs and stepped up onto the newspaper. This brought his shoulders to the level of the mermaid's waist. Peering upward around the table's central leg, Mordecai saw him lift one side of the mermaid's yellow wig and reach into the creature's cranium. He withdrew a glass jar filled with small red capsules, shook some out into his palm, counted them in one swift glance and returned the bottle to its hiding place.

He jumped down from the bar, went to the cigarette machine and put in two coins; it responded with ugly metallic clatter. Then, sitting at the bar with his white-clad back toward Mordecai, he secreted in the package of cigarettes the capsules he had got out of the mermaid. He turned so quickly that Mordecai had barely time to double up in the blackness under the table of booth two. He heard Carewe raise and drop the cushion of the next booth. Contracted within the shell of his dark garments, Mordecai realized for the first time that he was running a considerable hazard.

Whistling once more, the bartender strode to the rear of the Blue Grotto. A door opened, and Mordecai heard the soft hurried sounds of garments being changed. In a few minutes Carewe passed booth two toward the front door. He was muffled in a loose dark overcoat, and he was singing softly, a man well pleased with what the day had brought. The song was "I've Got You Under My Skin." In passing, he paused to fold the newspaper, tuck it into his coat's big pocket. When he reached the foot of the bar he stopped again. There was a click and all the lights went out. The front door opened, and shut again. It rattled as Carewe tried it from the outside.

Alone in blackness that smelled of stale beer and people's bodies, Mordecai crawled out from under the table and stood up with all his bones protesting the ridiculous posture they had been forced to assume for the past quarter of an hour. He started toward the door.

The telephone rang. As though magnified by the three walls of the open phone booth, it sounded unnaturally shrill and imperious. Mordecai's stomach dropped emptily, as though he were on an elevator which had stopped too fast. Could Carewe hear the ringing telephone in the early-morning silence? Would he come back and answer it?

While he thought these questions, Mordecai flitted as swiftly as a bat to the small booth to the left of the door. He had just slipped into the corner of the leather seat, which creaked, when the lock clanked and the door swung inward, admitting a cool gush of clean night air and a man's dark, bulky body. Mordecai crouched tensely in the booth's corner and told himself that since Carewe undoubtedly knew every inch of the barroom by heart, he would not necessarily stop to turn on the lights. The telephone shrilled a fourth time. A blacker patch of darkness, Carewe moved swiftly to the sound. The bell's fifth ring was choked off. "Blue Grotto." Carewe's voice was gruff. . . . "No, I don't rekanize the name. What does he look like?" . . . When he spoke again his voice had altered slightly. "Old gent in a black Homburg. Yeah, he came in a couple of hours ago.

Had a cognac. But he's gone home. We're closed up, see.
. . . I'd say he left about fifteen minutes ago. . . . O.K.
G'bye."

The telephone receiver clanged into place, and Mordecai
heard Carewe emerge from the booth. He walked half a
dozen steps toward the front door, then stopped. A pure
slim flame of yellow showed him standing with a cigarette
lighter in his hand, a cigarette in his mouth. He was facing
the booth which Mordecai had occupied. He lighted his cigarette and then pivoted slowly and faced the bar. It seemed
to Mordecai that he was counting a row of the glasses
lined against the mirror. He turned again toward the booth
where Mordecai had sat drinking cognac and now the lighter's small flame showed that he was frowning faintly. As
though on sudden thought, and still using the lighter as
a torch, he bent abruptly and looked under the table. He
straightened, shaking his head, wearing a slight blank smile.
With a minute click the flame went out. And Richard Carewe walked toward the front door—or the light switch near
it. The cognac glass in Mordecai's overcoat pocket felt as
large as a basketball. Doubled in his corner he crouched, not
breathing, so that his hatbrim hid his face, which felt very
large, very white, and slightly phosphorescent.

At the same moment that he breathed night air again the
open front door swung so far inward that it nudged the
high back of his seat. But Carewe did not leave. Mordecai
could picture him standing in the open doorway, one hand
on the latch, looking into darkness, listening to it. There was
a sound of movement, a click, and the blue lights sprang on.
Mordecai closed his eyes.

For a long moment there was utter silence, then the far
whir of a late automobile in the night outside. The lights
went off, the door sighed shut, clanked, and with a click the
latch shot home. Outside on the empty pavement Richard

264

Carewe's departing footsteps dwindled away into silence. But he was not whistling now, and his stride was less jaunty, as though his thoughts slowed his feet, as though he were less certain of what lay ahead.

When Mordecai pulled into a parking space in front of the dark façade of his apartment building he took the usual satisfaction in realizing that few other cars could have utilized that short stretch of curb. It was as he slid his key into the lock of the apartment-house door that he heard heavy footsteps just behind him. He half turned. The dark bulk of a man in an overcoat prisoned him against the blank door between two tall primly clipped bushes.

"We've been waiting for you," Richard Tuck's voice said.

Mordecai was startled to hear himself titter nervously.

"Hey, is anything wrong?" asked Brigit, looming up beside Tuck.

"I've evidently seen too many gangster films. Did one of you telephone the Blue Grotto half an hour ago and ask for me?"

"That's right." Tuck sounded puzzled. "But they said you weren't there. It was a little after closing time, but we tried it on the thin chance you might be. You weren't at home, and that's the last place we saw you. Brigit thought you might be tailing Carewe for some reason."

"I was."

"We think we've figured out most of this mess, and we wanted to see what you have to say about our ideas. But now it's close to three in the morning. I guess you're pretty tired."

"Tired? I am, on the contrary, exhilarated. Come up to my flat by all means, both of you. I shall be glad to hear whatever you wish to tell me. I have a few ideas too, but I'll let you two talk first."

# 24

Between the knowledge of the truth and proof of it lies a wide margin, which is why guilty persons sometimes escape what is known as justice," said Mordecai Fentwill.

"I have shown you that Richard Carewe, also The Bird, also Mr. White, had the opportunity to poison Eric Crone. He also had the opportunity to set the trap in the old house. He had more than that; he had the motive. Consider the shock he must have suffered when he learned that the police had, somehow, after a lapse of six years, learned of his appointment with the dead girl. What a dreary morning-after he must have faced. How terrified he must have been at the notion that the half-forgotten post card written so long ago might put a noose around his neck. Or, more exactly, send him to the gas chamber. But when he read of the mysterious attack on Mrs. Crone the bright hope occurred to him that by firmly linking in the minds of the police the crime he knew he had committed with one he knew he had not, the resulting confusion might accrue to his benefit. Using a timeworn device which would have occurred to any child of ten, he set the trap, sent the telegram and sat back to indulge in the illusion that he was a trifle more secure.

"To return to the attack on Mr. Crone, Carewe saw an

opportunity again to deflect suspicion from himself. His motive for this second attempt resides, I believe, in the fact that Carewe, by then, knew himself to be not only the killer of a young girl, but also knew himself responsible for the bullet which lodged in Brigit's shoulder. The latter and minor crime added its weight to the former and greater one, and instead of fostering a greater sense of safety, created a greater uneasiness. By now the alert newspapers had informed Carewe that the Briggs girl's diary had been found, and Mr. Crone, on the night he was poisoned, proffered in a rather carrying voice the information that the ownership of the murder car was known to the police. It was this piece of news which inspired the poison scheme. The precautions Carewe had taken to conceal the fact that he was Mr. White gave him, I am sure, the smug feeling that even though his presence in the bar was known to the police, his possession of the cocaine he used in Crone's drink was something they could never guess.

"But I do not believe he intended to damn Crone by what would be interpreted as a suicidal act. Cocaine is extremely lethal when taken orally, and Carewe must therefore have been infinitely cautious in slipping a very small amount into Crone's brandy-and-soda. Otherwise, Crone would not be with us now, nor would Miss Tripoly.

"For Carewe's next move was an apparent attempt on Miss Tripoly's life. Note the adjective. I am sure that the patent fakery of that attempt on her life did not escape you. Why, in the name of Aristotle, would a person bent on destroying her have blundered noisily over dry leaves, or rustle the bush he was standing beside? And that wild chase through the canyon! Really, it was rather insulting to one's intelligence. She was quite evidently fleeing to a place of safety; all her pursuer could hope for was to take a shot at her as she got out of her car. But why not do that in front of her secluded house, as she turned and fled? No, the only purpose in the mind of that creeper in the bushes was to frighten Lily Tripoly into the belief that her life had been in danger. And to convince us that it had. The necessity for some attempt on Miss Tripoly is evident when we ask ourselves this: What did the attempt on Crone's life accomplish?"

"Nothing, that I can see," Tuck said, "beyond confusion."

"It accomplished something very definite," said Mordecai severely. "The arrest of Desmond Grover."

"He wasn't arrested. He was held for questioning," Tuck corrected him.

"The delicate shadings of police nomenclature do not at the moment interest me. Suspicion was focused on Grover. That was the result aimed at. When Richard Carewe saw Grover and Crone together at that table in the Grotto he saw a perfect opportunity. He knew that Grover possessed cocaine, having, in the role of Mr. White, supplied it. He knew that Grover had been under suspicion. Since Grover also knew that Lily Tripoly was Eric Crone's witness, some menace had to be exerted in her direction, since Grover is not a fool and would not therefore eliminate Crone in hopes of suggesting suicide and also leave alive a witness who could clear him of any motive for suicide. Had you two not hauled Grover down to headquarters so promptly, I am fairly certain that an anonymous communication would have informed you that Grover possessed some cocaine and thus, inferentially, could have used some on Crone. But this, due to the speed of your cerebral processes, was not necessary."

"Why did Carewe pick Desmond Grover as his fall guy?" demanded Tuck. "As the killer of Ruth Ann, Carewe knew that Crone's car was the murder car, and he must have been fairly sure we suspected as much, since Crone was looking for a witness to his whereabouts. Wouldn't it have been far simpler to load the dice against Crone?"

"But he had nothing against Crone."

"What did he have against Grover?"

"His good fortune in having become the husband of Helene Crone. Oh, yes, I speak of love. Helene was Dicky's far, bright angel when he was a boy of twenty. He holds what he once felt for her close to his heart, as proof that fate is not on his side, and perhaps as a brave, impossible hope for the future as well. In an acquisitive culture like ours, this is a rather usual way of utilizing despised love: To excuse the corrupt and dishonest nudgings with which we prompt fate to favor us, in the form of good hard cash, and also to give those nudgings the flavor of romance. Did you ever read *The Great Gatsby*?"

"Love . . ." mused Tuck, doubtfully. "It isn't too clear."

"Carewe did not kill because of the crude and obvious fear that he might be jailed—or court-martialed—for using marijuana. Nor did he dread general social opprobrium for having attempted the conquest of a female three years under the legal age of consent to the more playful aspects of biology. It was Carewe's love for Helene Crone which impelled him to murder Ruth Ann. It was the knowledge that Helene would surely learn from Ruth Ann that he had not only 'borrowed' the Crones' car to drive another girl to the canyon, but tried to make love to her there—and failed. Adding the possibility that Ruth Ann also learned of the marijuana smoking in which he indulged, it is clear that he knew that all brief glimpses of his bright angel were to be snatched away forever. He feared being despised by Helene, but I am sure he writhed with agony at the thought of her contemptuous laughter.

"The broken andiron lay on the seat between them. As

Ruth Ann started to leave the car and walk to her home, he hated the back of that blond head. For an instant it symbolized his lifelong failure to be loved by anyone. From that implacable truth her rejection of him must have removed every trifling concealment—even, perhaps, the drugged euphoria which had enabled him to drive gaily off in Helene's car filled with the sheer, lovely belief that they were intimate enough to be that free with each other's possessions."

"You mean that he was in the car waiting for Helene when Ruth Ann got off the streetcar," offered Brigit.

Mordecai nodded. "And when he struck Ruth Ann down, I am willing to go so far as to say that he struck with such furious violence at the memory of another woman's head, the turned blond head of his mother, going away from him as she had always gone.

"The thing done, he could only get the girl from the car, clean the seat with a chamois, drive away from there. Only as he stopped the car at the place from which he had driven it did he realize, I think, how easily it might have been missed during the half hour he had been gone. This belated fear carried him as far as the act of opening the car to the cleansing rain. When he walked into the Blue Grotto the people there saw only one more besotted soldier. After a time he realized that he was safe."

From the pocket of his overcoat Mordecai drew out a small bubble of glass wrapped in a clean handkerchief. "I am very sure of myself, I know. Carewe's thumbprint is on this glass. It will match the one on the package of Lucky Strikes in the green plastic case."

"If it does . . ." said Tuck softly, and carefully wrapped the glass in a sheet of cellophane from his inner breast pocket.

Mordecai frowned, and closed his eyes.

"Are you asleep?" Brigit asked after a moment.

"No, my dear. I am merely putting myself in the position of a defense attorney confronted with one damning piece of evidence and little else. I was concluding that this damning piece of evidence could be refuted by one false statement, and one corroborating party, both all too easily come by."

"What false statement could Carewe make?"

"That he had left the cigarette case in Ruth Ann's possession some time before, and that it therefore must have fallen from her purse."

"But who would corroborate this?"

"His cousin Eloise."

"I think you have something there," said Brigit.

"It would mean changing her story from what she said about the green case six years ago," added Tuck. "But that's as common as fleas."

"And so," Mordecai said, "two facts must be proved without doubt. That Carewe was in Los Angeles on the night of February first—"

"Which is quite an order," said Tuck.

"—and that the Crones' gray convertible coupé was without doubt the murder car. Carewe had no car. It must be very clear how he drove Ruth Ann to the canyon. And that means that Mrs. Crone is going to have to be coerced into telling the simple truth about the glove at long last."

"And the love motive seems a thin place to me," Tuck said. "I believe it, but some people will find it incredible, in view of what Carewe has become."

"I see nothing incredible about it under any conditions," snapped Mordecai. "It is merely *An American Tragedy* minus consummation and a canoe."

"And Theodore Dreiser," said Tuck.

Mordecai drew himself to his full height. "When the case is presented to your superiors, I believe you will find my narrative powers entirely equal to the task."

271

Brigit said, "The trouble is there's not much psychology in it. For years now headquarters is nuts for psychology."

"I refuse," Mordecai said, "to throw in an Oedipus complex, a castration fear or any similar sop to Cerberus. The boy was never loved, and so he could not bear to lose the girl he believed himself capable of loving. And so Ruth Ann Briggs was impulsively killed before she could commit candor. I need not dwell on the fact that truthtellers, large and small, have been dealt with as unkindly before."

He was surprised when Brigit kissed his cheek. "I think you're wonderful," she said.

Pretending unconcern, he told her: "You won't in a few hours, if those thumbprints don't match."

But they did.

# 25

IT WAS at one minute past nine that Clare Crone stopped
the cuckoo clock. After the bird's last outcry the room
seemed oddly silent. Mrs. Crone smiled. It was strange to
think how many changes this symbolized; the cuckoo's
swan song had marked the end of one life and the start of
a better one. For peace now existed between her husband
and herself.

Her childish breakdown in the hospital had somehow
led to words and acts which had brought them closer together than they had been in many years. For the first time
in a decade he had telephoned her from his office for another reason than to say he would be late for dinner. How
kind of him to want her to know as soon as he learned of it
that Desmond was no longer under suspicion, that the two
big detectives were hot on another trail! Whose did not matter; a black cloud had passed, removing its threatening
shadow from her and hers.

A butter-yellow bar of morning sunlight warmed old
maple and melted in muted silver on a pewter bowl. The
narcissus which frailly filled it smelled of springtime and
gardens. Rising from her mind like a bright bubble of the
peace that filled her came a line of poetry she had loved

273

once, long ago: "And spring comes on forever, said the Chinese nightingale." She closed her eyes, felt a smile on her mouth, and saw, through the rosy haze behind her eyelids, a future full of many small gestures of affection for her husband, gestures which would gradually complete the restoration of their mutual trust.

The doorbell rang.

The young man on the porch wore a pink Brooks shirt and a dark-blue overcoat, bulky and expensive. Because of his little mustache and the way the cropped frizz of his hair had receded at each side of his forehead, she did not recognize Dicky Carewe.

"Is your husband home, Mrs. Crone?" he asked, and she thought of him as a salesman of the better sort when she replied in the negative, asked in the faintly patronizing tone she reserved for such strangers what was it he wanted, please.

"It was you I wanted to talk to," he said then, and added with a little laugh, "I guess you don't remember me. Dick Carewe? I used to be friends with Helene."

She felt a dim respect that the nervously laughing, not-too-bright high-school boy had somehow with the years attained the protective armor of such a good overcoat. But her recollections of his peroxide mother and his obvious uneasiness on the few occasions when he had entered her home made her reply exactly as though he had come to try to sell her a new vacuum cleaner or an insurance policy. "Oh, yes, I remember now. How are things going for you, Dicky?"

He stepped to one side and turned his clipped head toward the street. Directly across the street from her house was parked a long convertible coupé of a greenish-gray. It looked like a Cadillac, and it was quite new. "Not bad." He returned his attention to her with a swift motion that blocked her view of the street. His gray eyes under the anxious brows seemed cold and vacant, but oddly intense. "Can I come in a minute?" he asked and gave the little self-deprecating laugh she remembered as well as anything else about him.

There was no reason to hesitate, and yet she did. "Was it important? I'm rather busy."

"Pretty important. It won't take long. Just a few minutes is all." His flat voice seemed faintly strained.

She had the vague notion that he might have heard from some source that Helene was married but not getting on too well with her husband, and hoped to learn from her that this was true, that there was some hope in the future for him and his pink shirt and his new Cadillac. "Does it concern Helene?" she asked.

He paused before answering, as though striving for a scrupulous honesty. "You might say it does, in a way." His light eyes were looking past her shoulder at the front hall; the look made it seem as though that perfectly ordinary house represented to him the unattainable splendor of a palace.

Curiosity and the general feeling of kindness which filled her prompted her to step back and open the door wider. "Come in, then, for a minute. Are you married yet, Dicky?"

"Nope." He passed her and in the hall turned as smartly as a soldier toward the living room. When she shut the door and joined him he was standing in the room's center, tapping a cigarette on his thumbnail, looking around him and smiling with only one corner of his mouth. "Funny. When I was a kid this seemed to me the swankiest room, in a quiet way, I ever saw."

The smile and the tone of his voice faintly annoyed her. "I flatter myself that it is in better taste than most rooms one sees. . . . What was it you wanted?" She pointedly refrained from asking him to remove his overcoat or to sit

275

down. Already she regretted her impulse in admitting him.

He lighted his cigarette with a gold Dunhill lighter, thrusting his head forward to the flame. As he expelled smoke from the side of the mouth which had smiled he clicked the lighter shut. There was a sliver of time between that sound and the rather massive motion he made of thrusting aside the heavy flare of his overcoat and returning the lighter to his trousers pocket. He was looking at her steadily, and yet his eyes seemed withdrawn, as though he were thinking of the best way to put a difficult or delicate matter. His preoccupation did not make him timid. He seemed to have swelled a trifle inside his overcoat, and he seemed taller than when he had stood on the front porch. Finally his eyes sought hers, and again she was aware of their cold vacancy. He said, "I came to tell you that this time tomorrow there's a good chance you'll be dead."

After speaking he watched her impersonally. His thin lips wore a slight smile, as though he were well aware of all her inner reactions to his incredible statement. Before she could speak he said, "Siddown, and I'll try and explain how things are." He walked to the sofa and sank into its center. The down cushion sighed gently. He leaned forward toward the coffee table, flipped ash from his cigarette with his little finger into a milk-glass bonbon dish.

"Siddown, Mrs. C.," he said again, rather patiently. "This is gonna take maybe a little longer than I thought."

"I will not sit down," she told him icily, "and I warn you that I will give you just two minutes to explain this very peculiar remark before I call the police."

Her attitude did not seem to intimidate or alarm him; in fact, he scarcely noticed it. When he reached suddenly into the breast pocket of his coat she felt a pang of alarm: He was insane and was now reaching for a gun. What strange vengeance filled him?

But he brought out a wallet of fine soft brown morocco leather and from it drew a crisp new bank note. He tossed the wallet to the table before him and spread the green bill out with both hands, snapped it once. It gave out the sharp crackle of new money. She saw that it was a thousand-dollar bill. Then, before her astonished mind could frame more than a vague question about bribery, he held the bill up for her continued inspection with one hand and with the other reached into a side pocket to bring out a small brown paper sack of the sort a child might buy penny candy in. He spilled the contents out on the fine patina of the low table and she saw with vague astonishment a scatter of small capsules, red and white.

"You offer most people a choice," he said in a practical voice. "These?" He eyed the capsules half humorously. "Or this?" He flapped the bank note. "And which would a normal person take, every time? Why, the money. Every time. But you ask a certain type junky which he wants, and ten to one he'll grab the caps. I mean a panic man, a real boots-and-shoes dugout. Ten to one he won't even wait to count 'em, to see if maybe the dough would buy him more of the stuff. Because that's how a junky is, once he's really hooked and can't support his habit. It sounds real crazy; I know it sounds nuts to a lady like you, but you better take my word for it, because I know. And in a way it isn't crazy."

He put the bill back into the wallet and pocketed it. "Money buys people like us the things we need to stay alive. The only thing a junky needs to stay alive is junk. It's really kind of disgusting, the things they'll do to take care of their habit. I've heard a few of them admit they'd commit murder to get dope when they're hurting for it. I even know one who has."

His comments shocked her less than they might have because of remarks her husband had made down the years about the strange, lost creatures Dicky Carewe had for some reason talked of at such length. For the same reason she knew that Carewe had not exaggerated, and this made the angry and tremulous distrust she had begun to feel abate somewhat. It was clear that he was trying to warn her of something. As a sudden surprise she realized he must be a narcotics peddler. "Let me see if I understand you clearly," she said, sitting at the desk and rather pleased with her calm and level tones. "You are trying to warn me that my life is in danger from a drug addict, is that it?" Put so baldly, it sounded silly and fantastic; she thought how, with a few steps, she would be at her telephone, relating this bizarre incident to Eric.

"Right on the nose," said Dicky Carewe with satisfaction. "A fellow with a habit he can't handle, being broke, a panic man. He's been offered enough junk to take care of him for a couple of months—and that's like a couple of years to a junky—if, when he gets the go-ahead, he makes sure you're dead." He edged forward on the sofa so that he was sitting with spread knees, like a dark frog. "This kinda thing goes on all the time, only a lady like you probably don't know it. But you know you read every once in a while how a person is found dead in the front seat of his car with his head blown in and blood all over the place. That's one of the times it's done obvious. Other times, it's more like an accident."

"And who is behind this scheme you've come to warn me about—some enemy my husband has made?"

"No. . . . Me."

Her sense of shock and outrage jolted her to her feet.

He thoughtfully ground out the nub of his cigarette. Standing, he seemed a little bigger than he had a few minutes before. Her tone should have produced in him explanations, chagrin. But he seemed only resolute and immensely

278

certain of himself. He flipped the capsules into their paper sack and shoved it into a side pocket. "I say a couple of words—it's a kind of code we already fixed up, this junky and me—and your time runs out. He gets what he wants after he's done it—a few more words is all that'll take. The stuff's already hidden in a safe, kind of unusual place I figured out. The trouble is, I'm not a mean guy, and I don't like the idea of anybody getting hurt through me. I don't want this accident to happen to you, Mrs. Crone. So I also got another angle worked out. In case I tell him there's nothing doing, to lay off you if he wants to stay buddies with me, why, he also gets the junk he needs, and no harm done whatsoever. It's strictly up to you, what I tell him. And, believe me, I hope you'll see this my way." His head shot toward her and he spoke with passion for the first time. "Because I'm fighting for my neck, Mrs. Crone. I'm fighting to keep from getting railroaded straight to the gas chamber. And you're the only person who can keep that from happening."

For the first time he frightened her. The dim picture began to reveal itself. She started to the telephone.

"Go ahead, call your husband," he invited. Now he seemed weary, calm and amused. "Call the whole damned police force if you want. I got nothing to lose. You're the one who's got something to lose. Plenty. Your life."

His tone, rather than the stale threat, stopped her. "I don't understand how I can possibly help or harm you," she said. It made her angry that her voice sounded thin and petulant.

"If you'll just siddown a minute and stop tearing around like an old chick with its neck off, I'll tell you!" He waited, blotting up the sunlight with his big coat until she had returned to her chair.

She was thinking, with new calm, I must let him commit himself thoroughly. As soon as it's safe to I can tell Eric.

279

This man is dangerous. But he's playing a fool's desperate game. I won't be hurt if only I can be clever.

He returned to the sofa, leaned back with his hands shoved deep into his coat pockets. His shoes, she saw, were of very good quality, possibly handmade. "It goes back to the Briggs murder," he said, and this she had quite expected. "They got my name from this diary she wrote, and now I think they're out to pin it on me, being as every other angle's gone sour. And I come from the side of life where those things can happen to people, Mrs. Crone. You always knew I didn't belong here in your house, but you didn't know how much. That's because you've never found out about the part of the world where I live, Mrs. Crone. People like me, we got to make our own breaks. Or get broken." He leaned forward. "The way I figure it is this: To have any case against me that's gonna hold up in court against a smart lawyer, they got to prove your car was the murder car. Because I didn't have any car, see? But everyone knows there had to be one, otherwise how did Ruth Ann get taken to the canyon? So the police are going to try to prove how somebody borrowed your car that night, how your car was the one she was killed in. And if they also can prove I was anywheres near Acacia Street around the time the murder happened, well, it's gonna look bad for me. So bad it scares me." He leaned forward, as one who imparts a confidence. "Because I don't mind telling you I was in the Blue Grotto bar maybe an hour after it happened. I guess Jenkins remembers this, and maybe the singer who was there then, too. You can see how bad all this looks for me, can't you?"

The fear she had felt was increasing, devouring the security she had reveled in a little while before. She sounded shrill as she said, "But what can I . . ."

"I'll tell you what you can do. You can be a pretty fine friend to me, Mrs. Crone. A first-class witness. You can sign a statement for me. You can say you don't believe your car was the murder car. You can say you used it the day after the murder. You can say there was no blood in it. I read about that glove of yours in the paper. But you can explain that easy. You can say it turned up a long time after the murder, in the garage someplace, in a bunch of old clothes you were going to give away. You kept it, see, meaning to show your husband, and then you forgot and just happened to come across it the night that joker sneaked into your house and let you have it with the poker or whatever it was."

The fear inside her was a big tough bubble that would not burst. "How do you know it was my glove?" she asked.

He stared at her for a moment and then laughed. "Or Ruth Ann's. It doesn't matter. The thing is to explain it away so it don't seem to mean that the blood on it came out of the inside of that car of yours, get it?"

Now the sun was blaring through the south window, blinding her. As she stood up to close the louvres of the shade Richard Carewe walked over and pulled the cord that shut them. A dim twilight filled the room.

"That's not much to ask," he said.

The bubble of vague fear burst. Blind terror replaced it. With unbelief she realized that a few feet across her living-room rug a murderer stood looking down at her.

She got up swiftly, moved so as to put the frail ladder-back chair between them. "You wouldn't be asking me to do this," she said, "unless it was you who killed her."

He took a step forward—not toward her, but just away from where he was. "Figure it that way if you want to," he said, completely indifferent. Then his body seemed to swell a little more against the dull slats pushing back the sunlight. In the tone of one struck by a new idea he said, "Only if you do figure it that way, then you know I'm not kidding. I'm gonna go out of here with your signed statement in my pocket. Come here." Hands jammed in his pockets, he beckoned her with a jerk of his cropped head and started toward the front door. She moved forward with the notion that she could stand in the open doorway and scream or run down the steps calling for help. But he opened the door before she reached it, and stood with one arm braced against the lintel, barring any spontaneous burst toward freedom. She stared out over his shoulder at the sleek automobile parked at the opposite curb. He put the fingers of his other hand to his mouth and blew a sharp whistle. From the interior of the car came a croak of response. Something moved there under the low, black cloth top. Part of a gray fedora thrust itself out into the sunlight. She could not make out the face beneath it except that it was very thin and pale. Then a long dark sleeve emerged; the bony pallid hand at the end of it wagged a wave and then made a curious beckoning motion.

Carewe dropped his arm, seized her wrist in a cold, meaty hand and tugged her two feet forward; in a second the hand at the end of the sleeve wagged another salute and withdrew into the car once more. As Clare Crone started vaguely for the steps Carewe drew her back into the hall with a long strong tug. "Now he's seen you," he said placidly. "He knows who he may have to be looking for. Tomorrow. Next day. A week from now. When I give the word."

She realized her situation with a shaky dread inspired by the hat with no face under it and the disembodied arm. Carewe had killed Ruth Ann Briggs. He was not sane.

"Have you got a typewriter in this joint?" he asked, like one inquiring the time or requesting a glass of water.

As she nodded she saw how simple a solution lay before her: to write whatever statement he wanted of her and to telephone the police the moment he left the house. "It's upstairs," she said. "In my husband's room."

282

"Lead the way," said Carewe quite happily, having sensed her capitulation.

As she sat at the kneehole desk removing the black cover from the machine, he stood just behind her, frowning down at a paper in his hand. With startling clarity she remembered that she had sat as she was seated now on the day she wrote the long anonymous letter to the dead girl's mother.

"Date it!" commanded Carewe.

"I beg your pardon?"

"At the top of the page! Put this address and the date!"

Her fingers obliged; the keys clicked smoothly and precisely.

"O.K.," said Richard Carewe. "Now write "To Whom It May Concern.""

Again the obedient keys spattered and were silent.

"Now here's what I want you to say. I won't be sore if you change the grammar in case it's off." He read, in a labored way, from the folded and penciled sheet he held before his eyes. "Of my own free will, and in the interests of justice, I wish to make the following statement: First, it appears that there is an idea in certain quarters that the car which I then owned was driven on the night of February 1, 1945, by someone other than its rightful owners and that Ruth Ann Briggs may have been killed in it." He paused, frowning down at the next sentence, and she found herself thinking of her husband's face, and then, in rapid succession, of the faces of Richard Tuck, Brigit Estees and Mordecai Fentwill.

". . . glove in my garage, six months later," she heard him saying.

"I beg your pardon?"

He repeated himself. As the long lie unfolded she found herself aware that it differed in only a detail or two from one of the lies she herself had told—the last one, it seemed to

283

her. Would this written lie save Carewe's life? Had he guessed correctly where the weak spot in the police evidence would lie?

". . . and I am just as certain that there was no blood on either part of the broken andiron that happened to be left on the car's front seat."

As his voice stopped and as her eyes read the words her fingers had typed, terror again flooded her. She could not believe that she was doing what she was doing; she could not believe that two feet behind her right shoulder stood the older shape of a boy who had smashed in a girl's skull. But this was now doubly true. How else could he have known of the presence of that andiron? She felt dizzy, and a wave of incredulity almost closed over her head as she realized that the weapon with which a young girl had been killed had stood the six years since on her hearth.

She could not later remember the final words of the strange document; she returned sharply to the present when he said, "Now we get it notarized. Your signature, I mean."

She followed his brisk form down the staircase, going slowly and holding the rail for support. Below, he opened the door and this time whistled twice. As she reached the second step from the bottom she saw a small, ball-shaped man circle the long car across Acacia Street and come bouncing toward her house, his shadow following him in the morning sun. Carewe looked over his shoulder at her to say, "I paid him extra for this. I said you were a kind of invalid."

The round man came in blinking and performed his duty of witnessing her signature with mild pomp and an amazing lack of curiosity. When he started to the door Carewe held out a bill. "Here, walk down to the boulevard and get yourself a cab," he said. "I'm gonna be a few minutes here, and I don't like to keep you waiting any more."

When the door had shut after the notary Carewe turned to Mrs. Crone. "Now, was that so bad?" he asked.

She shook her head and forced her eyes to meet his in something like her normally frank stare; it seemed to her that her thoughts must show.

"I know what you're thinking," he said. "You're thinking that as soon as I've gone you can tell the police what happened here today. You're thinking that before I say those couple of words I told you about, I'll be in the clink." He shook his head slowly and wisely.

"You don't think you're going to get away with this, do you?" she asked, feeling more like herself as soon as she said the words.

He patted the cloth over a breast pocket. "I have." His slight grin faded as his head shot toward her. "Go ahead, Mrs. Crone. Tell the police about this. Tell them the truth, too. But the thing I told you about will happen." His tone was so absolutely sure of itself that she believed for the first time that the "accident" he had spoken of could actually occur; that she, Clare Crone, could one day walk out of her house into a sunny day like this one and never come home again. She vividly saw the bony hand at the end of the long dark arm raised stiffly, holding a gun. The skin between her shoulder blades prickled.

She looked up into his eyes, now slightly vacuous, as he stood before her in her hallway beginning to button his coat. His gaze met hers then. "But I think you're a smart lady," he said. "I think you know I'm not kidding. I think you know that the guy out there in my car who saw you just now isn't any joke. I think you'll take a little time to figure things out and be smart. And stay alive." He grinned at her, a conspirator. "Why be honest and dead? All it gets you is a funeral you aren't around to see."

285

Through all his banality, his clumsy cunning, his threats like those of a movie gangster, she sensed with an inner part of her mind that he had told her no more nor less than the truth. The peculiar horror which the unseen man who waited across the street had inspired in her was not, she felt deeply sure, unmerited. Panic rose in her swiftly, fluttering through the cave of her defenseless body with little black wings.

A darkness passed before her eyes, or else she closed them. When she saw Carewe again he was looking down at her with an expression that puzzled her. Rather abruptly he reached into the breast of his coat and pulled out his wallet. He drew out three bills—she saw that they were hundred-dollar bills. He held them out to her. "Here. Just to show I appreciate your help. Buy yourself a new suit or something. A good one. You got a nice figure for a chick your age."

She straightened, trying to make something important out of ignoring the three green bills held out to her in his hand. She tried to speak with dignity, but her voice quavered, as though what she had been forced to do had robbed it of the strength to bear such a load. The sound that came from her throat showed only the terrible hurt her self-esteem had suffered. "Do not add insult to injury," she said.

He tossed the bills to the table beside the telephone. "Then do what you want with them." And that was when she finally read the odd look on his face. It was pity.

She stood staring at the money, as though it held a secret message. She raised her head and looked toward Carewe. He had opened her front door and was now reaching in to close it after him. "So long," he said. His voice sounded oddly hollow. The pity was still on his face, and also another look—a kind of shame.

She took a sharp step toward him. Her voice was still

unsteady, only now it was shrill. "But how do I know you'll keep your word? How do I know I won't be killed anyhow, no matter what I say or don't say?"

His face turned carefully blank. "People who trust me," he said, like someone reciting a motto appropriate for the occasion, "I always treat them right."

"Like you treated Ruth Ann Briggs?" Her voice, she realized, sounded as though she were going to laugh or cry.

His face twisted a little as an expression started to form. But then he made it blanker than before. He stepped back from her, pulling the door slowly shut after him. "All that was a long time ago. It's right now you ought to be interested in. Buy yourself that suit. Have a little fun for a change. Nobody lives forever."

On "forever" the door clicked shut. She could hear his feet go down the steps quickly.

Later she could never recapture in words the bleak and lonely terror that filled her in that moment, and it was harder to describe her sense that the danger that threatened her was of her own making, as must be any escape from it.

And as though it had happened to another person, she remembered going to the hall closet and reaching up along the shelf for her husband's revolver. She knew enough to release the safety catch, but standing in her open doorway she had to fire three times, the gun held stiffly out before her, before he crumpled and fell to the ground, just where her front walk joined the cement of Acacia Street.

She felt the gun as it slipped from her hand and heard it thud on the floor, but she could not move. She could only stand there watching doors fly open, people running across the street toward her house. She felt no surprise when a large black sedan pulled to a stop at the curb. The big red-haired woman knelt beside the dark lump of the body, and it was the big detective named Tuck who continued toward her. As he reached her she looked up into his brown, sad, startled eyes. "Now I can tell the truth," she said.

"Evil condoned comes back to us," said a voice, but it was not Tuck's. The big man stepped aside and she saw the small and resolute form of Mordecai Fentwill. "A difficulty with which you have strikingly dealt, Mrs. Crone." He came to her side and took her arm in a kindly way. "I see you less as a killer than as a victim. You were prejudiced against your father and your husband through rather damning circumstances, and you supported an illusory loyalty with many foolish lies. But when the truth confronted you at last, you were brave enough to sacrifice your most precious illusion—that you are a 'nice' woman."

"I wasn't brave. I was only afraid," she whispered.

"Does courage exist apart from some degree of fear?" he asked with bright interest, as though they were about to embark on a philosophical discussion. Then he gave a dour glance at the crowd gathered about the other, fallen victim. "But there is little point, I think, in providing these gapers with the greatest spectacle in all their circumscribed lives. Let us go into your house, Mrs. Crone, and, for the present, shut the door."

THE END

www.ingramcontent.com/pod-product-compliance
Lightning Source LLC
Chambersburg PA
CBHW050354260626
47156CB00003B/720